OF NO CONSEQUENCE

E. HANNAVY-COUSEN

The Book Guild Ltd

First published in Great Britain in 2022 by
The Book Guild Ltd
9 Priory Business Park
Wistow Road, Kibworth
Leicestershire, LE8 0RX
Freephone: 0800 999 2982
www.bookguild.co.uk
Email: info@bookguild.co.uk
Twitter: @bookguild

This work is entirely fictitious and bears no resemblance to any persons living or dead.

Typeset in 11pt Adobe Jenson Pro

Printed and bound by CPI Group (UK) Ltd, Croydon, CR0 4YY

ISBN 978 1913913 885

British Library Cataloguing in Publication Data.
A catalogue record for this book is available from the British Library.

For my family, Richard, Benjamin, Eve, James,
Megan, Jacob and Pip

1

December

Her common sense told her that he couldn't have survived. It must have been the noise of him entering the water and smashing himself on the metal upright pole that was just visible by the landing raft that had woken her so suddenly. Several minutes had drifted by since then and the icy water strengthened the fatality of his state. Yet she couldn't just leave. At first she scrambled up to the road yelling for help. But by then the road was clear and the wayfarers had disappeared into the distance. Now time was of the essence – what if he was still conscious? She knew it was a stupid thing to do but she did it anyway. Adrenaline kicked in as she ran back, pulling off her backpack, her coat, her jumper, and hopping out of her jeans. Grabbing the water buoyancy aid that was lodged in the wooden fixture by the landing stage, she jumped into the freezing river. The icy water felt like knives that pierced her with a needle-like intensity. She gasped and could not breathe. Her attempts to swim floundered and she felt herself sinking below the surface.

In a timeless dream she forced herself to move her numb arms and legs, and seconds later her head came up out of the water and she gasped for breath. Totally disorientated, she used the buoyancy aid before her as a float and doggy-paddled towards the boat – her boat – and as she got closer she saw the body floating face down, cold, immoveable, dead. Nevertheless she made a grab for the floating hand; the cold fingers were rigid and stiff but the actual effort of gaining access to the body gave her momentum. Turning, she wedged her feet in the base of the boat and, using the little strength that she had left, pushed herself off and aimed for the bank. It was too far. It was too, too cold. She began to lose her eyesight, her face constantly dropping into the crystal burn of the freezing river. Her efforts were weak. She lost heart and accepted her fate. Her hand froze to the hand of the boy as they both drifted silently along with the flow of the river into the inky darkness. Her mind replayed an array of colours and sounds that echoed in her memory. She felt herself smiling as she gave in to the hope of another world and of finally meeting her mum. Then she was gone.

*

Earlier that day the weather had changed. Small flecks of snow had begun to drift in on the wind. The riverbank began to crisp up and take on the tiny flakes that sifted across the water. The wind took a hold, changing direction from the south to the north. The temperature dropped radically. A pretty last night, she had thought, but a worryingly cold one as she realised how very weak the shell of the boat had become. For inside, the soft and persistent wisps of snow had edged their way through the small splits in the cabin, covering the interior with a light powdery dust.

Her last few hours on the boat had given her time to reflect on what she should do next. She mused on her chances of keeping up with her escape, and thereby assessed the benefits of her so-called freedom. Rummaging around on the boat she retrieved from her rucksack a box of packet soups that had been part of her 'harvest haul'. Selecting tomato and chive, she hummed to herself whilst lighting the small camping gas stove. Tearing the packet open with her teeth she shook the pink powder into a saucepan, mixing it with the water she had saved from her water bottle. The glutinous material turned coral red and the aroma of tomatoes filled the cabin as the water heated. Sitting cross-legged on the makeshift bed, Joanna hugged the tin mug of the hot, comforting liquid. There was a definite air of disappointment, she admitted to herself, in how much time was taken up with just keeping herself fed and clean. That in itself had distracted her from the very purpose of her escape. With each tentative sip of the soup her thoughts flickered to the time when she had determined to find her roots.

At just eight years old Joanna had overheard her then-foster mother Pauline talking with her husband about how she felt for Joanna and inviting him to help her take on the project of discovering her true identity. The fact that she might still have parents out there was a mystery to her. She had already believed that her mummy must have died. But now the prospect that she had just been abandoned gave her very mixed feelings. The longing began as she considered that she had had a past – she had been conceived and birthed, but by whom? It wasn't until she was eleven that the home to which she had been assigned revealed what little they knew about her origins. The jumper that she had always carried with her she knew had belonged to her mother – at least she believed it to be, but here was a social worker explaining to her that the jumper was in fact what she had been wrapped in when she was discovered as a new-born of a few hours old. That jumper became so much more to her from that point on. Later, at fourteen, the ome gave her a small silver bracelet that had been found near where she had been abandoned. The police believed it had belonged to her mother as it seemed to have a loose clasp and dangling from the clasp a single thread from the jumper. The sum total of her heritage. The sum total of her identity.

Sighing, she dumped the empty cup onto the shelf – there was no water to waste in cleaning it. She was very much in need of a long hot soak in a bath or at least a decent shower; she recognised the perils of living like a tramp at the onset of winter. Three weeks was a long time in such conditions and to fight the dreariness that comes with isolation and near-starvation. Survival was just about what she managed to achieve, but her state of health and mind was pretty poor. Succumbing to a filthy cold that resulted in feverish hot sweats followed by freezing shivers, with aches in her limbs so painful that she had cried with the pain, her period of sickness had left her weak and low-spirited. She had not left the boat for four days, imprisoned by her lack of energy and illness. On the fifth day when returning to some semblance of normality she noticed how both the cabin and herself had begun to smell. To make matters worse she had had her period too. Using rags was unpleasant but with no means to use anything else she dealt with it as best she could. Added to which the constant sweating and lack of fresh water, along with her improvised toilet in the guise of an old paint tin, the boat assumed a sour acrid aroma that added to her misery.

Giddy and nauseous with lack of nourishment and water, she noted that her jeans were in peril of falling off her skinny body. Hoisting them up with a bit of old blue rope that was lying underneath the forward locker, she determined to make the effort to sort herself out. It was painful and long-winded as each movement took an enormous amount of energy, but eventually she emerged from the boat to be greeted by a downcast, frostbitten day. Standing on the prow, she took in some deep cool breaths. In some ways it was refreshingly beautiful. The crisp air, far from biting at her already cold limbs, seemed to cleanse and revitalise her. As she emerged she scanned the general area. Not a person in sight. Her eyes swivelled to the bus stop and noted that, though the clock had just chimed ten, it was probably more like a quarter past. There was no-one at the stop and Jo calculated that the ten o'clock bus had already gone, taking with it the one solitary passenger that she had observed boarding the bus each weekday. Feeling more confident and ramming her meagre toiletries into her backpack, she made her way under the bridge. Crawling up the bank she worked her way along the river's edge to the campsite. The Land Rover had gone and she estimated that she should have twenty minutes whilst the owner drove her children to school – ample time to get in the washrooms and luxuriate in a much-needed shower before it returned.

The washblock was an open-air effect, relatively new and made from pinewood. Each cubicle had a wooden door that locked from the inside. There was a gap at the bottom and top, and it would be fairly obvious if anyone was using it. Choosing the one furthest from the road, Jo felt it was the least conspicuous should anyone care to glance by. It linked to the central washing-up and laundry area where the sinks were huge and deep, reminding Joanna of the campsite she had once been to on the only real holiday she had ever had. It had been her and another foster sibling's job to wash up after the campfire supper. Turning her mind back to the present she considered that it being midwinter and closed until the spring, what were the odds that the water was even switched on? Fingers crossed, she prayed hard that it was (and if so, please God let the water be warm). Stripping off her dirty clothes, she tentatively turned the tap. One prayer was answered: after a brief splutter the water gushed in a torrent; it was icy cold. Shivering, yet with gritted determination, Jo lathered herself up as best she could with the scrap of soap that she had taken from the pub toilets. Washing-up liquid that she had found on the boat masqueraded as shampoo but was not particularly conducive to the task, matting her hair almost immediately and impossible to completely rinse out. The cold water limited the effect of the soap too. Though her body was tingling and red from the icy water and the rough cloth that she used for a flannel, the grime remained. Drying herself with the sweater that she had worn for the last few days, she pulled on her 'clean' clothes. Shivering and aware of her need to get back without being seen, Jo slowly unlocked the door, paused and listened hard for any movement or sign of occupancy from the house, with the drip of the showerhead exaggerated in the silence. Peeping round the door, she sighed with relief, as the car park was still empty. Making a dash for it, she glanced back, aware of the tell-tale wet stains on the tiled floor in front of the unit that she had used. They were a visible sign that someone had used the facility. Hoping it would miraculously dry pretty quickly before the owner returned, she shrugged her shoulders in resignation and niftily skidded back down the bank and to safety.

Entering the boat, the smell of damp, acrid sweat after the clean, fresh air gave her cause to gag and heave. It was disgusting. This, she realised, was all her. Her feet being grimy with a grey dirt that seemed to stick killed the euphoria she had felt from the shower. She knew she stank and her clothes had that musty, stale body odour that she had often found offensive when she had been too close to the homeless on the street. Her hair was a matted mess of felted knots, and she wore clothes so loose and baggy her skinny, skeletal appearance was exacerbated. And her hands – nails, broken and grimy, offset the dried callouses that were pretty ugly. Depression had been hard to fight. Giving in had been hard to fight. In fact she was now glad that Jamie had not answered her last attempted call, for she knew that had she heard his voice just at that most vulnerable moment she would have begged him to come to her. But he had not, she had not and it was time, it seemed, for the next move. She had ear-marked a potential spot, a substantial-sized barn.

Well off the main road and tucked in a field behind a row of elderflower trees was a fairly dilapidated but massive metal structure seemingly forlorn and neglected. Full of straw bales and broken bits of farm equipment, it lay hidden from passers-by in a large crop-yielding field. Working on the barn had given her a positive focus (and the callouses). The straw smelt clean and there lingered the memory of summer. It was a warming substance and she could bed herself in, tucked away from the elements, and keep dry and warmish. Yet, she reflected, that alone was only a minor element. It niggled her that she had not managed to get any further with her searches. In fact it had taken her all her wits to keep herself fed and hidden. Knowing for some time that she was going to run and escape the institutional homes that would be her inevitable fate, she was still shocked by the unexpected and unplanned speed whereby she had upped and run. When it had become clear that her latest foster home was giving up on her she did just have to get out immediately. Recalling how tough it had been to avoid the perverts that haunted her care home, she couldn't risk being put in their way again. Not all gave in and many were strong enough to avoid the bullying and sexual harassment that they met on the streets, but it was a tough call. Her one hope had been in staying with a family until she was old enough to be able to work and get a place in a young person's hostel. Sally Whitworth had made it clear that she and her daughter Alex despised her, and with the threat of being placed under the supervision of her social worker, that chance had gone. With no ID, no address – in fact, nothing that could prove she existed or that she was a legal citizen – her options were very limited.

Frustrated by the complexities of the legal system for the abandoned child and by the lack of anyone actually discussing her existence with her, along with the blatant lack of autonomy she had over her own life, giving her no rights at all, her anger rose. Wanting some answers to questions that were surely the right of everyone to know – her origins

– was evidently not a priority for the courts. Vaguely she had thought about researching old newspapers that might well have logged her abandonment and she also had hope in the Salvation Army. A boy in one home that she had stayed in had used them to find his father. Hope had dwindled until now. Ironically, having been pushed into the rash move of running in winter and camping out on a rotten boat fed her desire for the truth.

Post-shower and on her boat with the snow gently pushing its way through the cracks, Jo had lain down for the last time on the bunk bed and drawn up a plan of action. Glancing at the raw but still dirty skin, she realised that her attempts in the shower had not worked. Perhaps if she paid to go into the leisure centre for a swim she could get herself a decent, hot shower. Surely soap and hot water would do the trick? However, a further scan of her scraggy, grey body told her that realistically she wouldn't be given the chance. Did receptionists turn away filthy clients? You bet they would. In the broken mirror a haunted face glared back at her. Dreadlocks, she mused, that is what her hair wash attempt had given her. Anyway, she wouldn't risk being turned away. That left the Salvation Army; they were good at keeping confidences, and meeting down-and-outs. Maybe they would have somewhere she could clean up, though she had no idea where to find them. Positive thinking had to be the order of the day. Get to her barn by midnight and tomorrow pick up the bus into Tenterden – something she hadn't done since the day she had arrived. Go back to the Gateway, find the address of the nearest Salvation Army Hostel, and then she would indulge herself in reading – find a book, sit in the corner and luxuriate in a novel. The library did free coffee on Tuesdays. Comforted by those thoughts, Joanna dozed off and dreamt of nothing.

*

A noise abruptly woke her. She jumped up quickly, trying to ascertain what it was. Freezing and covered with a shadow of grey snow that melted and stuck to her clothes, Joanna fumbled for the latch and peered outside. The church clock chimed midnight, but it was always fifteen minutes out so it may have been just before or just after. Something had disturbed her. There was nothing to see on the river or the bank. The sky was bright, the moon was almost full and myriad stars brightened the sky to an eerie saffron yellow. Joanna took one last look around the boat, gathered her backpack, rolled up her sleeping bag and stuffed it in its bag, and ended her packing by attaching the bag to the backpack, then stepped out of the boat onto the freezing bank. Hoisting the pack onto her back and pulling her collar up to try and keep out the cold, so began her walk to the edge of the mooring where the gate would lead her to the bridge. Crossing the bridge took her by the pub. In the deep silence of the night and just as she reached the edge, Joanna heard the calls. Shouts and high-pitched whistling tore through the heavy silence – eerie and definitely close. Looking up a group of young people were peering over the bridge and then staggered up the road towards Northiam, still calling out. Silently she crept along the bridge in the opposite direction. They had disappeared as she reached the gate.

Archie. That was the name they were calling for. With ease she flicked the catch on the gate and sentimentally turned to look one last time at her boat, her first home, when the moonlight picked out a shape in the water...

Now her frozen hand melded to Archie's and they floated together in the dead of night.

*

Mike had been pleased with the night's takings. He had hopes of a fruitful Christmas period to help relaunch the pub from just a spit and sawdust relic to a thriving traditional pub and gastro bar. He had worked hard for this and taken out a serious mortgage to pay for the bold move. A country pub nowadays was either the thriving hub of the community or a dead loss. For the first time in this two-year makeover, it seemed to be coming together. His new chef, expensive but worth it, balanced his quirky bespoke menus with tasteful, traditional pub grub, pleasing both the local oldies and the newcomers from the London commuter belt. What made him leave the pub, as he went to lock up and scan the amazing night sky, he could not be sure, but it was with horror that he heard the call for help and the sound of someone entering the water. In a matter of moments he had grabbed his mobile phone and, without waiting to check, dialled 999. When he reached the river's edge he could just make out two bodies drifting along in the middle of the undercut by the bridge. He ran and hammered on the door of the boat keeper's cottage, yelling out to anyone who could hear, then skidded back to the river and tried to unleash a small open row boat that was tethered to the fence. He struggled to release the rope and chain by which it was secured and cursed at the length of time it was taking.

Eventually, with the help of Guy, who had understood the situation and had come from the boathouse with rope and bolt cutters, they released the boat and launched it into the river. Both men were strong and were able to channel the boat into the right direction. With extreme effort and great difficulty they hauled both bodies over the front, releasing their faces to the air but with feet still in the water they straddled the front. The effort they had to put in to get back to the bank was extreme as the overloaded weight made the boat awkward to manoeuvre and difficult to guide. They had to follow the drift of the river that meant they pulled up to the right of the bridge – awkward in the extreme as there was little leverage to be had. But now help had arrived. The friends of the lost Archie had returned from their fruitless search for him on the road and they sobered immediately with the intensity of the scene that they met. Villagers from the nearby houses had awoken to the sound of sirens as the police, firefighters and paramedics turned up with all lights and sounds carolling in the cold night air. Both retrieved bodies were given mouth-to-mouth. Both were wrapped in foil blankets and both were air-lifted to Maidstone hospital. It was unclear whether either would survive.

The mountains are now hidden by the mist. I can no longer see the gate that is padlocked at the end of the drive. I close my eyes and envisage it open. In my mind I leave, running through the gap onto the deserted road and aim for the junction of the pass. The mist comforts as it hides the chains on the gate. Still visible are those around my left ankle and leg. He calls. I turn and go. The haar drifts and rolls towards me. I take a deep breath. In time, in time I will be free.

2

Two months earlier – October

School for Joanna had always been somewhat farcical. With so many placement changes she was now expected to take her GCSEs with three different exam boards. Friendships, she had learned, were almost impossible when entering a ready-made society. The older you were the harder it was, and so of late she didn't bother to try, aware of the precariousness of her placement. At the whim of the foster parent she could be whisked back to residential home care in the blink of an eye. Stability and security did not exist for the LAC (looked-after child). The shrill sound of excited chatter greeted her late arrival to the form room followed rapidly by the scraping of chairs as all students responded to the buzzer indicating the first lesson. Joanna's daily reluctance to converse or respond beyond a cursory monosyllable to any of the students had ensured that she was left to herself, apart from the considerable efforts of Jessica and Clarissa, who had made it their mission to draw her into their social group. It half irritated and half amused Jo to see how hard they tried to include her even though she had made it blatantly obvious that she wasn't interested.

The monotone voice of the maths teacher drifted around the airless room. Joanna made play at responding by fiercely staring at her book and doodling with her pencil. It gave her time to think. Her morning had begun, as it had for the past few weeks, with her being the butt of unpleasant and cruel jibes and comments from her foster mother, Sally Whitworth and her real daughter Alex. Earlier that morning their vibrating voices, music and the boiling kettle had penetrated Joanna's dreams. Annoyed at this interruption she had turned over in bed, bleary-eyed, and glanced at the clock. Evidently it was time to move. She had screwed her eyes tight shut – listening. She recalled the morning ritual whereby Alex made every attempt to enter her locked room; clearly Alex had hoped that Jo would have mistakenly left it unsnibbed. However, the lock held while Joanna sank deeper into the bed. Alex's cold, insistent voice grated as she endeavoured to bring Joanna to the attention of her mother. Hanging on to the safe space of her dreams Joanna had gripped the duvet tighter round her skinny body. She recalled hearing the retreating footsteps that had given her a small reprieve. Inevitably a tirade from Alexandra's mother would reach her ears soon enough. Two more minutes of private heaven and then as expected, Alex's voice was joined by another, an equally cold but more tired one, that demanded she 'get up immediately'. Dragging herself from the comfort of her solitude she flicked the snib on her door and opened it.

She had eyed the grim face belonging to Sally Whitworth and, sneering behind her, Alex's smug one. Sally had grabbed Joanna by the shoulder and shaken her aggressively and hard. The tenor of Sally's voice had heightened as she off-loaded her enmity towards her. Again she expressed how sick of her she was and how fed up she was of having to haul her out of bed every day. The final threat of sending her back if she didn't behave was always the conclusion of the one-sided conversation. In controlled disdain Joanna glanced over Sally's shoulder and registered a satisfied smirk on Alex's face. Responding with nothing but a half shrug she found herself being aggressively pushed aside by Sally, who continued her tirade by grabbing clothes from the floor and back of Jo's chair, frustration being heard in unpleasant comments. It wouldn't be the first nor the last time that 'strangers' voiced their opinions about her 'sullenness', her 'slovenliness' and her 'ungratefulness' at their *kindness* towards her.

Back in the sleepy drone of the classroom Joanna pondered how tired she was of other people who were meant to have her best interests at heart. Glancing round the classroom she consciously observed how the rest of the class were using their time – not many were actually working on the maths questions. Mr Jackson was hanging over the two whiz kids in the far corner of the room.

Joanna slipped back into her own world as she recalled Sally's irritated voice screeching, 'Are you listening to me?', with Sally sounding and looking like a squawking bird, her thin lips spitting out, 'Three minutes, girl – organise yourself, get washed, dressed and eat your toast.' Both mother and daughter had left Joanna to it. 'And don't leave the tap running again!' came the final warning from Sally as Joanna moved purposefully to the bedroom sink. Joanna had buried her face in the wet flannel whilst overhearing Alex complaining to her mother that she wasn't firm enough and it wasn't fair that Joanna would get away with it yet again. *Get away with what precisely?* Joanna had wondered as she scrubbed her teeth. She glanced up at the mirror and noted her reflection. Sage green eyes stared back at her, along with a strong, pointed nose and mousy dark hair. Musing yet again on which of her parents she most resembled, she paused with her brush full of foaming white froth. The answer to that question would not be forthcoming any time soon. Her hair curled unhelpfully around the frame of her face and soaked up some of the foam. 'JOANNA, HERE, NOW!' echoed from the floor below. Joanna had thrown the brush into the sink, pulled off her nightclothes and yanked on the faded dark green uniform of Mary Rutherford College. Within seconds she was dragging her school bag behind her and as it hit each stair with a bump the tap, not fully turned off, dripped steadily. The whiff of toothpaste floated around her nostrils as a niggling thought troubled her – had she indeed turned off the offending tap?

She was jolted back to the here and now by the laughter of the class sniggering as she had failed to hear and respond to her teacher's request for an answer to a question he had directed to her. She jerked her head up to face the wrath of Mr Jackson. A strong whiff of mint reminded her that she still had toothpaste clinging to her hair. And absentmindedly she hooked the stray strands into her mouth with her tongue sucking off the residue. Her failure to reply to Mr Jackson had opened the doors for another dressing-down – this time about her inability to catch up with all the work she had missed on this particular module.

Idling down the corridor towards her next lesson, she teased herself over and over again as her mind exercised the possibilities of how she could discover her roots, and then she let the thought go. A fairy-tale scenario of a glorious reunion was her hope but the stark reality for her was much more basic. Her being born (obviously) then wrapped in a grubby jumper and placed in a plastic Woolworths bag before being dumped by a litter bin at the back of a park gave Joanna all the clues she needed as to how her mum had felt about her. That was her real drive to stay alive – the possibility of discovering these parents and demand to know why they had abandoned her. No matter how much she badgered the care home and her various social workers, none were in the least interested in helping discover her ancestry. And today, after the showdown that morning, her prospects were even more bleak as she recalled the drive to school earlier.

Eight thirty, belted up in the back of the battered Fiat Bravo, her eye had focused on a speck on the right window that drew her thoughts away from the babble in the car. Squashed in the back with a baby seat on either side, she had glanced at the child in the occupied one containing Jack, a pretty two-year-old boy whose murmurings disappeared into the hubbub of the engine noise and radio chatter. But the noise wasn't enough to drown out Sally promising Alex that she was not to worry as they would soon be rid of 'the pain'. Lost in thought about what that meant, Joanna had felt the violent sting of Sally's hand flicking across her legs. They had arrived at school. Most of Sally's final instructions were lost in the cold breeze that tore round her face, but the gist of it as far as she could gather was to ensure that she used her free lunch ticket as Sally was not cooking tonight. Nothing new there then. With that Joanna dragged herself out of the car and onto the pavement, where Alex already stood, holding her two bags and raising her eyebrows at her mother's instructions. Joanna watched as Sally Whitworth's face visibly relaxed as she leant over and retuned to 'Classic FM' and drove off without a backward glance, a trail of black exhaust fumes following her up the road.

Her arm had been gripped in a cruel vice by Alex's left hand while she dropped her bag onto the kerb with her right. She'd hissed at her, 'Loser, keep out of my sight'. Turning, she had stalked off in the direction of the main entrance hall where she joined the throng of students idling into the building. Pausing, aware of the group of giggling girls on the grassy bank, sniggering and whispering about her, Joanna bent down and dragged her bag from the pavement, then slung it over her shoulder, firmed her step and strode away from the gate. Once she had turned the corner and was out of sight she slowed down and dragged her heels, reflecting on her situation. Desolate and lonely, she didn't blame people like Alex for hating having a stranger foisted onto her family every few years and Alex had made her feelings known from the very beginning. It was all very predictable. Previous foster parents had all had their own problems and concerns, and Joanna was at the bottom of their list. They even had an acronym for her sort now – an LAC kid. This, her 'last chance' (as her social worker had put it), wasn't exactly working out. Sally Whitworth and her delightful daughter were not going to be her saving grace. Only Jim, Alex's father, had shown her any respect, but he was weak. The fear of being returned to an institutional care home haunted her.

The wind had begun to pick up when Joanna noticed a bedraggled dog skittering up the road that suddenly shot off the pavement and went under a car. The car skidded and stopped. A weird silence took over for a few seconds and then she observed, as if outside the bubble, horrified glances and audible gasps of people who had seen the accident. Watching the driver, a young man in a smart suit, opening the door and crouching by the front wheels desperately trying to drag the dog out, she felt pity for him, having to face that nightmare in his dreams forever more. With resignation Joanna had turned away and slowly walked back towards the school, leaving a small crowd of tearful and concerned onlookers. The dog, she mused, might survive, and so, if she were clever enough, might she.

Lining up for her next class, Joanna brightened up. English lessons had always been her solace. Bright and well-lit with many encouraging posters on the walls and ceiling, this room was a safe thinking place. Mrs Harry liked the sound of her own voice and hardly ever picked on anyone who didn't raise a hand. It was a chance to relax and listen. Today was no different; in front of every student was an onion. This was a poetry lesson, Mrs Harry informed the class, and the onion was a key factor in the first poem they were going to study. The reaction of the students was predictable, but they were also intrigued. A calm drifted over the class as Mrs Harry explained how she wanted the girls to proceed. Following the instructions, Joanna sniffed the onion. 'What do you notice?' encouraged Mrs Harry. She really expected it to smell like an onion, but it didn't. It smelt earthy and musty. Reflective suggestions continued and the students became closely involved in the minutiae of the onion, scribing their thoughts and responses. By the end of the lesson most of the girls had written a substantial commentary, culminating in a few of them (including Joanna) biting and eating into their onion. Mrs Harry, meanwhile, had collated the words and phrases from the students' musings, completing the lesson by reading from their intensive writing:

> It makes you cry
> It is encased in a paper-thin shell
> It is tough on the outside but soft and fragile on the inside
> It bruises
> It weeps
> It has deep hidden depths
> It repels, yet it is tangy
> I hate it – it smells it stings it hurts my throat
> You can't get rid of it…

Reading Carol Ann Duffy's poem 'Valentine' Mrs Harry emphasised the use of the onion as a metaphor for love. Handing out copies of the poem, she explained that their task was to recognise the sheer brilliance of rejecting superficial emblems of love (the 'satin heart' and the 'red rose') and experience the hard reality of what Duffy was exploring as real love, real commitment.

It was, though, an unexpectedly brutal reminder. 'You can't get rid of it' hit home. Real love. Commitment. Vulnerable and as if ripped open like a parcel, Joanna lost her equilibrium. At the buzzer she flew out of the classroom and made for the toilets. Flinging open the door, she shoved her way through a group of smokers about to light up in the interim between lessons.

'Bloody hell, what's that stink?' spat a tough-looking, angry, curly-haired blob of a girl called Mel. Sue, a fat, spotty-faced bully, made to grab Jo's arm but Joanna was in no mood for their petty jibes. Ignoring them all, she aimed for the far cubicle and bolted herself in. Clarissa, who had tried to keep up with Joanna's dramatic exit, burst into the toilet just as Mel had made her comment.

Having been on the receiving end of Mel and Sue's verbal racist jibes for many years, Clarissa recognised the cruel commentary being verbalised on their new focus. For Mel the choice between yelling at someone behind a closed door or attacking a body standing in front of her was an easy one to make. Clarissa was yanked by the arm and swirled round to face them all. Breathing hard and facing the group, she was about to say something when Sue coughed, recoiled, spat and said, 'You smell vile. You really do stink.'

Clarissa pulled her arm from Mel's grasp and said, 'Well, just be grateful that it covers up the stench of your cigarettes – Larkfield's on the prowl!'

Something flickered in Mel's eyes; she had history with Mrs Larkfield and they were already late for science. If they were much later Old Capson would give them hell. Mel made a quick decision, nodded to the others and, on leaving, turned to Clarissa and commented, 'Just you two watch it, okay?' The door slammed shut at their exit and a silence returned. Silence – except for a deep breathing, wheezing sound coming from the cubicle, where Joanna was tearing her nails along each arm in a frenzy, opening old scars, watching pin pricks of blood pop out of her skin, tears stinging her face and eyes. The pain of ripping at her tender skin offset the pain ripping through her head.

December

Following Joanna's dramatic attempt to save a life the area of the river was sectioned off. It was unclear as to how the boy had died or when; the authorities were treating the incident as a potential murder. So it was that in the early morning, runners and dog walkers of the village found their paths blocked by investigating officers and blue and white incident tape. Joanna's clothes and backpack had been gathered and taken to be reunited with her by a dutiful young police officer. It was his first 'on-site' investigation and he was determined to do this properly. His cursory examination of the backpack told him very little. He switched on the phone that he found and scanned through the numbers for some indication as to who Joanna was. Within seconds the battery died. Frustrated, he managed to note down the first six digits of the last number called. This might be a lead as to her name and her family. He threw the items into the back of the police car ready to take to the station for further examination with the hope of recharging the phone. On reflection, he mused as he drove towards Ashford Central Headquarters, her backpack did seem to hold an odd collection of items.

Mike had not slept. He and Guy had been taken by ambulance to the Conquest hospital in Hastings to be checked over, though neither had actually been in the river; they were soaked from their efforts in recovering the bodies, leaving them both shaking and shivering with shock. Guy's wife, Jenny, took the children to school as normal and then, mid-morning, drove to Hastings, where she collected two very saddened men. The knowledge that the boy had not been saved and that the girl, though alive, was in a critical condition numbed their emotions. Mike supplied coffee for the investigating team and sandwiches as well as answers to myriad questions with which he was being bombarded. Focus was now on the pub, as that was the last place the boy had been seen alive. Had Mike noticed how much he had been drinking? Was there a drugs problem that Mike may have been aware of? Was Mike aware of the age of his customers? And so on and on it went. The euphoria of the evening before dissipated and Mike felt more and more disheartened as well as totally distraught by the unnecessary death. The pub soon filled up as the morning wore on with people anxious to discover the truth of the previous evening's events. Some were morbidly curious, others just wanted to catch what notoriety they could from the surge of reporters and television crew that had assembled into the car park of the pub. Admitting that they had not witnessed anything, there still seemed to be a need for the world to know what they had heard – which just happened to have been the sirens and wail of the emergency services. Camera teams from local news stations turned up in their droves and reporters from all aspects of the media made their way into the tiny village and disturbed the inhabitants' peaceful and somewhat uneventful lives. Six hours later the police (having satisfied themselves that Mike had not knowingly sold to underage drinkers) began to take a different approach and thanked him for his heroic and brave attempt at saving lives. The boy sadly had died but certainly the girl, if she survived, would owe her life to him. Just a few more moments in those conditions and she would have gone too. However, she was not out of danger yet and it was taking some time for her to regain consciousness – if she would at all.

October

Had Joanna known what was to occur over the next few months of her life, she may well have not taken to the streets in the way that she did. It may have been the opening of old desires to hunt down her parents that gave her the stoic resolve to go walkabout. Or perhaps she had met enough damaged people in her short life that she recognised in Sally the early signs of derangement that would put her real daughter in danger and open up the cracks in her own life. Who knows, but clearly Joanna felt unsafe at her foster home. Having relieved herself of the two girls that morning, Sally had headed straight for Martha's Nursery in Elphinstone Street. Her sponsor, Martha, had been a true friend, though recently there had arisen an unspoken animosity between them. Martha couldn't quite put her finger on it, but Sally was always on the defensive in every issue. Martha, dependable and supportive, never charged Sally the full cost of nursery care. Even so, the price of a full day was prohibitive and ate into her foster payments. Sally only used her services when desperate. Her intended visit to social services was just such desperation and she didn't want to be encumbered by Jack.

Martha welcomed Sally like a long-lost friend and immediately offered coffee and toast. Accepting, Sally looked with envy around the beautiful, state-of-the-art kitchen. The slam of the back door broke her thoughts when a voice spoke from under a red rain hat. 'Weather gets you down, sunny one minute and streaming the next.' This was Elsie, the kindly but fussy play leader. Sally, conscious of time and anxious to 'do the deed', blurted out her need to drive to Bexhill to meet up with her social worker. Sally knew that without an appointment this seemed to be a desperate call. Martha had understood what that meant.

Frowning, she glanced at Sally but only stated, 'You are her last hope, you know.' Sally let out an exasperated sigh. Martha could never understand how Sally had been lulled into this situation and that it was torturing her. And really blast the woman – who was she to be so judgemental?

In her head Sally fumed. *It is all wrong. She is wrong. Wrong for me, for Alex for Jim and for herself. I can't help her. I don't like her and I want rid.* But all she actually acknowledged to Martha was, 'Yes, I am well aware of that fact, thank you.'

Martha turned and handed Sally a coffee whilst hoicking her ample body onto the stool by the breakfast bar and staring quizzically at her.

'Oh, come on, don't look at me like that,' said Sally, shaking her head somewhat despairingly. 'You don't know what it's like. I cannot like the girl and I don't want her messing up my family anymore. What is wrong with being honest?' Martha sipped her coffee and said nothing. Martha's look and earlier comment was too much for Sally; she reached for her bag, opened it and placed a ten-pound note on the side then said, 'Thanks for having Jack – I'll forgo the coffee, Martha. I'll be back within two hours, but now I must dash.' And with that she flew out the door, unlocked the Bravo, stepped inside, belted up, turned on the ignition and reversed out of the drive. Martha, observing her from the window, watched until the car vanished from sight.

*

'Look, Joanna, come on, open this door.'

'I'm not here for my health, you know. Jessica told me to come after you or I wouldn't be here. So please just come out now.' Silence.

'I am going to be in real trouble, I am now twenty minutes late for history and you know what Lappin's like.'

'Well, you're going to have to come out sooner or later – so why not now? What did we eat it for? You stink, I stink and now I feel sick. I only ate it 'cos you did. What is it with you? Can't you just be normal for once?'

*

Sally, at thirty-six years old, was a mess. Inside she felt empty and a dark fog often drifted into her head. Finding the daily routine of kids tedious and uneventful, she became resentful and bitter. Jim as a provider was able enough, but he was so boring – she often questioned whether she really loved him. Bullied at work, he never aspired to anything much and missed out on promotion opportunities because of it. Basically he was a good man but with no life in him. Alex was born the year after they had married. It had been a birthing experience so traumatic Sally emphatically refused to repeat it. Jim wanted more children. The compromise was obvious – fostering. It would bring in some income and provide siblings for Alex. Sally could stay at home and get paid for looking after little tots. It was okay at first – nothing too long-term or permanent as they were the transition between birth parents and prospective adoptive parents – perfect. Yet as Sally began to reflect she found it boring and frustrating being stuck at home. She needed a career – a focus in her life, something to dispel the darkness that often entered her head.

After a review Yvonne had suggested they take on older children closer to Alex's age, creating less pressure during the day. It could mean friendships for Alex and free day-time hours for Sally. That was just the worst suggestion ever. Sally found the teenagers difficult to handle and very needy, and Jim was far too soft. Not surprisingly Alex resented them one hundred per cent. The house became a place of misery. Ironically the empty day-time hours were the worst thing for Sally and she began to have darker and darker moments of despair – a feeling she hid from everyone. Then came the offer to take Jack, a toddler, for a short-term stay whilst his mother went into hospital. The money had increased and would be useful so she had agreed. But they had complicated the issue with Joanna. 'She has been in seventeen different homes, a few care homes and is now almost unplaceable,' Yvonne, the social worker, stated the night she rang Sally in desperation. 'We want to give her one last try in a family home before returning her to the care home. She's a lovely girl but very quiet and withdrawn. She seems to have given up on herself. I think that with Alex, you and Jim, there is the home that she has never had.' Something in that sad statement had moved Sally, who had replied in the affirmative, yet even as she did so she had known that it was not what she wanted at all. To this day, Sally had no idea what had possessed her in that dark moment to agree.

With a grim determination to end this awful situation she drove along the crowded busy coast road. The sun hung low and glinted on the sea that lapped at the pebbles. A cold yet beautiful sky gave no hint of the rain to come. Waves shivered to and fro, hushing as they swept through the fragments of stone and shingle. It was brightening up, though Sally hardly noticed as she crawled through the slow-moving traffic, frustrating her efforts to get to Bexhill. Two months overdue, the bypass construction mocked the queue of commuters as they were teased by its outdated completion time, heralded by posters and signs. Nagging in the back of her mind was the fact that neither Martha nor Jim understood what she was going through. Her irrational thoughts and rages that she shared with no-one frightened her. Joanna had to go. She convinced herself that all she needed was to be the three of them again – a happy family, then all the disturbing thoughts she had would dissipate and life would go back to normal (she had forgotten how much she had hated what 'normal' meant).

Reversing into the only space left in the car park, she opened the window a fraction and then it did what she knew it would do, what it always did – it flew right down to the bottom and refused to wind up again. Further frustration welled. Clouds had drifted over and the sky darkened. It would only be a short shower, but enough to soak her driver's seat if the window stayed down. Pulling hard on the two centimetres of glass protruding from the opening, it shifted a tad, then slipped back again. Glancing at her watch she furiously grabbed a 'bag for life' from the back of the car and, after scrabbling through the glove box, came out with a blob of blue tac. Ingeniously she sealed the gaping window space with a Sainsbury's bag and the blue tac. She neither knew nor cared if it would hold but left the car to the mercy of the weather and entered the foyer.

Reception was buzzing with energy: phones ringing, computers clicking, voices reverberating and people queuing. Her eyes were drawn to a boldly printed notice above the receptionist's head: 'Zero tolerance. No abusive language or behaviour.' To the right of that a further notice declared, 'An appointment is essential. Please queue to make yours. No appointment – no interview.' In no mood for queuing or being turned away, Sally's reaction was explosive as the girl behind the glass window asked for her "'pointment details, perlease'. On realising Sally didn't have one, without eye contact or another word, the girl pointed to the notice. Calling out 'next' in a clipped voice, she dismissed Sally with a wave of her hand. Furious and boiling with anger, Sally created a scene by threatening, to anyone who would listen, that she would return the foster children in her care that very afternoon if she wasn't able to get an interview with Yvonne Peralta as a matter of urgency! Yvonne, as it turned out, was in a meeting and unavailable. Such was Sally's belligerence that she was invited to wait until Yvonne's deputy would see her. The murmurings that followed made her smile inside. How dare they! A heaviness flooded her mind and she stared at the floor. After what seemed like an age a young, fresh-faced girl – could she really be old enough to work here? – proffered her hand to Sally and invited her into the office.

Thirty minutes later, mostly satisfied with the outcome, Sally left the building with the promise that Yvonne would call on her way home that evening after she had finished her meeting. The car awaited her with the Sainsbury's bag still intact, though the drive back was remarkably cool and draughty. Stoically she drove back to face the wrath of Martha that she knew would be hostile and unforgiving, but she held a sense of some relief inside her. The dark cloud – the one in her head and the one in the sky – abated briefly.

*

The toilet door opened and a voice whispered, 'Clarri, Clarissa, are you in here?'

'Yep, I sure am – over here, Jess.' Clarissa beckoned Jessica over to the cubicle door that was held fast shut.

'What's going on? Where is Joanna?'

Clarissa jerked her thumb towards the toilet door. 'I tell you, this girl is barking. She's been locked up in there almost thirty minutes and there's not a sound from her. Honest, she is totally off her rocker.'

Jessica knocked on the closed cubicle door. 'Jo, it's me, Jessica.' Silence.

Clarissa shrugged her shoulders in an 'I told you so' kind of way. Looking at her nails and back up to Jessica, she uttered, 'She won't come out. I've told you, she has refused to budge.' Jessica spoke to the closed door. 'If Larkfield finds us we'll all be in trouble. Come on out.'

Clarissa raised her eyebrows and screwed up her face in a grimace. Suddenly the door swung open and, as predicted, in strode Mrs Larkfield. Her immediate response had been surprise. She had expected to catch girls smoking, then when she realised that they had just skived lessons her anger rose until the cubicle door clicked open and Joanna revealed herself. Larkfield was incandescent; her voice became shriller than ever. The inevitable followed. Mrs Larkfield frogmarched all three girls to wait outside the deputy head's door, where she left them while she retreated to the staff room to clean herself up from the onion that Joanna had vomited over her shoes.

He had wiped the smile off her face again. An attempt to get into her head was futile, she told him. Her inner voice, her real self was there and he couldn't ever prise it out. Then he struck.

That night she buried her third.

3

December

Having decided on her imminent move Joanna had taken most of her food stash to her new 'home', the barn at the end of Toad Hill. Returning to her boat for the last time she packed her rucksack with her scant clothes and cooking equipment, plus the lamp and other odds and ends that she had found useful on the boat. She spent the afternoon sleeping and eating, running over in her mind her planned course of action. To move out at night was the best option and preferably as late as possible. The boat was now a stinking hell hole and bitterly cold, with wind, rain and, at times, snow drifting in through the weak casing. Added to which there was an increase of pedestrians wandering the village from the pub, the village hall and the church as the events leading up to Christmas seemed to be in full swing. With that in mind she decided that around midnight would be the safest time to leave the boat. Anyone reeling out of the pub would hardly be curious or bothered by her wandering along and she could just slip away from the heart of the village to the barn, no questions asked.

Observing the activity around the barn for some weeks Jo had deduced that it was mainly used to store straw and hay, of which there was a substantial amount. An added bonus was a cold-water tap at the far end, which, as long as it didn't freeze, would be very useful. A tangle of farm machinery, both good and broken, was stacked at the other end. It was a big space but seemingly neglected and badly in need of refurbishment. The doors at the front were half broken and one part entirely missing. The wind hurled through but it was big enough to hold a straw wall that Jo had built from the bales, affording protection from the elements. It hadn't been easy, for they were extremely heavy to move. She had pulled and pushed and heaved for many hours in order to get the tiny cave-like 'room' together. Then there was the added job of surrounding it with a higgledy-piggledy bundle of bales to disguise her hideout. No-one had been in the barn for several weeks. The only activity seemed to be on a Saturday morning, when a man pulled up in a jeep, jumped out and loaded the first bale of straw he could grab onto the trailer and drove up the hill to the field on the left, where he then entered a small chicken run and scattered the straw. What else he did to the chickens Jo didn't know, for she tried to keep well out of sight. Clearly staying there she wouldn't be disturbed so long as she ensured there was a handy bale left close to the entrance each week. At least she could be safe for the winter. She hoped the farm machinery might not be required until spring.

*

At the police station Dennis, the novice police officer, had read out his observations to his sergeant and itemised the contents of Joanna's bag. He also informed his sergeant that he had written down the last number that she had called on her phone, having charged up the battery. He had rung it once but it went to answerphone. Both he and his sergeant had examined what little they had on the girl and came up with nothing much. But then the sergeant quizzed Dennis over why she would have been there at that time of night in such a remote place. He also quizzed him on what he felt about her as a person, for it was Dennis who had supported her body as she was dragged from the boat. He had initially laid her down on the frosted grass where he had placed his jacket. He had wiped her hair back from her cold, cold face. With great intent he had initiated mouth-to-mouth until the paramedics arrived. In the cool light of the day Dennis found it hard to control his emotions. What if she didn't survive? What if he had not used the appropriate action and procedure? It had been his first fatality and mouth-to-mouth on a real human being. Yet she felt as cold and unresponsive as the dummies in training school. Back in the office he was now being berated for having not used the obligatory mask over her face in the resuscitation. The first point of any contact with another body had to be protection of one's self. Especially, so the sergeant went on, when it was clear that the girl was a down-and-out. This comment startled Dennis and he raised his eyes to meet his sergeant's in an act of defiance. 'I don't think that is a fair comment, Sarge,' he responded.

'No? Didn't you see the state of her hair, her nails? Didn't you smell the contents of her bag? And come to that, how would you account for the contents? Or the lack of them? What was she doing, clearly packed up, ready to fly, at that time of night? And more importantly, where had she emerged from?'

Dennis looked away. He hadn't given any of those pointers a thought. What a police officer he was turning out to be. Of course the sergeant was correct. Her bag was full of items that would suggest an outdoor adventure – but at this time of year? No, this was definitely a runaway's survival kit bag, added to which there lacked any paperwork, any identification as to who she was. Not even a name.

'Right then, Sarge – shall I call the number again and see what we get?'

The sergeant nodded in agreement and then asked Dennis to tell him exactly what he was going to say to the recipient of his call. Dennis thought about it. Basic training. What did he desire from the conversation? Information. How was he to get the confidence and assurance of this Jamie person to reveal who the girl was? Especially if she was homeless or a runaway. And there was the other option that the phone was not hers anyway and might well have been stolen. First Dennis suggested that they contact the hospital and get an update. If she had died there would then be all the more urgency to discover who she was. The response from the hospital call left him no option. The girl was still unconscious and on a ventilator. Her body temperature had risen and she had a stronger pulse, but the doctors were not holding their breath for a full recovery. They had no idea how long she had been in the water but if it was anything like as long as the dead boy her chances were small. She also seemed to be undernourished and emaciated which would also hinder her recovery. He was then informed that the post-mortem on the boy would be delayed due to pressure of an NHS in financial crisis, lack of staff and time of year. All they would say was that he had a deep wound to the back of his head. Whether it was inflicted before entering the water or as he entered, they couldn't say for sure at present, meaning it was still a murder enquiry.

October

Her shirt sleeves now pulled down over her wrists to cover up the reopened scars her nails had caused, Joanna was now in control of her emotions. Reeling from the effect Mrs Harry's lesson on 'love' metaphors had had on her, she determined not to be caught unawares again. Robert Bentley had entered the area via the office door and startled all three of them. Clarissa had begun to verbalise their excuses but he just turned and headed off towards his room, requesting them to follow. Robert sat down in his swivel chair clasping his hands in front of him. Jessica stood by the filing cabinet, looked him straight in the eyes and smiled. Clarissa, breathing heavily and constantly mumbling under her breath, shuffled her feet and side-glanced at Jessica. Joanna just stared vacantly at the picture on the wall above Robert's head.

'So', he began, 'would each of you in turn like to give me an explanation of what exactly you were doing this morning and why you took it upon yourselves to miss period 2?'

Robert Bentley was a good man. A teacher for thirty-three years and deputy head for two, he had found the task of dealing with sad cases onerous and gut-wrenching. He was a sucker. All his colleagues said so, but he wouldn't have it any other way.

'It's people we are dealing with here,' he used to say. 'People, not animals.'

The obvious retort always followed: 'Well, when they behave like people I'll treat them like people.'

He couldn't get it through to some of his staff that all children needed was to be understood and loved. There were times, however, when even his temper was tried. Swearing and foul-mouthed, disrespectful abuse he found very hard to tolerate, and unfortunately that was becoming more common, but when he came across an unfortunate like Joanna, he was a softy. Joanna wasn't like anyone else he had come across. She didn't scream abuse, nor attack other students, and by reading her file she had every reason to feel aggrieved. No, Joanna just didn't *do* anything. There were reports of 'incidents' with her foster sister Alex, which, it seemed, were mainly screaming outbursts of complaints from Alex towards Joanna.

Bentley interrupted the words spilling out of Jessica's mouth and asked her to clarify the reason why it took both girls forty-five minutes to make sure that Joanna was 'okay'. Clarissa looked down at her feet and then at Jessica. Robert Bentley turned his full attention towards Joanna. She never moved her gaze from the photograph above his head. Her silence became loud and, along with her refusal to look at him, belligerent. Bentley sighed and picked up a file on his desk; glancing through it his attention was caught by the stark information about her laid bare in front of him. He began reading a letter from the file to himself. Jessica and Clarissa took this opportunity to glare at Joanna and raise their eyebrows as if to encourage her to say something.

Bentley scratched his right ear and said in a soft voice, 'It states here that you have moved into this area from London just a matter of a few weeks ago. Furthermore, I see that you have been to several other schools – this being, what, your sixteenth placement?'

Joanna dropped her eyes and, staring straight into his, as if in defiance, corrected him. 'Eighteen. Eighteen schools and now twenty-one homes – if you can call a "care home" home.'

She had caught their attention. The shocking fact of what she had just uttered struck home. Resuming her pose of neutrality Joanna stared at a space on the wall, the bit between the certificate for excellence and the school photograph of ten years previous, where Bentley looked a much younger and more handsome man.

Robert Bentley, formally but kindly, dismissed Jessica and

Clarissa, leading them by the gesture of his hand towards the open door that he firmly closed behind them.

'Joanna, what shall we do with you?' he mumbled as he returned to his chair, crossing his arms and sitting back. 'Tell me,' he soothed, 'what can we do to help you?'

Joanna turned her head and with a wry smile shrugged her shoulders and said in a winsome voice, 'Find who I belong to… find my mum.'

*

Following her interview with Bentley Joanna was sent to the school nurse to attend to her now-bleeding arms. Consequently she did not turn up for her PE lesson. There was no chance for Clarissa or Jessica to talk to each other the whole of the double lesson as they were in the throes of circuit training. Jessica was hoping to get picked for the county athletic trials and so she put her heart and soul into her efforts, leaving Clarissa to join the 'almost made it' group alongside Mel, Sue and gang. Clarissa had forgotten the altercation in the toilets and was annoyed at having given them ammunition to fire at her. Inheriting her South American father's skin tone ensured that Clarissa was the butt of these nasty girls' venom. In fact, she was proud of her Latin connections, but these particular girls tried to make her feel abnormal and dirty. Hastings, she felt, was a bit like that. Though there were many international language schools and immigrants from all walks of life in the town, a few families were resistant to anyone non-white. In fact, Hastings was an island that few born there ever left.

Now as the girls turned the rope for her to skip she knew they would take this opportunity to hurt her. For each turn of the rope Mel, in a low and menacing voice, grunted, 'Two-tone bitch, go home, bitch, two tone no home, skank.' With each turn Clarissa tried to jump, allowing Sue to lift the rope higher and retort, 'Jump, bitch, jump'. Clarissa was desperate to keep up with the movement of the rope, for failing to do so would result in her tripping and being whipped by the rope. By the fourth round Clarissa could no longer respond with efficiency and at the final jump, her toes caught and she went face down in a heap at

Sue and Melissa's feet. Both girls circled round her with the pretence of helping her; their feet pummelled into her ribs and toed her viciously.

'Hey, girls, what's happening here?' queried Miss Johnson as she leapt over towards their group. 'Ah, Clarissa, you were doing so nicely. Do try to keep the momentum going. Now, let's see what you can do, Mel, whilst Clarissa and Sue hold the rope. I'll be back to check on you in a mo.' And with that she turned and blew her whistle in the direction of the next group of girls, who were wall climbing.

Clarissa pulled herself up from the floor and grabbed one end of the rope. Mel, with a cocky grin on her face, stated, 'Say one word, Miss Latin-tino, and you're dead meat.'

In contrast, Jessica's morning had improved with the confirmation that as long as she attended the trials on Thursday she was almost certain of a place in the school team. Clarissa was as good a runner as her but her skills were never seen in school. Outside both girls met up regularly three times a week and ran around Alexander Park on several circuits, racing against each other, with each other and against the clock. At times Clarissa showed more stamina than Jess. But in school she never bothered. Vaguely aware that Clarissa had what she called 'issues' with some other students, Jess never questioned it. Invariably they both vied with each other in the park run along the Hastings seafront, both within seconds of each other. Clarissa bolted as soon as the lesson ended but Jessica had to wait to get information about her forthcoming athletics event, missing the opportunity to talk to Clarissa about the disturbing revelation they had both heard in Bentley's office.

Rushing her shower, she scurried towards the dinner queue, which she scanned until it was evident that Joanna wasn't in it. Outside the weather was blustery and uninviting, but Jess had a hunch that that would be where she could have headed. Grabbing a sandwich from the snack counter and paying at the till, Jess stuffed her lunch into her bag and aimed for the back entrance, eyeing the ever-growing crowd of faces swarming into the canteen for Clarissa, but with no luck.

The air was slightly chilly and the north-easterly wind found the gaps in her T-shirt, jumper and skirt, drying the residue from the shower on Jessica's body. She headed up towards the oak trees that stood proud against the science labs where very few students ventured due to them being locked over lunch, and in this weather no-one wanted to be outside. 'At least anyone in their right mind,' muttered Jessica to herself. She turned round and, as she had predicted, spied Joanna sitting at the base of the tree, hugging her knees, her eyes fixed straight ahead and tearing her dinner ticket into tiny pieces.

Throwing her bag down on the grass she sat herself beside Joanna. 'Budge up so I can lean against the tree too,' she demanded.

Joanna did so. Dragging her wiry, reddish brown hair behind her ears, she pulled her bag towards her and took out the sandwiches. Both pairs of eyes were honed on the bullies, Mel, Sue, and their gang, as they huddled against the school fence trying to light up cigarettes in the prevailing wind.

'Class idiots – want some?' Jess asked Joanna. She tore open the cellophane on the sandwich wrapper and, without waiting for a reply, rammed half a sandwich into Joanna's hand. Joanna made as if to ignore her, but then, after one look at Jessica's 'no-nonsense' face, took the proffered food. She bit into the bread and tasted the tomato and grated cheese. It covered the sour taste of the onion that had clung to the roof of her mouth all morning. Gratefully, she finished the half and then waited for the expected usual questions people always asked. Jessica did open up a conversation but not quite as Joanna expected.

Showing no inquisitiveness towards Joanna, Jessica instead focused on her own worries. Jessica revealing her dislike of school was an eye-opener for Joanna. Her dreams of being a real athlete she felt were hampered by the continuing focus on her GCSEs, in which her parents expected her to achieve high grades. On top of which, they couldn't afford for her to join a decent running club and so all her training was reliant on school clubs. Taking out the second sandwich she tore that also in two and handed over a half to Joanna, who was fully engrossed in listening as Jessica revealed how her older sister had got into York University and how her parents now had similar hopes for her in following in her sister's footsteps.

Both girls ate in silence for a time and then Jess mentioned how Clarissa, her best friend, was bullied because of her race which they never mentioned as there was nothing either of them could do about it. She wished that Clarissa would get a grip and get on with living – it was so frustrating. Jessica found Clarri's stubborn resistance to achieving in school a pain, when she clearly had the ability to be a brilliant athlete.

Further silence followed. The weather became inclement and drizzly but neither of the girls seemed bothered. A small pause broke the tension when, having dropped in a comment about her brother Jamie's aspirations to be a musician, Jessica slipped in the question Joanna knew would come. 'Now what about you? Why did you run out of class today?' Jessica turned her head towards Joanna, who, having concentrated hard on all that Jessica had said, was caught slightly off guard.

Her impromptu reply of, 'I dunno, scared, I think,' gave Jessica the opportunity to face her and urge her to open up.

'Go on,' she prompted. Dropping her gaze, she watched the pieces of torn dinner ticket that were beginning to take flight on the breeze swirling around them.

Joanna spoke. 'Look, it is obvious I won't be here much longer and I have no idea where I will end up this time. This was my "last chance", as they say.' She continued with little emotion, 'And it has gone, but I'm not going to let them put me in the home again – ever. I'd rather die,' she uttered. Suddenly she gritted her teeth and stood up. 'You don't get it – being "looked after" is a joke. There are too many of us and not enough of them... easy money for a while until you've saved up for the holiday or the car – short-term placement so you don't have to commit – I'm sick of it.' She stopped, and before Jessica could respond, with hair blowing in the cold wind, running up towards them blundered Clarissa. The moment had passed. With the drizzle turning into heavier waves of cold rain all three grabbed their bags and ran towards the entrance back into school.

*

Joanna wasn't wrong in her assessment of how she had been passed from minder to carer to parent. As if to support the careless way LAC children were placed, Robert Bentley, in consultation with Sybil

Larkfield, had had to circulate a round robin to all Joanna's teachers in response to a request from social services as to how Joanna was performing. This coming so soon after her last appraisal had all the signs of her being on the move again. Robert Bentley shared with Sybil what little information Joanna had proffered earlier. 'And now after umpteenth homes it looks like she is going to be placed back into an institutional care home. It doesn't bear thinking about.'

Sybil coloured slightly and crossed her legs, straightening her skirt as she did so, avoiding eye contact with Robert Bentley when she said, 'I do believe that some staff here have misjudged that girl.' Knowing that Sybil was one of them, Robert just smiled ruefully.

However, the reason that Joanna did take flight and run that very evening was because of an accumulation of events that no-one could have predicted, heralding the total breakdown of the Whitworth family, pre-empting Alex's disastrous encounter with Assef and the despicable revelation of child slavery. The accumulative course of events began with Sally.

*

On her return from social services Sally had parked some way from the nursery. Pulling on the hand brake, ignition off, the radio silenced, she sat and took in her surroundings observing the road. The 'posh' end of Hastings. A smile, albeit cynical, stretched across her face. *Look at this place – how the other half live.* She stretched her legs, shook off her shoes and leant over, fumbling through the glove compartment, retrieving a packet of cigarettes that she had confiscated from Alex. The crumpled packet was wedged at the back. She grabbed one out of the six that was more or less whole. Her fumbled, shaky attempts at lighting up finally worked. She drew in a long, deep breath of smoke, until, angry with herself for being so pathetic, she wound down the passenger window and chucked out the offensive stick. Burying her head in her hands she almost screamed out loud. She felt an abject failure on every count. Her head ached and the 'black dog' loomed over her.

A knock on the passenger window made Sally leap out of her skin. She looked up and saw Elsie standing there in her coat and gloves, smiling. Sally wound down the window.

'Thought it was you,' Elsie said. 'Just left your little one in a lovely sleep. I'm off home now, no point in staying as there isn't that much to do today. Martha can cope now and it's my afternoon at bingo. Wish me luck and then we can all go on a cruise. Bye, love.'

'Oh, yeah, bye.' Sally smiled and Elsie waddled down the road, her 'save the world' bag swinging at her side.

Leaning back, Sally glanced at her mobile phone. No messages. Further up the street Sally watched as Becky then left the house. Martha was alone. With a deep sigh Sally went to face the music. Locking the car she reflected that the window on the driver's side could stay open, with the bag taped across it; there was no chance that anyone would want to nick it and besides, the rain had stopped.

*

Having managed to persuade Martha to support her in her pleas to get rid of Joanna, she arrived home in a better frame of mind. Placing Jack in his playpen with an encouraging pat on his head, she turned to go up the stairs to make the beds when her foot squelched on the stair carpet and water oozed around her shoes. She put her hand down to touch the mark. It was wringing wet! As she glanced up the stairs she realised that the whole lot was sodden. Running up the stairs to Joanna's room and pulling open the door, it was just as she knew it would be. The sink was overflowing and water cascaded over the bowl and out of the door, soaking the stair carpet. The toothbrush was bobbing about on the surface of the full and overflowing bowl and the flannel was acting as a plug. As predicted, the cold tap was running. Sally was seething. She yanked the tap closed and dragged the flannel out of the sink, whereupon the water stopped dripping over the side and plummeted down the plug hole. 'I'll kill her, I'll bloody kill her'. Had there been any chance of Yvonne persuading Sally to keep Joanna, that had now been quelled. Spending the best part of two hours extracting and mopping up the water from the stairs and bedroom floor had further inflamed Sally's chagrin.

*

Joanna was debating quite what to do. Deliberately dawdling down the now empty corridor, she was thinking hard. She recognised the whispered interruptions in her classes, the furtive looks at her and the writing in the report book as signs of her impending departure. Past experience validated her thoughts. Dithering in the entrance hall and dragging her bag down the steps and with no control over what her near future held, she dragged herself up the path. At what speed would she be extricated from the Whitworths she couldn't imagine. It was risky to even go back to them as her previous placement had ended abruptly and this may too. Inside she felt a dread and anger at having to leave yet another school and another attempt at belonging. Looking up she recognised Jessica was waiting at the school gates. The rain had stopped but there was an icy wind coming up from the sea end and Jessica looked frozen.

'Hi, Jo.'

'Hi.'

Jessica linked her arm through Joanna's and they began to walk down the hill. The wind was too strong to enable them to hear themselves speak so they pushed on in silence until they turned the corner and into the alley. The wind lessened and Jessica invited Joanna to hers for tea. Joanna smiled and shook her head; in an exasperated but flat tone Joanna explained how she couldn't as her foster parent would have to make the 'arrangements' with her mum first and then other complications would set in.

'Okay then, perhaps I can come back with you then and meet her? That would be a start. Then I could get my mum to phone her later?'

Joanna, horrified, shook her head…

They continued to walk in silence until they reached the park. Light was fading in the October dusk and there was a keen sense of winter in the air – the forecast had been for snow on higher ground, which sent hope through all the students, but it was rare for Hastings, being so close to the sea, and being 'snowed in' never actually materialised. The wind chill was bitter and both Joanna and Jessica were feeling it through their thin school uniform. Nevertheless Joanna directed their path to the bench by the pond and sat down staring at the water, clearly not in a rush to get home. Jessica, feeling very cold, didn't want to stay in this freezing, open space, but before she could protest a dull whisper emanated from Joanna that chilled Jessica more than the wind.

'You won't see me again.' Joanna began in a monotone. 'I'm not wanted at the Whitworths' but I'm not going back to the home. So I'm off – one way or another.' Then she turned and stared Jessica in the face. 'You are the only person I have told and if I get prevented I shall know why.' Joanna looked into Jessica's eyes and the cold glint that sparked in them sent a shudder down Jessica's spine. 'This is no game,' Joanna continued. 'It is my life for what it's worth. I really liked the sandwich, and the chat, but the idea of us being friends is ridiculous.'

Joanna was ready to run off in a moment, but Jessica, shocked by the severity and determination of her voice, was semi-prepared for such a move. She grabbed Joanna's bag and then her arm and pulled her back to the bench.

'Listen to me, Jo.' Grabbing Joanna by both shoulders, as they were face-to-face she stated, 'You cannot just up and go – not like this, not in this weather and not without my helping you. I won't let you do it. If you must go away, then let's plan it together. I can help. Please, please don't do this,' implored Jessica. A lump of mud came hurtling through the air and just missed Jessica's ear.

She turned to face Mel, Sue, Carla, Becky and Tracy. 'Bloody hell, Jessica, never took you for no lez,' Mel retorted. The others laughed and spun on their heels, ambling towards the entrance, kicking a can as they went, filling the air with abusive and derogatory comments all the way out of the park. Joanna took the opportunity to escape from Jessica's grasp. She grabbed her bag and belted off in the opposite direction. By the time Jessica had gathered her wits she realised Joanna had reached the far exit.

*

Back at the Whitworths' Jack had sensed the panic and had begun to at first whimper then scream. Ignoring him, Sally set to with a vengeance. Manic rage overtook her and only when she had sufficiently cleared most of the water did she relent and take him in her arms to pacify him. Jack's large eyes were full of fear and his hiccoughing tears filled her with guilt. 'Nasty girl, we'll be rid of her soon, Jack, it's all her fault. Nasty, vile girl.' Automatically Sally patted his back and murmured soothing words. They sat together on the settee, Jack sucking his thumb and leaning on Sally's arm as she flicked through a picture book with him.

Ten minutes later the front door opened and Alex entered, calling out that she had brought Laura home for tea. Too late, Sally heard Laura's giggles and knew that she could hardly say no with the girl actually in the house. 'Blimey, Mum, it stinks like wet dog in here.'

'Lady muck left the tap running,' spat Sally.

'When are you going to get rid of that stupid bitch? Ah, wet dog, bitch – do you get it?' Alex doubled up at the doorway with laughter. 'I told you she was a waste of space.'

'She ate an onion in English and chucked up on Larkfield,' Laura preened.

'Ate an onion? Where did she get an onion from? And where is she? Didn't you walk home together? Alex, take Jack from me a moment.'

Sally informed Alex that she would have to make do with sandwiches for tea as she had the social worker calling round. Alex raised her eyebrows at Laura, nodded and put Jack in his highchair.

'Laura and I have a bit of homework to do then we thought we might pop down to the youth club in Warrior Square at seven – okay?' wheedled Alex.

Sally paused, looked at them both quizzically and then agreed. It might be advantageous not to have them around when she handed Joanna back to Yvonne. Both girls raided the kitchen for tea and biscuits then disappeared, giggling, up to Alex's room. Sally's anger further built once again towards Joanna as she wondered where in hell was she?

4

Frustrated and rather irritated by the government official's dismissive attitude, social worker Yvonne Peralta had been unable to get the support she required. The 'target' and the 'focus' and the paperwork that was now a major part of her job was overwhelming. How was she supposed to get it all achieved and still find time to place all her children in viable homes? Mr Eckersley had no answer to that. 'But,' he assured her, 'I am sure that you will manage, as you always do.'

To top it all, on arrival back to her office she had the temporary replacement of her assistant tell her that she had to visit Sally Whitworth on her way home. 'It's something to do with Joanna,' was all the information she could glean. Joanna! Yvonne's eyes had rolled and she immediately got on the phone to the school that Joanna had been placed in. Requesting a written report on her progress, she half smiled when she heard that she had actually vomited on Mrs Larkfield. Poor kid. It would be dreadful if she were to be moved again. Yvonne, though, was confident that Sally and her family would hang on to Joanna for the duration of her care. Another move would be bad news and Yvonne was trying to avoid her going back to the home where she had (if she were to be believed) a torrid time. Yvonne began to tackle the shedloads of paperwork piled on her desk, floor and filing cabinet. She sighed – when were they going to move into the twenty-first century and go paperless?

*

The atmosphere at Joanna's 'home' was fraught. The group of faces that met her indicated quite clearly that she was in real trouble – again!

'Where the hell have you been?' came from Alex.

Sally, who was standing by the fridge with Jack in her arms, wheeled round and turned on her immediately. 'You left that tap running this morning' she hissed. 'Just as I knew you would. I warned you. I remember telling you to make sure you turned it off. But no, Miss High and Mighty doesn't listen. She NEVER listens! And what did I come home to? I'll tell you what. A stinking, soaking, wet house, that's what. It took me two sodding hours to clean it up. And I had to put the heating on early to dry it out, costing me a fortune. It's still not dry. Well, you've done it now. Yvonne's on her way and Martha here is going to back me up. You are going to have to leave! And God help anyone else who is fool enough to take you in.' The cruel venom in her retorts was electric.

Alex and Laura grasped the moment, laughed, stood up, grabbed their coats and pushed past her out the back door. 'Bye, Mum, we've finished our homework. Going to collect Claire and then we're off to the club.' Alex then turned. 'Bye, Martha, and cheerio, Joanna, I don't expect you'll be here when I get back.' With a flourish both Laura and Alex exited the house.

Sally, with Jack in her arms, left Joanna with Martha and stormed upstairs. Joanna said not a word, her head a muddle of confusion; she was transfixed to the spot when Martha heaved herself from the chair and came at her, giving her such a bear hug Joanna could hardly breathe. 'You're half frozen. Come and sit down here by the radiator.' Martha held out a plate of cheese sandwiches. 'I bet you could do with a nice hot chocolate too. Let's get these wet things off you,' she soothed.

Joanna allowed herself to be coerced into obeying. But her mind was whizzing. How long had she got before Yvonne was to arrive and shunt her off to the home? She needed to gather her things and get out, now, fast. 'What time's she coming, Martha?' asked Joanna.

'Not till seven thirty – you've plenty of time, it's only six. Now get that sandwich and chocolate down you before you freeze to death.'

Having succumbed to Sally's pleas to support her in her bid to get rid of Joanna, Martha felt guilt and concern for the girl. Recalling nasty, unpleasant jibes and short-tempered comments that Sally had showered on Joanna lately was unsettling and disturbing. Alex too had changed with the ever-increasing volume of children that had passed through their home. The Sally of old that she'd known had a heart of gold but the Sally she'd encountered today was a very different person. Bitterness and resentment towards both Jim and the foster children had seeped into and altered her personality. Sally's propensity to fly off the handle and even lash out now and again with her hand whenever situations got tight gave Martha grave concerns. The ever-increasing nasty intolerance towards Joanna in particular was appalling. Martha was seriously regretting how she had encouraged Sally back into fostering.

Lurking outside and convinced that she was at the right house, Jessica watched from a distance. Her guess was confirmed when she noted Alex and Laura leaving together. But what she overheard as the girls walked by, Alex crowing over how she had 'got rid of the pain at last', made her decide on her next action. Joanna had been clear that she was going to run before she was taken away, which could mean only one thing – she would really be going tonight. Taking a deep breath, she strode up to the Whitworths' front door and rang the bell.

*

Yvonne had made it home through the driving wind and rain, observing the students from various schools as they plodded along the pavement in their school jumpers, no coats – obviously it was 'uncool' to wear them at the moment. She marvelled how they didn't all succumb to pneumonia! Pulling into the drive, she was aware that her youngest, Clarissa, wasn't home. Yvonne liked to be there for her arrival whenever possible, especially now, as her two other children were away on a school trip. Unlocking the front door, she flicked the central heating switch to override the pre-timed 'turn on'. Smiling to herself, she recalled her husband's constant comments of, 'It's not winter yet – think about global warming!' In the kitchen Yvonne opened the fridge door and took out three chicken breasts. Switching on Radio 4 she began to prepare the meal. Chopping onions, she pondered over the fact that Joanna had apparently eaten a raw onion. What was that all about? Surely Sally hadn't flipped to that extent and just given her one for her lunch? She continued to cut up smoked bacon and chicken. Her ears pricked up though when she heard, 'Police would like anyone who was in the vicinity of Warrior Road, Square or Avenue at ten thirty last evening to contact them...' Another stabbing! Yvonne froze over her chopping. Where was Clarissa? She looked at the clock and then with relief heard the front door's latch click and in she walked.

'Hi, Mum, I'm starving. What's for dinner? What can I eat now?'

With a smile Yvonne nodded towards the cake tin and decided that she would definitely be taking Clarissa with her tonight, however unprofessional it might be.

*

Jessica knew that the kindly faced lady who opened the door wasn't Mrs Whitworth, as she had heard Sally call down the stairs for Martha to 'get that' as she was putting Jack to bed.

'If you want Alex she's just left on her way to the youth club, the one on Warrior Road. If you run you should just catch her,' was Martha's greeting. Inadvertently letting slip that the youth club had closed until further notice because of the latest stabbing, Jessica was invited into the kitchen to see Joanna. The two girls faced each other.

An awkward few moments passed while Martha hovered expectantly. Joanna had shot off her chair as soon as Jessica uttered the betrayal of Alex and, with a cold voice, asked, 'What do you want?'

Martha, sensing the tension and knowing Joanna had very few friends, decided to leave the girls to it.

'Oh, great – now Alex is going to do me for this. What are you doing here? If you breathe a word I'll, I'll—'

'Listen to me,' interrupted Jessica. 'We haven't much time. I know you want to get away but you need help if you are going to run you need a plan – so get yourself to the Rock-a-nor chippy for eight thirty. I'll bring you what I can, but you must wait for me. I'll let you have my mobile. I don't suppose you have one? No, I thought not.

Well, it's no good without the charger, so I shall have to go home and get it. Okay?'

Before Jo could respond the door swung open and in strode Sally. 'Yes, may I help you?' Her eyes fixed on Jessica's with a hard stare.

'Sorry, I was just returning Joanna's book. She left her maths homework in the classroom.' Jessica faltered.

'Kind of you, I'm sure, but Joanna won't be needing it. She's leaving. Now I am going to have to ask *you* to leave. It's getting late and I am expecting someone any minute.' And with that Sally ushered Jessica towards the back door. Both Jessica's and Joanna's eyes met, Jessica's with a plea of 'be there' and Joanna's with an empty, cold glare.

*

Robert Bentley had just left the school and unlocked the pride of his life – a magnificent, British racing green Aston Martin. Always he succumbed to that moment of pure pleasure as he moulded into the leather seats, flicked on the Debussy CD in the CD player and breathed in the scent of luxury. Belting up, he turned the key and pressed the retro 'start' button and heard the engine smoothly rev into action. Mentally the woes of the day metaphorically dropped off the tyres as he took control and drove away from the school site. His journey was not long, but it was therapeutic driving through the outskirts of Hastings, unwinding and getting a decent distance in, before returning home. Tonight was no different and he chose to drive off into Rye, where he could grab a meal at The George before going back to his large and very spacious but lonely house. He left Helen's Close and drove out onto the A28, where he managed to avoid the cluster of students hanging around outside Tesco's. Putting his foot down, he drove out towards Beckley.

For some reason he decided to venture further, and instead of turning right in the direction of Rye and The George, he went straight on and found himself, twenty minutes later, outside the Old Wharfe Inn in Cranenden. He turned into the car park and pulled up decisively by the oast house adjacent to the pub. Stretching as he left his car in gear on the slope, he decided to walk across the little quaint bridge he had just driven over and view the river before going into the inn for his evening meal. He felt strangely disturbed as events from the day jumped around his mind. The biting wind cut through his jacket and he regretted having left his overcoat on the passenger seat of the car. He spent some shivering moments reading the sign stating boat trips were available up to Bodiam Castle and, making a mental note that he would take a trip in the spring, he turned around and made his way back to the inn, an ancient building that reflected a long and distant past, with thick black tar glistening on the walls of the massive inglenook fireplace that blazed with logs burning red and smothered in drifting smoke that found its way up the twisted chimney. Customers perching on stools swivelled their heads as he entered and his polite nod received gruff 'evenin's from those with beer glasses raised to their lips.

Mick, the barman, acknowledged Robert's arrival with a, 'What can I get you, sir?'

Robert eyed up the local beers on offer. He always felt slightly uncomfortable when entering unknown territory. He was the outsider and he didn't really want to stand out as a loner, but sadly, since his divorce, that is exactly what he was. 'I'll have a pint of Level Best and a look at your menu, please,' he stated, and perched by the fire in the well of the fireplace, amongst the day's newspapers and magazines. It was rustic with a friendly atmosphere and he gladly sat and reflected on the choices.

Sipping his beer and retreating into the background the voices of the regulars took over and Robert was forgotten. He relaxed at last. He always chose places outside of the school catchment area as he found it quite intimidating 'bumping' into parents or, worse still, students who were underage and in places where they shouldn't be. Sitting by the open fire didn't distract him from how disturbed he was by the broken specimen of humanity that had sat before him in his office. He had noticed the fresh cuts on her arms – why had she done that? Reading her file was disturbing enough. It seemed quite likely that the girl would be gone anyway by tomorrow. Yet the plea in her voice haunted him. 'Find who I belong to. Find my mum.' Staring at the flames, he tried to imagine her situation. To have no-one, not a single soul to whom you had any connections, was dreadful. My God, what had he read? Seventeen different homes, or was it eighteen? That's more than one for every year of her short life. Of course there were the institutions as well. Calling them care homes didn't make them sound any better. Robert shivered, but not with cold. He pushed his half-finished pie away, downed his beer, acknowledged the barman and those who were facing him with a nod, and left.

*

Jessica had left the Whitworths knowing that she would have to act on her promise to help Joanna run away. Unaware that she had been caught out, Alex and her friends had entered the 'Black Cove' club on West Street, the other side of town, completely the opposite direction of the youth club. A neon sign flashed on and off stating ID required for all customers, but clearly not for the girls. Alex and her friends just flashed smiles at the bouncers and walked through the door, passing the illuminated sign stating '18 years and over'.

Martha had sat at the table and cupped her hands around a hot chocolate. The clock ticked pensively and Joanna, sitting opposite her with hair dripping wet, teeth chattering, attempted to dry out and thaw. Her hands too were cupped around a mug of hot chocolate, but she didn't drink it.

Sally had returned to the bedroom with Jack after screaming wild accusations at Joanna about her trying to get Alex into trouble over the supposed closure of the youth club and getting her feeble friend to call on her. The vitriol was totally uncalled for and Martha felt it was just short of verbal abuse. It pained her to see how Joanna just accepted whatever was thrown at her and how hard and cold her eyes grew with each slanderous sentence. Suddenly Sally had faltered and her face coloured up as though she had become aware for the first time of what she was actually saying to a child! She left the room, leaving a silence that was painful. Martha didn't know quite what to say. She couldn't defend Sally's outburst and she felt she couldn't support her either, so she said nothing.

Meanwhile Joanna sat outwardly pensive but inwardly wildly thinking of her escape. She mentally planned how to get her very few possessions together, change into dry clothes and leave without being challenged – it would not be easy. She pondered on what Jessica has said about meeting her at the Rock – she had said she would help her, but could she trust her? What if she told her mum? It was a stupid thing to have done, to have told anyone. Yet as she was without local knowledge of train times or anything she realised that she couldn't do it alone. She would have to get out of Hastings fairly quickly as once they realised she had run off, there would be a search. Runaways were often traced easily because they returned to a place where they had been happy, or to people they had known. Not an issue for her, though. That she was aware she would have to go somewhere fresh and into the unknown filled her with trepidation. She wouldn't have a clue how to exist. In fact she was beginning to panic. It was all wrong and a really stupid time of year to just up and leave. As if to echo her thoughts the rain started to teem down and ping on the windows.

Feeling quite sure that it wasn't going to work, she jumped as Martha interrupted her thoughts. 'Penny for them.' She had stood up and was rinsing the cup and mugs in the sink. She had her back to Joanna.

'Oh, err, nothing…' Joanna drawled. 'I think I'll just go and get changed. Thanks for the chocolate.' Leaving the half-full mug on the kitchen table, she tentatively made her way up the stairs.

Aware of the heat, steam and smell of wet carpet, she shrivelled inside. What a stupid thing to have done. Tiptoeing by Jack's room, Joanna heard Sally reading a bedtime story to him. Her voice was wobbly and Joanna knew that she had been crying. It was all her fault. She turned on the landing and walked by Alex's room before entering her own. Pushing the snib across, she slumped behind the closed door and leant into it, panic rising within her. Getting a grip, she steadied her heaving breaths and began to reflect on her options. Pulling open the wardrobe door, she dragged out the one bag that she had had since her babyhood. It had been bright red once but was now a dirty, dull brown. Joanna emptied the contents onto her bed. The last item to fall out was the jumper that she had been wrapped in at birth. Joanna took it and tightened it around her hands and drew it towards her face. Her mum must have wanted her to survive at least. She had wrapped her in this. Lying on her bed and closing her eyes, she breathed in deeply. It calmed her. It always did. She tried to recognise a smell that was unique to the jumper, albeit only imaginary. She had traced the words on the label many a time with her finger, always hoping for a clue. They were shredded and almost unreadable yet she still traced each letter. Imagining how her mum had given birth to her and then removing her jumper to wrap her baby in it. She played out the scenario many a time – perhaps she had talked to her and told her softly how she loved her and hoped she'd find someone good to look after her. But then the reality always set in – if she loved her that much why had she been shoved in a Woolworths carrier bag and dumped by a bin?

Haunted as ever by the stark reality of her life, she replaced the jumper in the bag and carefully sifted through the rest of her stuff. A silver bracelet – the metal was so thin that she was too scared to wear it in case it broke – found near the bin. Of course it may have had nothing at all to do with her mother, but it might have… A book of fairy stories she had been given at the home one Christmas and the one photo of her six-year-old self in a school snapshot, running to the line in a skipping race. Allowing herself these moments evoked a lump in her throat and the sick, empty feeling of nausea. Inside she cried, but outwardly there was no sign of the torment she suffered apart from the gouges on her arms and bruises on her thighs where she had nightly pinched herself mercilessly. Physical pain enabled her to override the mental torment and emotional hunger for love that she earnestly craved. The family she remembered best had presented the photograph to her when they emigrated to Australia, their parting gift. She wished that they had been in the picture too, for her memory of them was fading. It always made her feel so alone seeing that photo, a stark reminder that she was. It was the last family that had given her any semblance of love at all.

Year on year she was no longer seen as a 'wanted' child and her mini spells in short-term foster homes interspersed with longer episodes in the children's home culminated in the most humiliating advert in the local press. *Can you give one of these children a home?* There it was in black and white, a begging plea for someone – anyone – to take pity on herself and the five others in the advert. Few would-be adopters had actually responded so it was with stark embarrassment when she had been exposed to the scrutiny of those that had. It isolated her all the more and hardened her resolve to get clear of the system whereby she was just another outcast, a no-one, a loner. And of course she was.

Except… Jessica had said that she would help her.

Joanna bit her lip and tried to work out the time. She had no watch and there wasn't a clock in her room. Hooking her hair behind her ears, with a swift shrug of her shoulders, she scrambled all the rest of her things together. She took her toothbrush with a wry smile and stuffed it into a toilet bag that was split at one end, along with the toothpaste, the flannel and a bar of soap from the sink. Strictly speaking they weren't hers, but tough. Sally wouldn't miss them. Opening the drawers, she rammed as many of her clothes as possible into her bulging bag. From the wardrobe she grabbed her trainers. Her school shoes were down by the radiator in the kitchen drying out. Dumping the rest of her uniform in the bottom of the wardrobe, she scanned the room for anything else she might need then reluctantly she let herself out of the room and crept down the stairs to retrieve her shoes. As she reached the bottom stair the doorbell rang. Without a second thought, seeing as she was closest, she turned the key. Her intake of breath was audible when to her utter amazement Yvonne stepped over the threshold with none other than Clarissa.

*

Voices were rising and falling from below. Clarissa, feeling totally embarrassed, found herself sitting on the chair in Joanna's room. Joanna herself was standing staring out of the window. Neither had spoken since they had been ushered upstairs. Perched between them on the bed was the stuffed bag. Joanna, cross that she hadn't managed to retrieve her shoes, felt betrayed. How long had Clarissa known?

The awkward silence raised the tension and caustic atmosphere in the room. The one and only time Clarissa's mum had included her in her work and it had to be with someone she knew. Half-hearted attempts at stating that she had no idea, or that this was a first, or that she was as shocked as Jo, fell on deaf ears. The ping of her phone indicating a message broke the silence. Flicking it open, she read Jessica's message.

'You need to read this,' said Clarrisa, and threw the phone over to Joanna.

Joanna jumped and just turned her head away.

'Just read it,' urged Clarissa.

'I want you to go away – go to Alex's room as your mum suggested in the first place and do your homework. Leave me alone,' Joanna coldly responded.

'Okay, okay, I'll go'. Clarissa stood up and made to leave. 'But you'd be wrong not to read that text. It's from Jess and she has no idea I am here or that my mum is involved. But if you want to make a good get-away you'd better read it.' And on that note Clarissa left.

Joanna stared at the blank, dark screen. She stretched her arm across the bed and retrieved the phone, flipped the lid shut and open again, revealing the message. It read: *Hi, gotta help Jo. Meet at Rock before 8.30. Scared Jo will do a runner. Get money, food anything you can think of – don't tell anyone.*

Joanna opened her door. Clarri was waiting on the other side of it. 'Well?' she asked. 'Can you cut the sore feelings routine and let us help you? We have about forty minutes before we meet Jess.'

*

Clarissa had been annoyed at being forced to go with her mum. 'I'm not a baby,' she'd retorted. 'I can look after myself for an hour or so,' she'd argued when her mother suggested she had to. Yvonne raised her eyebrows, mentioned the stabbings and apologised to her daughter but was adamant that she wasn't going to be left on her own. Her rattling on to Clarissa, as she had so many times in the past, that she dealt with 'neglected' children all day in her work and she wasn't about to make her daughter one of them, incensed her the more. 'Leaving me on my own for an hour is hardly neglect,' argued Clarissa. 'I am nearly sixteen'. But Yvonne was having none of it.

On their drive to the foster home Clarri had received a call from Jess. Her breathless, broken comments confused her.

'What are you doing?' demanded Clarissa. 'Why are you so out of breath? I can hardly make out what you are saying.'

'I'm running home, and I haven't much time. Listen, you and I are going to have to do something tonight for Joanna. She is in a real mess and it's down to us… r… g… rt… th… n… w…'

'Can't hear you, you're breaking up. Text me'.

*

Meanwhile Jessica had entered the underpass and sprinted like crazy to the other end. She always hated going through there, especially in the dark. She was also beginning to panic, having received another frantic text from her mum demanding to know just where she was and when she was going to get home. If she weren't careful, she would be grounded. Her face red and steaming from the biting wind, rain and exertion, she automatically checked her watch to see her running stats.

*

Her mother was standing by the open back door with a bag of rubbish that she was dividing up between the recycling boxes. 'I was just about to phone around to see where you were,' she stated. 'Get in and get those wet things off, you must be frozen.' She gave Jessica a swift peck on the cheek and ushered her into the warm house. Though small and insignificant from the outside, it was snug and homely, or 'cluttered', as Jessica viewed it, but her friends all seemed to find it a 'nice' place to go.

Her brother was sitting by the fire playing his guitar, which echoed through the house. It was worse when he sang along, but tonight he was just practising his chords. 'Glad you're back, I'm starving,' was his greeting.

'Aren't we waiting for Dad?' Jessica asked.

Her mum responded with a resounding, 'No!'

Jessica glanced at Jamie and he shrugged his shoulders and lowered his head so that his hair fell over his forehead as he tried to complete a chorus from the Leatherheads.

Her mum seemed intransigent when it came to her father and his late nights. Jessica left the room to get changed. She had no time for her parents' silly, pathetic and childish angst with each other when there were real problems in the world. It made her cross that they would get het up over such trivial things. Her mum knew that they were struggling to keep Sandi at university, yet she moaned every time her dad worked overtime. In her room Jessica rummaged through her drawer until she found the brick of an old mobile phone that she had had two years previously. She plugged the charger into the wall and noticed with relief that it was charging. Grabbing warm, clean clothes, she ran a bath and put in her favourite bubble bath. The bubbles grew as the water fizzed out of the tap. Sitting on the edge of the bath texting Clarri the rendezvous point with Jo, Jess felt excited and enthralled at what she was hoping they might do to help Jo. She wrote in the message that it was a matter of urgency and that she was to be at the Rock at 8.30. That would give them time to plan what they would do with Joanna, because at that precise moment Jess had no idea what that could possibly be.

*

Downstairs the voices were becoming extremely agitated. However, for once it wasn't about Joanna. Sally had just heard about the closure of the youth club and realised that her only daughter, Alex, had both lied to her and done so with ease. Knowing that Hastings had been the centre of further knife crime exacerbated the fear that Alex was wandering the streets and no-one knew where. Naturally she blamed Joanna for Alex's behaviour. Storming about the kitchen she yelled at Yvonne that if it hadn't been for Joanna then Alex would never have lied, that Joanna had taught her to be deceitful and that she had deliberately flooded her home. The ludicrous comments and her raging was disturbing, making it clear to Yvonne that Joanna could no longer stay in Sally's care.

Meanwhile Martha took it upon herself to go out in her car and try and locate the whereabouts of Alex. Though she didn't have a clue where to begin, at least she felt she was doing something. Yvonne did her best to calm Sally down with the assurance that she would take Joanna away as soon as Alex had returned.

Amidst all this commotion, the two girls had snuck out of the back window of Alex's bedroom, jumped onto the shed roof and down onto the garden path. Joanna had her bag, her treasured birth jumper secure at the bottom, and Clarissa nothing more than her mobile. The garden was one of many interlinking the back of the terraced houses. It meant that the girls had to climb across several gardens till they reached the last one in the row. It was with some ease that they managed to make it to the end as most of the fencing was broken or non-existent. The final garden proved the trickiest. The owner was having a cigarette outside the back door that was lit up with fairy lights. Silently both girls hunkered down in the darkness by a small shed, not daring to breathe. Finally with the last drag the dog end was flicked into the fish pond. After a cough, followed by a spit, the smoker returned to the back door, entered the kitchen and turned out the lights.

Whilst both girls adjusted their eyes to the darkness out front Martha revved her car and drove along the street. As she focused her view in the mirror, she thought she saw two females jumping over the end fence and scampering up the alley. Preoccupied with her quest to find Alex, she thought nothing of it and sped off.

Joanna, aware that the next few hours were crucial, found the girls' enthusiasm to help her comforting, as with no money and no idea of where to go, facing it alone would be rather bleak and terrifying.

*

Alex's return home was under the most humiliating circumstances that she could have imagined. She cringed at the memory of it and furthermore the vicious slap she received from her mother when she finally did arrive left her face stinging and red. But it was the audacity of that bloody woman Martha that really wound her up. Clenching her fists, she paced about her room in abject fury. Seething with anger, she went over in her mind the horror of the embarrassing moment when Martha had pulled up in her pathetic little car and demanded that she 'get in'. What followed was beyond belief. Her new friends had witnessed how Martha had virtually dragged Alex into her car right outside the club they had just left. Ignoring her had only ended up with the dreaded woman virtually kerb crawling as she trawled beside them. Even now in her bedroom Alex flushed with indignation as she recalled all that Martha had said. It was Mark's face, his raised eyebrows and hurried release of her arm when he realised her real age that had finally made her get into the car. Having lost face with them all, she couldn't get away quick enough.

Martha had lambasted her with a torrent of abuse such as she would not have thought possible during the drive back. She said nothing until they were fifty yards from home, when she pulled the car over and faced

Alex, who then received the full force of Martha's pent-up concern and frustration. According to her Alex was pretty unpleasant and that do-gooder Joanna was suffering because of her. Martha calling her spoilt, selfish and a bully angered Alex most. She just glared at Martha, eyes streaming and mascara dripping over her cheeks. But the best bit that came out of the mad woman's raging was that Joanna was going!

On and on she went about her 'selfishness and inability to share her parents, a home and security'. Well, and why should she? She refused to accept that she was spoilt and cruel. She acknowledged that knowing there had been a knifing in Warrior Square and choosing to pretend they were going there had been a mistake. But really it was a bit much that this old biddy was reading her the riot act. Martha concluded her speech by driving up to the house and unlocking the door. Breathing heavily and with a racing heart, she realised she may have gone too far. By the expression of loathing on Alex's face she felt, regrettably, that she may have done. When she turned off the engine, Alex opened the car door without a word and ran up the path to the front door. Martha shifted her body out of the car and followed.

Both stood silently on the step as the doorbell finished its trill. Immediately it flung open and Sally stood there, eyes wide and desperate-looking. 'Mum, I'm sorry,' began Alex. But before she could say anything more a slap found itself landing across her face.

'Get in,' hissed Sally. 'Get in and explain yourself.'

Martha winced at the ferocity of the hit and the hurt that Alex had felt. She slowly followed the two of them through the hall and into the kitchen. Pandemonium broke out. Alex screamed out at top note to her mother about what a bitch Martha was and how Sally's busybody of a friend had humiliated her. Sally returned the screams with just as much venom and vitriol. Both seemed to have forgotten the presence of Yvonne and Martha until the key turned in the lock and Jim walked into the room. His entrance muted the pair of them. The look of disbelief and shock on his face made both mother and child drop their defences. Sally sat silently with her face in her hands whilst Alex stormed from the room and fled upstairs to her bedroom. The silence that followed was deafening. Jim moved over to where

Sally was rocking herself back and forth. Martha bit her bottom lip and didn't quite know what to do next.

It was Yvonne that made the first move. 'Evening, Jim.'

'Well, who's going to explain what's going on?' he asked.

*

Flinging herself onto her bed Alex pummelled the pillows with her fists. She kept hearing Martha's speech over and over in her mind. How dare the woman! What right had she to lecture Alex on her behaviour and social life? But the more that Alex screwed up the pillow, the more she felt a nagging sense of truth. She almost blushed with the reality of Martha's comments. How could she face any of them again? But she did despise Joanna. She was jealous of her and of the way everyone took pity on her. No, she wasn't jealous – she was angry at how Joanna had been shoved into her life, her home and her school without any consultation at all. Why should she share all she had with a complete stranger anyway? Feeling totally righteously indignant, Alex rolled over and flung her arms behind her head and stared at the ceiling.

It was only then that she realised her bedroom window was wide open and a freezing wind was rattling through. 'Bloody nerve, someone's been in my room,' she angrily said, and strode over to close and lock the window.

A few seconds later there was a tap at her door and she heard the voice of her father tentatively calling through the shut door. She smiled inwardly. *Dear Dad, never raising his voice, always so gentle and infuriatingly passive.* 'What?' she demanded of him.

'Please, Alex, come down and bring Clarissa with you. I'll be waiting in the kitchen – take Clarissa into the living room and put the telly on for her.' Alex heard his steps retreat down the stairs.

Who is Clarissa? was the first thought that ran through her head and did her dad really think that she was going to go down and face all those interfering faces in the kitchen? *Not on your life.* And she turned towards her wardrobe, took out her jacket, grabbed her bag and exited out of the very same window that Jo and Clarissa had left earlier.

*

Outside the Rock a group of young people huddled together in a concentrated hubbub of trouble. Joanna wasn't listening to sense. It had taken Jessica all her wits and wiles to get out of the house with her mother's permission – and even so, she only had a little time left to achieve her goal before she would be at risk of being grounded. To top it all she had to bring Jamie in on the act. So now here they were, the four of them trying hard to get Joanna to see some sense and not to disappear into the cold of the night totally alone. Besides which, as Clarissa kept reminding them all, how could Joanna possibly run away when she had no money at all?

It was now 8.40 and all of them were at risk of losing their parents' goodwill should they stay out much later. What Jessica had managed to do was pack a backpack under the guise of her 'weight training' for the trials. This she had rammed with bits of food and toiletries, a box of orange juice, along with a recharged mobile phone, a candle (why she put that in she didn't know, but it seemed right at the time), a lighter and the full contents of her savings. She nearly took the fiver that she'd noticed sitting under the coffee jar in the kitchen but just couldn't bring herself to actually steal. It had taken Jessica all her wits to ensure that Jamie would support her and do a training run with her. At least that's what she told her mum. Jamie himself really had no desire to run around the streets in the dark just in order for Jess to train. However, her whispered explanations intrigued him and he felt curious enough to go along.

The sky was dark and the wind began to blow in from the sea, adding to the chill factor. Joanna felt herself distancing her mind from this group of well-intentioned people. She knew it would be hard and she also knew they had got themselves into trouble for her, but that couldn't be helped. Time was running out and she had to make her move. She stood up, leant across Jamie and grabbed her bag. 'I'm going now,' she stated.

Jessica began to remonstrate, but it was Jamie who butted in first. 'No,' he said, 'you will not be going anywhere unless it is with our help.' He glanced at his watch. 'Now, here's the plan...'

5

Robert Bentley had just settled down to read his latest political tome on Disraeli and how the government of the day began to corrupt the machinations of parliament when he was disturbed by the Debussy ringtone on his mobile. It was a number he recognised immediately.

'Sybil, to what do I owe the pleasure?' he uttered.

There then followed a long and drawn-out tirade of how the police had been in touch over several 'missing' students. The whole thing had seemed bizarre to start with, for the fact that a couple of girls had gone out without permission and not apparently having returned home yet, hardly seemed to be a worthy police matter, though of course everyone was tense since the spate of knife crimes had hit St Leonards.

He glanced at his watch. 'But it isn't even nine o'clock yet. It is hardly a big mystery at the moment – what is the problem?'

Robert stood up from his chair and looked out of the window. The sky was dark and leafless trees that bowed under the strength of the wind blocked the view down to the sea. He caught glimpses of twinkling lights that glittered through the moving branches. 'Find who I belong to. Find my mum,' echoed through his mind. Her voice, forlorn, lost and dull. 'Poor kid,' he uttered as he drew the curtains, put out the light and, walking to the hall, grabbing his thick, woollen overcoat, hat and scarf, let himself out into the night. His footsteps fell quick and crisp on the pavement as he made his way down to the coast road.

*

It wasn't too long after her exit that Alex was beginning to wish that she hadn't left the house in such a dramatic way. She was cold and felt stupid. She had nowhere to go. Laura would still be with Alan and there was no way that she could face Mark after what Martha had done. Pulling her jacket tighter around her, she began to regret the skimpy clothes that she was wearing and longed for the warmth of her bedroom. She was also hungry and in trouble at home. But now she was too far in it to go back. What to do now?

As she sidled down the alley she noticed the police presence by the Square. Another knifing, she supposed – it chilled her, as the reality of all that it meant sunk in. Her mum would be frantic! But then perhaps she wasn't that bothered – she was too busy sorting out Joanna. What a creepy girl she was, reflected Alex as she touched her still-stinging cheek. Of all the people that her mum had fostered Joanna had to be the weirdest.

Fumbling in her pocket for her mobile she was brought up with a start. It wasn't there. Like losing a limb! Alex, feeling bereft, alone and isolated with no means of contact, walked on. Disturbed by her isolation, she wandered into the nearest pizza house and ordered a Coke and chips. Standing at the counter, tucking into her chips, pondering what to do next, she glanced up at the overhanging mirror above the counter and noticed a crowd walking past the entrance reflected in the glass. She swung round and ran to the door. Yes, there was no mistake – it was Joanna and her two gumpy mates with a bloke. Grabbing the last of her chips and swigging down the dregs of Coke, Alex sped out of the pizza house and legged it up the road to follow while wondering what 'that crazy loser' was up to.

*

It had to be admitted that Jamie had no idea as to what should happen next, but what he did know was that they couldn't just let this frightened, disturbed girl go off into the night alone. He knew that there would be real trouble if they didn't all get home fairly sharpish, but what to do with Joanna? Realising that she might just run off like the timid rabbit she seemed to be, he had made a decision.

Alex watched from a distance as the two girls split and went in one direction and the boy and Joanna went off in the other. Curiosity overcame her and she decided to follow Joanna. She quite enjoyed leaping behind lamp posts and in and out of shop doorways as Joanna kept turning round and looking up at the street cameras. *How weird*, she thought, *it almost seems as though she's trying to be caught on camera.*

Reaching the station, Joanna stopped walking and she and the boy got into a huddle. He seemed to be giving her some kind of lecture, for Joanna just kept nodding and listening without comment. Alex wished she could hear what was being said. Yet all she could think was that somehow that geeky girl had got herself a boyfriend and he seemed pretty cool too. Alex felt angry and jealous at the same time, then in a flash Joanna had gone – she just flew into the station. The boy turned and ran up the hill and onto the bridge and watched her.

Alex ran into the station also and scanned around until she saw Joanna get onto the train to Rye. *Blimey*, she thought. *What is she up to?* Alex turned and exited the station, not noticing that Joanna had slipped out of the carriage further down the train and back-tracked along the inside of the platform, hugging the wall with her face turned inwards. She had also removed her coat and had pulled Jamie's running hat onto her head. Reaching the road Alex looked for the boy on the bridge but he was no longer there, and so, having come this far and with little else to do, she decided to go home and face the music.

Robert, meanwhile, idled down the road and searched in all the doorways and eating houses in vain. He knew it would be like looking for a needle in a haystack, but nevertheless he felt compelled to do something. There was certainly a larger police presence. Suddenly he thought he caught a glimpse of Joanna being escorted along the street by a boy who had his arm around her. But then she was gone – he couldn't be sure that it was her at all. He began to pick up pace and, dodging in and out of the crowds, finally caught up with them. But was it her? Was he mistaken? He called her name. 'Joanna! Hey, Joanna!' he shouted. The boy seemed to hold her tighter and the girl never turned. Perhaps he had been mistaken.

*

Jessica, in a heightened state of agitation, was astounded on arriving home to discover Robert Bentley standing in the doorway nodding and smiling at her mother as she invited him in. Too late to avoid the encounter; her mother had spotted her and called for her to come in, where she caught her mother quizzing Mr Bentley as to what Jessica had to do with a missing student. Rudely, so Jessica thought, he ignored her mother and went straight for Jessica. Not unkindly, but with a definite no-nonsense approach, he attempted to interrogate Jessica about her movements in the last couple of hours.

Fortunately for her Jamie came bursting through the door, out of breath, slapping Jess on her back and congratulating her on her speed in the last lap of their training run. Robert's questioning glance to her mother was answered by Jamie as he confirmed that Jessica and he had been out running – a regular occurrence – and had seen nothing of Joanna. Jamie squeezed Jessica's elbow as she looked uncomfortably down at her feet which did nothing but confirm in Robert's mind that they had some knowledge that they were not prepared to divulge as yet.

'Ah well,' he said as he then apologised for disturbing them, 'I can but hope that the police will find the poor girl soon – especially in these rather turbulent times, not to mention the dreadful weather. Goodnight, all, and should you hear of anything that might be of interest…' and he handed Jessica his card. 'My mobile number – good evening.' And with a nod to each in turn he left.

Robert felt he knew his pupils quite well and had never had any reason to think that Jessica was up to no good, having always admired her strength of opinion in ethics class that he sometimes observed. Furthermore, he recognised her athletic skills as exceptional. 'An all-round good egg,' he would have said. She couldn't lie easily, this he knew, but he let this one go for now. Robert started the engine and pulled out of the road and onto the main high street, narrowly missing a dustbin that was precariously balanced on the kerb, and drove to Joanna's foster home, where he found the unfortunate Clarissa facing the music on her own.

In front of her were her mother, Sally, Jim, Martha and a very young community police officer. All made attempts to 'get the truth' from her, but she stuck to the cobbled-together story that they had all agreed to. She explained that she would stand a greater chance of changing Joanna's mind if she went along with her and try to make her see sense and return home.

'But where is she now?' questioned her mother.

'I don't know,' was all Clarissa would say. 'She was determined and I lost her near the station. That's all I know. I turned around and the next thing I knew she had gone. I decided then to come back here and tell you.'

The atmosphere in the room was electric. Jim, his usual ponderous self, had sunk into the armchair, frowning deeply. Martha just glanced from one person to the next, avoiding eye contact. Sally was ashen, with streaked tearstains on her face, mumbling, 'But where's Alex? My Alex?' The community officer importantly wrote down every word that was being said, repeating it for clarity.

'So,' she began, 'you say you lost her at the station?'

'Err, no – I said that I lost her *near* the station,' responded Clarissa, then she turned to Yvonne and said, 'Mum, I think she might have been aiming to get to London. All I know is that Joanna wants to find her parents. She knew she was being moved again and she said she couldn't take anymore.' There was an uncomfortable murmur at that comment and all shuffled in their seats apart from the police officer.

'That's all very well,' commented Sally, 'but no-one seems bothered about where *my* Alex is—'

As if on cue Alex came bursting in the front door and into the living room, gasping, 'Hey, Mum, Dad, you'll never believe what I have just seen… What are the police doing here?' Scanning the room, she noticed Clarissa. 'Hey, how did you get here? I've just seen you down by the Rock with Joanna and your gumpy mates.'

That was all the police officer needed. She wanted to 'interview' everyone separately, calling in on her walkie-talkie, suggesting that a squad car should go to the train station and check out for sightings of Joanna and a group of youths on any significant and available CCTV.

By the time Robert arrived the kitchen was an improvised interview room with everyone else gathered in the living room.

Two hours later Yvonne was driving Clarissa home, having spent a most harrowing couple of hours realising that her daughter had been an accomplice to an orphan's runaway and that she had a serious situation on her hands. The police, meanwhile, had scoured the area where Joanna had last been seen and were, to their credit, avidly trawling through CCTV camera footage of the station and the street cameras close to the vicinity. Sally and Jim were both suitably concerned about their daughter and her behaviour. Jim was secretly distressed over Joanna's unhappiness and obvious loneliness in his care but didn't dare voice his thoughts at present. Sally took two sleeping tablets and sunk into a disturbed but much-needed sleep. Martha spent the night driving round and round Hastings, not convinced that Joanna had left and determined that she would take her into her own home when she found her.

Jessica, in the safety of her room, wondered what Jamie had done with Joanna and where she could possibly be. Trying to ring the mobile she had given her was fruitless as it went straight to voicemail, as did Clarissa's. In the end she just texted a message: 'ring me wen u can J'. Jessica snuggled down in her bed and wondered. Fifteen years of being ignored and being totally unhappy and alone was cruel and wrong, and where was she now? So much for her big adventure! Jessica realised that she had been excited by the idea of running away with Joanna but in reality when it came down to it, all they did was get cold and rely on her brother to sort it all out. What a mess.

She stared at the fluorescent stars on her ceiling and listened as her dad turned the key in the lock and called out that he was home. Unusually she heard her mum call back and state that she would have a meal ready for him in ten minutes. *Oh, good, maybe she will be nice to him for once,* was her last thought as she turned over and drifted off into a troubled sleep, where she dreamt of onions chasing her through the streets of Hastings, being supported by Mel and her gang dressed as knives.

*

At precisely 1am Jamie, still dressed and alert, quietly opened his bedroom door, crept along the corridor and listened at his parents' door that stood ajar. He heard the quiet, soft, steady breathing of his mum and the regular heavy breathing of his father. Convinced they were both asleep, he went down the stairs and unlocked the front door. He whistled softly and from behind the bin that was precariously perched on the edge of the kerb, jammed next to a bush, crept Joanna. His finger on his lips, though Joanna needed no hint to be quiet, they stealthily crept back in. Jamie locked the front door and led her up to his room. Safely inside, Jamie wedged a chair against the door to prevent anyone entering. It was bitterly cold outside and she had been wedged between the bush and the bin for several hours. Shivering, pale and unable to feel her fingers or toes, she was clearly chilled through.

'Right,' said Jamie, 'I can't put the heating back on as it would wake everyone, so get into the bed and wrap yourself up in the duvet while I go down and make a drink – don't move and if anyone should come in just stay perfectly still. I'll make it look as though I've just piled up the bedclothes as I left it.'

Without saying a word Joanna tumbled into the bed and curled herself into a ball, ramming her hands under her armpits trying to induce some life back into them. Jamie took her bag and put it in the wardrobe. He ruffled the duvet over her and dented the pillow. It looked at first glance like a heaped duvet on his bed. 'That'll have to do. Now keep still and I won't be long. Don't panic if you hear voices. Chances are me moving about in the kitchen will wake someone – but that's not a problem.' And with that he removed the chair from the door and made his way down to the kitchen.

Putting on the light and filling the kettle Jamie wondered how he'd allowed himself to be part of this ludicrous situation. He again pondered over whether he should just hand Joanna over to the authorities. But, as he now realised, it was the authorities that had got her in this state and certainly wasn't an answer for her.

As he bustled about, heating milk and water and making hot chocolate and toast, the kitchen door opened and his dad walked in. 'Thought I heard a noise down here.' He yawned. 'What's up?' he asked his son.

'Nothing, Dad, just felt hungry and wanted a drink, haven't been to bed yet – been studying,' Jamie retorted.

'Yeah, well, you mustn't work too hard – you need your sleep,' his dad responded.

What Jamie hoped was that his dad did too, for all he needed now was for him to decide to have a father-son chat and join him in tea and toast, as he had done on other occasions. With relief Jamie noticed his dad turn to go back upstairs, saying, 'Well, don't stay up too late. I'm off to bed now, night, son.'

'Night, Dad – sleep well.' And Jamie placed the toast and chocolate on a tray, giving his dad a few minutes to go ahead of him. He heard the bathroom door close and the flush of the loo and took that moment to return to his room. Once inside he replaced the chair and acknowledged his dad's knock on the door as he returned from the bathroom to his bed. 'See you in the morning.'

'Yep, night.'

Joanna hadn't moved. In fact, Jamie wasn't sure that she was still there. He pulled back the duvet to discover an empty bed. Aghast, he began to panic when he noticed a foot poking out from under the bed. In her fear at hearing Jamie's dad go downstairs, Joanna, in a panic, had slipped out the bed and rolled under it.

Still half frozen with cold, she cupped the hot chocolate and drank, in sips, the delicious silky liquid. She ate the toast slowly and deliberately as though it was her last meal. 'Thank you,' she whispered. 'Thank you so much.'

'That's okay.' Jamie smiled in return but didn't voice his biggest concern. *What happens next?* For he had absolutely no idea.

'Sorry, Jamie, but I need to pee.'

And that was just the first problem.

6

Jamie waited until his dad had left for work before attempting to leave his room. He told Joanna that no-one would come in and she wasn't to be afraid. Giving what he hoped was a reassuring smile, he turned and picked up the water bottle that had improvised as a toilet for Joanna then took it to the bathroom and flushed the contents down the loo. Throwing the bottle in the bin he began to reflect on the responsibility he now felt for this virtual stranger. Had this been Melvin, the drummer in his band, who had 'helped' Joanna, Jamie could only imagine how he would have taken full advantage of her by now – and by the look of grateful thanks in her eyes, Joanna would have had no choice but to let him. Jamie felt sick at the thought.

*

They had argued over taking the food Jamie had offered her and the sleeping bag that he had taken from the back of his cupboard, but she was truly grateful for his insistence that she have them when later that day she found herself on the freezing waters of the River Rother. The small boat she had chosen to break into was tucked up on a slight bend just under the small, quaint bridge, wedged tightly into the bank and so unseen from the river walk at Cranenden. Jamie also insisted that she take the twenty-five pounds that he had saved towards a new guitar. It was with a determined mumble of, 'I'll pay you back – I promise – one day,' that she took the proffered money and rammed it in her back pocket. They had walked into the town together and she split from him when they were both in the midst of a melee of students gathered at the bus station. Joanna assured him that she would contact him as soon as she could and when she had found somewhere to go.

She watched from a distance as Jamie stepped onto the school bus that would take him to the Ridge. Once the bus had turned out of sight Joanna ran out of the station and made her way to the centre of town. Pulling Jamie's beanie hat down over her head and avoiding the CCTV cameras, she headed out. On her back Jamie's rucksack fitted nicely, with her own bag strapped at the bottom and the sleeping bag strapped to the top. Getting out of Hastings was her purpose. Scanning the bus headers she went for the one whose destination she had never heard of called Tenterden. Joanna bought her ticket, climbed the stairs and settled down at the front of the bus, where she had a good view of the route the bus was taking her. Painfully slow and laborious, it dribbled away from Hastings, and the further it travelled the more she experienced a sense of freedom and independence. At each stop various schoolchildren got on and then a few stops later dismounted. At times the bus was heaving and then within twenty minutes her company was reduced to a few individuals.

Taking in the change of scenery Joanna began to plan her next steps. As always at the forefront of her plans was to research all she knew about her birth. For that she required access to a computer, but that would have to go back on hold (as it always seemed to) whilst she endeavoured to find some shelter. Jamie had told her of neglected and abandoned caravans along the Military Canal road near Rye. He also mentioned holiday homes and chalets that were spread around in Hastings, but all were pretty obvious places that would be easily checked out. Jo immediately ditched those choices. However, Jamie's suggestions had given her an idea that she was about to explore. The bus took its course as she took in the scenery, which altered from that of the busy seaside town to rural hills and dips. The roads themselves became narrower and snake-like as the bus coiled around tight bends, pursuing the winding track towards the rural outskirts.

Eventually the bus crossed over a steam train railway track and then a small stone bridge that denoted the border between Kent and East Sussex. The river flowed either side and exposed stacks of canoes chained to a holding area, secured for the winter. She spotted (tucked down at the edge of the riverbank) a small boat that seemed to be tethered by a rope to a boarding ramp. Furthermore, just at the side of the river, was a camping and caravan site – empty now but with the promise of washrooms. Opposite these sites on the south side of the road stood a lonely kiosk supporting a kebab and coffee stall. Just as the bus trundled past it pulled up outside the one pub that the village boasted. Two people alighted and took their time to amble up the aisle of the lower deck, giving Joanna the chance to scan the area as the bus slowly drove off up the hill.

Terminating at Tenterden, Joanna felt the chill air as she alighted. At first she just wandered around the town to get a 'feel' for the place. Though she had not been out for long, Joanna felt hungry – it was an unusual sensation for her as she often denied herself meals and took pride in refusing the grudgingly offered food from Sally. Now focused on controlling her own destiny, there was a sense of exhilaration welling up inside her and she was ravenous. For the first time she felt as though she had autonomy over her own life, which made her laugh. Totally homeless, adrift from any security at all but still she felt strangely liberated. Her backpack felt heavy and the weather began to drift in with chill winds and soft rain. Spotting a café conveniently situated on a busy corner and adjacent to the main bus stop, she decided to get some sustenance. The warm, aromatic air of the café tickled her tastebuds as she opened the door. Steam filled with aromas of coffee, bacon and sweet pancakes. It was abuzz with people of all kinds and she could see why. The main attraction was a £2.50 meal deal of a bacon roll and as much tea as you could drink. Relieved to take off her backpack, Joanna picked a table by the shop front where she could observe the street. Oblivious to anyone else, she felt comfortable, anonymous and safe.

The roll and tea went down easily and, relaxing over her second cup, she formulated a plan. While the owner allowed her to she sat and wallowed in her own thoughts. The next 341 bus back to Cranenden wasn't due for another hour and a half. Her plan wasn't much of one, but it was one that she felt would keep her out of the public eye as much as possible. She and Jamie had talked in the night of what her options were and he had been extremely practical in his perceptions of what the police may or may not be aware of in her escape. For instance they would (as she had realised) check the obvious places where a runaway might find shelter: holiday homes, caravans, outdoor sheds, etc.; in fact, all the places that Jamie had suggested. But what she hoped they wouldn't expect was for her to slip into the small out of the way village and break into a boat on the river – a river that she had noticed was closed for the season. The ferryboat that took trippers up the river to the castle was shut until the spring and it was highly unlikely that anyone would be using the river for their own personal pleasure trips in the short, darkening winter days. Moreover, the village had no shop or place of public gathering – apart from the pub and a church, neither of which she would need to enter. This was the place for anonymity.

Finishing her third cup of tea, Joanna left the café. A decision made not too soon, she noted, when she crossed the road and glanced back to see a uniformed police officer entering the café. Coincidence, probably, but nevertheless, she kept her head down and wandered in the opposite direction until she came to the recreation ground and toilets. It was awkward trying to negotiate the small cubicle with her backpack and bag and at the same time trying to use the loo without dragging her stuff onto the sopping wet floor.

Ten minutes later she was sitting on the park bench and scanning the mobile phone that Jessica had given her. She made a note on her bus ticket of Jamie and Jessica's numbers that were listed. Reluctant to destroy the phone altogether, she removed the battery and the sim card. Keeping it gave her a kind of hope – someone who seemed to actually care about her would be at the other end of the call if she ever needed to ring. That would be a first. The rain zipped across her face in a sharp, icy blast and mingled with the salty drops that had emerged from her eyes. She swung her hand across her nose and wiped away the snotty drips onto the back of her hand and down her trousers. Looking up, she watched a woman drag a collie dog away from the trees in an attempt to get home before the rain drenched them completely.

Realising just how damp the bench was and feeling the wet seep into her trousers, Joanna stood up and hoisted her backpack onto her shoulders, wandering away up towards the other end of the high street; she still had another hour to go before her bus came. People were bustling, charging along, avoiding eye contact, being busy with so much to do, but Jo was at a loss as to how to use her time. Her bag felt heavy as it too absorbed the rain. With still fifty-five minutes remaining until her bus was due, she entered the 'Gateway', a library-cum-post office and council information centre. The place was inviting and buzzy with various people queuing for the counters of the three areas. Joanna merged with the hubbub and found herself a corner seat by the crime section. She grabbed a Henning Mankell novel and began to read. *Faceless Killers*, not the most encouraging title she could have chosen, but it wasn't long before Joanna became fully absorbed in the story.

'I love his books. Did you see the TV series? Liked Kenneth Branagh better than the Swedish version – can't stand subtitles.' A woman of about fifty sat down next to Joanna and heaved a heavy shopping bag onto her lap. 'It is so horrible out there today. Thought I'd wait in here until my bus came.' Joanna's heart sank but she managed a swift smile back at the woman and bent her head further towards her book. But the woman persisted. 'On holiday?' she enquired, nodding at the backpack.

Joanna, flustered and reddening nervously, responded, 'Err, kind of – I'm staying with my cousin, just arrived from Tunbridge Wells.' She faltered. Now what? Could you get from Tunbridge Wells to Tenterden? And where was she supposed to be staying? 'I am getting the bus later,' she added, and buried her head in her book.

The woman would not go away. 'How lovely,' she said. 'Whereabouts are you staying?'

Joanna raised her head, rolled her eyes then said, 'Excuse me but I really must dash.' Shoving the book back on the shelf, Joanna grabbed her bag and flew out the door. Angry at losing her warm, free seat, Joanna crossed the road from where she could observe the woman when she left the library. It was imperative that she did not get the same bus. This would only work if she was insignificant and now that woman would know her. Easily describable and angry with herself, Joanna sulked under a tree getting really quite wet and cold.

At last the woman left the Gateway just as Joanna realised that she needed to head along to the bus stop to pick up her bus. With a sense of relief Joanna surmised that the woman was not going to cross the road and was in fact perching herself on a pop-up seat in the opposite bus queue. Hoisting her bag back onto her shoulders, Joanna headed towards her stop and leant against the café wall while awaiting its arrival, going over her plans. She decided that if she couldn't use the boat to sleep on she could dump her stuff and then reconnoitre the rest of the village looking for other suitable places to stop over. A holiday cottage would be hopeful. That would at least provide her with some means of comfort, though there was bound to be weekend visitors even at this time of year and that would mean a cleaner popping in to ensure all was up to scratch. She would have to take it carefully, stage by stage. Yes, the boat must be the first choice. It was a farming village, she had noted, and so there would be barns and tractor sheds to offer some means of cover. It was with renewed hope that Joanna recognised her bus as it pulled up at the stop and she settled on the seat, journeying to her new destination.

*

Grateful that neither she nor Clarissa knew what Jamie had done with Joanna, Jessica had struggled to keep to their story The police had footage of Jamie and Joanna walking through the town and then Joanna getting on the Rye train with Jamie leaving her and walking home. From then on the girls could give them no more information, as they had no idea where Joanna had gone nor whether she had actually caught the train. Not convinced that she had boarded any train, police were irritated with the inconclusive CCTV footage.

Jamie's interview with the police was equally galling for both him and them. His story that he and Jo were dating soon fell apart when he could not tell the police anything about her. He had not thought that through. He struggled to respond to the barrage of questions that was hurled at him as to where they had met and how they had actually carried on a relationship. The police, not seemingly bothered by his false story, tried to impress upon him how vital it was that he should tell them where Joanna had gone. But in all honesty he could not. Part of Jamie's hurried 'plan' had been to give Joanna various options of where to go and not say which she had chosen in order that, when questioned, he could be honest and not land her in it. In that respect he felt as lost as the police, and perhaps a trifle more concerned. The really disturbing encounter was from his parents. His mother was furious at the fact that 'someone' had taken the newly stocked contents of the cupboard and fridge. His father was hurt that he had lied to them. Neither had taken in the real tragedy of the situation – Joanna didn't touch their radar.

*

Robert Bentley, twenty-four hours after Joanna's disappearance, had got no further in finding her. Neither of the two students, for whom he had felt some respect, had bothered to respond to his invitation to help and he was totally convinced that both they and the brother knew something. And so he did what he always did on these occasions. He got into his car, belted up, placed a CD in the player and, releasing the clutch, headed for the little village of Cranenden, where he knew there would be some excellent pub grub waiting for him in The Old Wharfe Inn.

*

Jamie was still trying to placate his parents. He hadn't realised that they would have taken it so hard. It was as though he had done something terrible instead of helping someone out. They had gone on about him being a liar and cheating them and abusing their home and stealing their food, and as far as Jessica was concerned, it seemed as though he had led her astray. Really he felt utterly bewildered at his parents' lack of compassion and perception over why he had done what he had. They did not see Joanna as a desperate girl but only as someone who had blighted their comfort zone. For the first time in his life he felt alienated from his parents and their moral compass. It disturbed him. Jessica too had avoided him, refusing to discuss what she felt was his betrayal of her, with his insistence that he knew nothing. Frustrated at her complete lack of belief in his denial, he felt annoyance and anger at how this whole sorry mess had developed. The girl had gone, he had helped her escape and yet it didn't feel very comfortable not knowing how she was or why he cared so much.

*

It was just before nine and the sky was dead black – no stars, little evidence of any moon and an icy blasting wind flew across the river. Joanna lay on the tiny bunk bed and pulled the sleeping bag up under her chin and settled herself down for the night. The boat was bitterly cold and the lapping of the icy water didn't help. The condensation made the air wet and small globules of water ran down to the edge of the ill-fitting window, forming small rivulets which bubbled up then dropped to the shelf below. On this shelf Joanna had rigged up a small wind-up torch that she had found at the bottom of her sleeping bag. She guessed that Jamie had put it in there, or it had been left and forgotten after his previous camping trip. Joanna had enjoyed her first day of escape. She had successfully found this hidey-hole, having broken into the small boat earlier. It was easier than she had imagined. After having left the bus on her return from Tenterden, Joanna had wandered up the side of the riverbank, whereupon she had found herself amid a few dog walkers and runners making the most of the late afternoon sun. But that dropped out of sight early and the heavy night sky dimmed all spark from the lurking stars. Joanna scoured the underbelly of the bridge and scanned the availability of suitable boats. She had very little choice, for most of the moorings were empty, bar one that was a fairly robust-looking dinghy type. It was called *The Hapless and Last*. Not the most inspirational name she had ever seen, but the boat was easily accessed. It had a small but rusted chain linking through the two plastic handles that she had easily pulled off from the wooden shutters at the entrance to the cabin.

Inside the boat was cramped and damp, but there was a small primus stove and a kettle. On the shelf above the stove were two mugs and a caddy containing teabags. In the tiny cupboard below the gas tank she found a saucepan and various plates, bowls and a motley collection of cutlery. There was also a small screwdriver which Joanna used to screw back the handles on the shutters, linking the chain back through as though, to a casual observer, it was still linking the two together.

Having dumped her baggage, Joanna left the boat and wandered along the riverbank and onto the main road. She ventured far along both ends of the lane until the houses were out of sight. She felt comfortable and somewhat safe. There was no-one about and those that were seemed to be oblivious to her wanderings. She checked out the deserted campsite on the other side of the river and noted where the shower facilities were housed. Turning from the bridge, she made her way across the cricket pitch towards a dilapidated village hall. Looking back over the river, she noticed the low setting of the sun that picked out the top part of 'her' boat. Hugging herself, and with a skip in her step, she wandered along the lane when, turning back towards the pub, headlights flashed and to her horror she saw… no, it couldn't be…

Ducking behind a Range Rover parked at the edge of the lane, peering out, her heart pounding, she saw Bentley! But how? Calming herself, she watched as he left his car and walked straight towards the pub door. Coincidence – it must be – but didn't someone (she couldn't remember who) once say that there was no such thing as coincidence? Now what to do? She decided to be bold and just check out the car park. Maybe she was mistaken. Then she spotted it – racing green and sitting on the far side of the car park, as spotless and shiny as it always was – the Aston.

Joanna pulled up her scarf and covered her mouth and, with as much bluff as she could muster, wandered by the window of the pub and peered in. Half covered with a drab curtain, the window view was blocked, but on tiptoe she could just make out the back of Bentley's head – a few centimetres from her own. Two men in overalls were opening the door to the pub. Joanna followed them in and made her way to the ladies' loo, snatching a furtive glance at Robert Bentley, who was sitting at the table by the window nursing a pint of beer and reading a newspaper. The warmth from the huge log fire enveloped the bar area and the aroma from the kitchen tantalised the ever-hungry runaway, who made use of the toilet facilities and gave herself a good wash.

Glancing in the mirror, she studied her appearance and decided to leave off the hat, which she stuffed into her pocket. A girl of about eighteen joined her in the washroom and redid her makeup whilst Joanna fiddled with her hair and planned her next move. She really needed to know why Bentley was here in this remote village. It was bizarre to think that he had just turned up. Convinced that he knew she was there, she waited until the girl with the makeup left and she was alone. Reflecting on what she could observe from the crack in the door that she held open, she was able to watch Bentley without him being aware of her. He had now replaced his paper on the stool by the fire and was tucking into his meal, a meal that she envied. For some moments she felt sorry for his obvious loneliness and all at once realised that this was nothing more than just a real coincidence.

Relieved and more confident, she waited until he had taken a sip of his beer and was about to fork up another mouthful of his pie, when the door opened and two women came into the washroom. Taking her chance, she followed them out on their return. Keeping to their right side she managed to sneak past Bentley and out the door without being noticed.

Or so she thought. Robert had just put down his knife and fork and was about to go for the sticky toffee pudding when he became aware of the attractive woman who had walked by him earlier. Volunteering a smile, he caught just a fleeting glimpse of another person, a girl in a bit of a rush who skedaddled out of the door in a flash. His stomach churned. He had no idea whether it was her or not, but there was certainly something familiar in the bowed head and scurrying figure. But he was seeing her everywhere he looked.

Twice today – he could have sworn that she was at Rye station when he had made the attempt to search for her among the commuters before school. That turned out to be false, as he knew to his embarrassment, after yelling and running along the platform only to grab a young girl by her backpack that turned out to be a very amused New Zealand tourist. The second time he was less bold about challenging the 'would-be' Joanna. He had driven through the town and caught sight of a girl waiting at a bus stop. This time, however, he just drove up to the roundabout, did a complete turn and cruised back by the stop only to discover a bus had pulled up and crowds of young students were piling on. Now he tried to remember what the destinations were from that stop. But, not being a regular on public transport, he had really no idea and decided to check it out tomorrow. He was probably wrong. After all, this would be a crazy place to try and hide – it was a bit of a backwater and certainly had nothing going for it as far as action was concerned, as there was none. So Robert simply picked up his spoon and enjoyed the syrupy, sweet and warm comfort food that mingled beautifully with the astonishingly cold vanilla ice-cream.

Her heart still racing, Joanna leant against the outside wall of the pub. She took in the air and the night sky, then, in fear that Bentley was about to step out and see her, scooted across the road into the darkening shadows of Petty Lane. This escape was not how she had envisaged her great move out of care and into the world. Sick of the constant change of do-gooders and hardnosed 'carers', the bitter, disaffected and lonely disturbed youngsters like herself, Joanna had made a conscious decision not to become embedded in drugs and prostitution like so many before her. It had been very hard. Fighting off despair and the cheap thrill of getting high enabling her to forget it all and drift into drug-induced oblivion had worked once – but the after-effect was horrible.

She had had no recollection of what occurred in her trancelike state and had woken in a stranger's room with her 'friends' lying comatose in various states of undress and dishevelment. Disgusted with herself, she remembered almost passing out, her head throbbing and her stomach retching. Like a frightened rabbit she had taken in the disastrous effects of the room. The vomit on the bed, the strange litter of hypodermics, burnt foil, spoons and shot glasses spread across a coffee table disturbed and frightened her. There had been no sign of the men that she had vaguely remembered enticing her to the house the day before, with their promises of fun and excitement. Well, that was not what she had envisaged as 'fun'. In a panic in case they returned she had attempted to wake the others, but they shrugged her off and told her to clear off in no uncertain terms. Grabbing her things that she had found scattered around the room, she had staggered to the door and fumbled her way across a filthy landing and tripped down a wooden staircase, dodging the excrement and regurgitated food as she fled to the front door.

The sunlight had blinded her as she drew in great gulps of fresh air. She had run until she felt far enough away to be safe from the guys. Bending double, she tried to control the cramps in her stomach and the urgent need for water to drink. Horrified, she'd noticed a needle scratch on her arm and a bruise where the needle had failed to engage with the vein. What had she taken? Staring wildly now, she'd attempted to make her way up Lavender Street to the main road, hoping to get some idea of where she was.

It was then that a car had drawn up beside her and the front passenger door had flown open. Miss Grigson, from the home, had leapt out and grabbed Joanna forcefully by her wrist. There then followed the usual tirade of verbal abuse and threats that had followed Joanna throughout her life. Having bundled her into the back of the car, John Foyle, Grigson's sidekick, turned the car around, whereupon Joanna had to guide them back to the house that she had just exited. What followed she couldn't make up. Both Foyle and Grigson had locked her in the car while they rampaged through the house, dragging the other three girls from the place. All four were then wedged into the back of the car and driven back to the home, isolated from each other and interviewed individually. Then... nothing. That was the shocking part. No consequences, no police, no search for the men responsible. Even when Joanna was beaten up the following evening by the girls for snitching on their whereabouts no-one did a thing about it. At that point Joanna resolved not to trust anyone (especially those in authority or under the umbrella of 'carer') and to never again be dragged into the kind of drug, alcohol and sexual perversity of street life. Three weeks following that incident she was fostered into a home in Norfolk – far away from Barnet, another short-term placement.

Now two years down the line she was wandering the cold, windy heights of Toll Hill, her torch guiding her to examine every outhouse and shed that was available. Darkness drew on. Realising it was a hopeless task in the bitter cold and without streetlamps to assist her and the cloudy sky obliterating the moon and stars, Joanna turned and made her way back to the boat, resolving to explore further in the daylight. Glancing at the pub car park on her way back she noted with satisfaction that Bentley's car was still there and surmised he had not made a connection to her at all. The approach to the boat was slippery, requiring both hands to steady herself down the bank. A swift look to left and right, she once again removed the simple chain and lock and clambered back on board. Knowing that by its location, anchored under the trees by the bridge, she could not be observed easily from the road, she felt relatively safe. Even so, she carefully wedged the blinds into place and rammed her socks in any suspect gaps so that when she lit the lamp any light would be safely harboured inside the cabin.

The cabin smelt stale, damp and fusty. It certainly wasn't built for living in and the galley was a cramped glorified cupboard, housing a camping gas stove and ring. But to Joanna it was perfect. Having sealed off any chinks of light, she switched on her torch and rummaged around in the drawers until she found a lighter. She flicked the top and it ignited. Checking that there was enough fuel to use it again, she did a further search through the cabin. On the back shelf there was an old Tilly lamp. Picking it up she realised that there was nothing left of any fuel with which it might light. It did seem to be extremely rusty and unused. Perhaps it was just for decoration. However, the stove looked more promising as there seemed to be a fairly sturdy-looking calor gas bottle directly underneath the appliance. Joanna switched on the taps, but nothing happened. After fiddling with the main lever on the actual canister there came a hiss from one of the burners and she quickly flicked the lighter and the burner ignited with a loud pop and fizz and a smell of burning dust. Immediately she rifled through her bag and brought out a can of beans. A can opener was wedged in the corner by the basin and once she had relieved it of its place she could see why it was there. Its main function had been to support the flimsy top shelf that was precariously balanced in the corner. Once removed the whole section came crumbling down with a clatter.

Joanna froze, praying that there would be no-one outside passing by to hear the noise. After a few minutes her heart resumed its usual steady rhythm and she breathed again. Removing all the broken bits of shelf and stuffing the debris into a plastic bag, she opened her can of beans and heated them. The scrappy piece of cheese she had was dobbed into the saucepan as well, where it bubbled and reduced to a melting puddle in the midst of the beans. The aroma was wonderful! Hoicking herself up onto the seating platform, with satisfaction and a semblance of happiness, she ate from the pan the most lovely, delicious meal ever. Dipping into her bag of goodies that Jamie had given her, she pulled out a sachet of minty chocolate drink. This was the icing on the cake as far as she was concerned, and by nine o'clock she had straightened out the sleeping bag to fit over the very short bench seat, curled herself up, cuddled her jumper, switched off her torch and slept.

*

Meanwhile Clarissa and Jessica were having a truly hard time. Both sets of parents were furious with what they saw as an immature and childish prank involving a vulnerable and highly strung young girl, who would be 'God knows where' and involved in 'God knows what' and evidently the two girls were clearly part of the scheme. Neither would believe that they had no idea where Joanna had gone. For, as Jessica's mother had suggested, the girl knew very few people, had very little connection to the area and would have no-one to whom she could go to for support. That gave little comfort to Clarissa and Jessica, who felt furious at their parents' total lack of sympathy for Joanna's plight and were solely concerned for the betrayal that they had felt from their own daughters. School was even tougher. Bentley seemed to take it upon himself to corner them at every moment and demand that they advise him on what Joanna had planned. Larkfield took every opportunity to find fault with their every movement, from lateness in class to the length of their skirts – it was only a matter of any pretext being used to get them in her office with the sole intention of giving them the third degree over what had happened on the night of Joanna's escape. But funnily enough the interest from the police seemed to have dissipated.

Inevitably both girls were beginning to feel betrayed by their adventurer. Annoyingly their attempts to make contact via the mobile they had given her rankled when it was continually unavailable. They felt cheated. To top it off Jamie was being particularly off-hand both with his parents and the girls. In fact he was hardly ever home, spending most evenings searching the back streets of Hastings, St Leonards and even Rye, in the hope of finding the girl with the dark hazel eyes.

The disturbance in the Whitworth household was worse. Sally was appalled at how Jim had suddenly turned on her and made her feel as though it was all her fault. Alex hardly spoke at all except to scream some verbal histrionics on how hard done by she was. And social services were on her back arranging enquiry after enquiry; they hadn't even paid for her looking after Jack!

*

As if in accordance with everyone's feelings the weather turned truly nasty and winterish. Heavy rain and north-easterly winds kept the temperature down and the sky grey. This alternated with heavy fog and dull, heavy days. Life in Hastings was shrouded in ever-increasing gloom and life on the boat was cold.

7

As time went by Jamie had wistful moments of wondering about Joanna. She became something of an iconic figure, a girl with whom he had spent the night in a feverish state of fear and protective collaboration – and now she had gone – vanished into the foggy winter of drizzle and chill. He carried on as usual, of course, and put up with the constant nagging from his parents and sister (that was only after they had decided to get back to actually talking to him once they had got over the fact that he had taken Joanna in on that eventful night) and their constant echo of, 'But you must have an idea of where she is, Jamie…?' But deep inside he was disturbed. He kept telling himself that Joanna was just surreal; it was an event that had happened and now no longer existed. How could he be so smitten with someone that he didn't know? Yet smitten he was, and he found himself totally distracted in school to the detriment of his studies. He found it difficult to concentrate – gazing out of the window, searching lines of faces in crowds, in bus queues, outside shops and strangers in parks, just in case she was there. His mother noticed all this and didn't help by pushing him to confirm every few moments that he was 'all right'. He knew that he would have to 'do' something. He couldn't just allow her to drift off into oblivion.

As each day moved into another, time was taking him further and further away from her. He was ineffective. He was ridiculous. He was losing her face in his mind. Now he was scared that if he did see her in a crowd then he would no longer recognise her. Often he closed his eyes and tried to bring back the face that had lain on his bed. The way her hair curled around her face with just a hint of toothpaste sticking to the ends. They had talked in whispered tones on and off throughout the night. He was disturbed by her coldness towards herself and life in general. He was appalled by her history – again told in such matter-of-fact terms – no dramatics, no emotional slants or woe-is-me anecdotes, just the plain, simple truth of her sad life. He was also very angry with Sally and how she had callously given up on her.

In his pondering and deliberation Jamie recalled something that Jessica had said the day after Joanna had disappeared. Mr Bentley had turned up at the house again 'out of the blue', according to Jessica, and had given Jessica his card, which was odd, but even odder was that he had written on it that he could help and could be trusted, and to ring his personal number on the card. Well, Jess hadn't, and she had thrown the card in the drawer in the coffee table, where restaurant cards, takeaway menus and the like were shoved. With very few options left, Jamie felt that he might contact Bentley and see what he could offer by way of tracing her.

Not really thinking whether it would be of any value or not for surely, as a teacher, there was very little that he could do and in fact there was not much that he could keep to himself. Jamie knew from past experience that teachers had no right to keep students' confidence. His best friend John Wilkie had confided a personal problem to his head of year and within a matter of a very few days after that confidence had been breached, John was in serious trouble. The police had come to the school and John was suspended for several weeks. When he returned he had changed and refused to share with anyone what had truly happened, though rumours were rife. All Jamie could get from him was, 'Don't tell the bastards anything.' Embittered, failing his studies, he eventually left school altogether, resulting in John Wilkie being just a memory. Would it be different for Jamie if he contacted Bentley? He was, after all, a student at a different school and technically Bentley had no jurisdiction over him – but on the other hand…

Several times he had gone to ring the number on the card and then shoved the card back in his pocket. He deliberated over what help this man could be. In actual fact neither of them knew anymore than anyone else, but it was just the mere fact that he could share his concerns with another person outside of his family that made Jamie finally press the keys of Bentley's number.

*

It was another Friday evening – my, how quickly they came round. Not wanting to wish his life away, Robert Bentley had mixed emotions on another end to another working week. He relished his Friday nights, his one evening of total absorption in his music and sometimes his gastronomic 'treats' in various restaurants and pubs. There was something special about this precursor to the weekend that gave him pleasure. Saturdays were different. They highlighted his isolation and loneliness, and Sundays were always then spoilt by the oncoming dreaded Monday – a time of marking and preparation and lesson plans that took up most of the day and evening.

On this particular Friday, Robert had left school early – well, early for him. It was getting on for five and the weather had brought in a seeping fog which rolled off the sea and created a damp, chilly and wintery end of the day. Robert didn't fancy driving far and felt a little bit snuffly, having been fighting the various viruses that had spread around the school for the past few weeks, he didn't want to go far. So for once in a very long time he drove straight to Sainsbury's and quickly grabbed a ready meal, a baguette and a decent bottle of Rioja. At the checkout he noticed Barack Obama's *Dreams from My Father* on special offer, a book he had long wanted to read, so he grabbed a copy and stuck it in his basket. He was quite looking forward to his evening in, away from the pressures and stress of work, winding down with peace and quiet and Obama for company, when he felt his phone vibrate in his jacket pocket.

The conversation took place in Sainsbury's car park. By the time Robert had put down his basket and fumbled for his phone the ringing had stopped. Not bothering to check who had called, Robert completed buying his goodies at the self-service checkout and made his way to the car. Sliding his bag of goods onto the passenger seat and closing the car door against the now-drizzly fog, Robert relaxed and checked his phone. Number unknown! Ah, well – if it was important they would ring again, and he slid his car into reverse, taxied carefully back out of the parking space and then rolled into the space opposite in order to stop and answer his now-ringing phone – clearly it was important and he thought he had better respond.

Jamie was annoyed when, having at last deciding to ring Bentley, he received no answer, and more infuriating was that Bentley's phone had no message option. In pent-up frustration he gave it a few minutes then pressed redial – if there was no response he would have that as a sign to leave Bentley alone.

On the second try Jamie was about to give up when he heard Bentley respond with his deep sonorous voice stating, 'Bentley here.'

Robert was staggered; he had all but given up hope of ever finding anything out about Joanna, and here was his first link. They arranged to meet the following day in the Old Town. Jamie said it would be better at lunchtime as he was working in the kitchen, the Saturday shift at The Stade. He had taken the job to supplement his meagre allowance but resented how it encroached on his evenings and weekends. However, it did give him a bit of independence and freedom to be outside of his parents' eyes. The conversation had been very awkward. Jamie had insisted that Robert swear to absolute secrecy anything that they discussed. He pointed out to Robert that he was not under Robert's tutelage nor was he a member of his school, and if he didn't agree to his terms then there would be no chance of them sharing their ideas and concerns and attempts to find Joanna. Robert agreed to everything. He knew that should the moment arise when he had information that should rightly be given over to the police he would struggle to do what was right – both morally and personally. He also knew that should this go too far he could lose his job. Yet he was prepared to commit.

His drive home was steady and ponderous. He absentmindedly took his shopping into the kitchen, popped the ready meal in the cold oven without waiting for it to heat up, opened the bottle of wine and poured himself a large glass, which he swallowed in large gulps – something he never did. He poured himself another, threw his jacket on the back of the sofa and slunk down in the armchair, musing over all that Jamie had said and being intrigued by what he failed to say. Obama was forgotten. Robert did what he always did when disturbed: he went to his piano and sunk himself into playing as loudly and as vibrantly as possible the Tchaikovsky overture that he loved so much. His ready meal coagulated in the oven, forgotten.

*

Joanna was taking a risk. It had been so long since she had conversed with anybody that even she was feeling rather isolated and alone. Several times she had toyed with the idea of switching on her phone and contacting Jessica or Jamie, but something always held her back. Having prided herself on her independence, the very fact that she needed (and wanted) to hear their voices disturbed her. There would be questions that she wouldn't be able to answer. But more importantly she didn't want to admit how much she wanted to see them, to be a part of them and to have a sense of their friendship. She was also ashamed of how little she had accomplished since running away. Time had run by and the struggle of just keeping alive was taking its toll. Conversely she was also scared that they might have given up on her and moved on – that was the most likely scenario. Making the decision to move out of the boat and change her location gave her courage and something to share, so she planned to contact whoever she could later that evening, when her new plan had been fully formed. The lack of means by which she could feed herself was becoming a more dire problem. Last month her luck on that score had been realised, whereby she had managed to obtain much-needed food.

The ancient church across the river was open to visitors during daylight hours but unmanned. Joanna had often spent time in the relative warmth at the back on weekdays when there were no services. Religiously each morning at nine thirty a woman from one of the cottages unlocked the door, and as soon as it was twilight she returned to lock it again. Jo always ensured she was well out of the way as soon as the clock struck three. She had noticed that there was a small plug-in heater amongst the debris of flower-arranging bits and pieces and candle ends and other flotsam and paraphernalia. It had been useful to wander in about midday and hunker down behind the back pew, plug in the heater and warm herself up as well as drying her socks and underwear that she had rinsed through. The fan heater was effective and blew out like a hair dryer, and like a hair dryer the air was hot and furious when flicked to the top speed. She had to be quick and used the fan heater in short blasts so as not to become too noticeable to the outside world. Considering the thickness of the door that Joanna ensured was closed behind her, it was really not credible that anyone could hear, but she wasn't intending to take chances.

On one occasion the door latch was lifted – fortunately just as she had turned the heater off. A middle-aged woman and man entered and made their way to the front of the church and let themselves into the vestry. Joanna dived down and hid in the under part of the back pew, the cushions and hassocks blocking her in and out of sight. For some time the couple were heard walking to and fro and opening and closing the door as they made several trips back and forth. Eventually the door closed for the final time.

She waited for several minutes until she felt sure that they had truly gone. Slowly she pulled apart her hideout and it was then that she realised the purpose of their visit. Bags and boxes of food were heaped by the altar in readiness to display for the forthcoming harvest. Joanna was sure that they wouldn't leave all this produce in an unlocked church. In her panic to get out she tripped over the heater flex and smashed her knee on the edge of the stone font step. Sharp, electric pains shot up through her thigh and she yelped in agony. Distressed now, Jo limped to the boxes and heaps of tins and cartons and fruit, and grabbed one of the bags. Boldly, she hugged the bag to her chest, along with her now-dry washing, and limped out the door. As she made her way down the path she recognised the two incomers on the path opposite by the pub, who were just about to re-enter the church with arms full of flowers. That was a near miss!

Back on the boat she searched through her bag of goodies. Did she feel guilty? Absolutely not! This was food for the poor and needy, and who was more needy than her at this point? No, this was an ironic gift from God. She had paid for it with the pain in her knee and the swelling that had now arisen in a throbbing red welt above the kneecap. Her attempt to call her friends failed when she realised that the phone had died. A final visit to the church enabled her to charge it up as she lay on a pew cushion staring up at the stained glass window where she watched an entrapped butterfly dance between the rafters, amazed at how the light from the sun merged with the glints from the coloured glass to the creature in flight.

*

Time went by. Joanna survived a few more days on the boat but had begun to plan her next move. The weather was horrible, wet and very windy, making the boat rock about and bash into the bank. Little leaks appeared and each morning a puddle emerged in the centre of the decking which meant nothing could be safely left on the floor, and with such little space it was all rather cramped. Not only that but the dampness had created a smell that was ingrained into her sleeping bag and clothes. It was all pretty horrid. After her escapade with the harvest goods, Joanna had put together her now fully charged phone. However, she had no idea of anyone's numbers, having lost the scrappy piece of bus ticket on which she had written them down so many weeks ago, but by scrolling down the contacts list she soon found names that she recognised.

So at about the same time as Jamie had set off for his 5K run Joanna punched in his number. Her heart thumped with anticipation and her mouth was dry. But panic over, she needn't have become so concerned, for it went straight to answerphone. Joanna pressed delete. Then she paused, thought about it and rang again. This time she responded to the invitation to leave a message. Just hearing Jamie's voice inviting her to do so made her feel even more lonely. She quickly and clearly explained to Jamie that she was okay, that she wasn't too far away, that she would try and ring him again, that he couldn't contact her as she would be turning the phone off immediately. Which was precisely what she did.

Now, five days later, as Joanna packed up her things in anticipation of her next move, she felt comfortable and happy, excited by the thought of moving on and speaking to her friends. That was the night of Archie's tragic death.

December

Robert had heard the news of the tragic drowning in Cranenden. It struck a chord with him, for he had grown strangely fond of the place and especially the pub, with its comforting fire and home-cooked food. It distressed him to think of the wasted young life. He watched as, on the local south-east news, police cordons separated the death scene from the rest of the village. The reporting of the tragic last few moments of the boy's steps was ghoulish as they were traced by his friends who whimpered and sobbed through the heartless interview. Had they been aware that he was drunk? Why had they not all walked together across the bridge? Had they fallen out with him? Was it a fact that his best friend had fallen out with him over a girl? Was the girl in the pub last night? Was the girl, who he was found with, his girlfriend? On and on it went.

'Quite inappropriate,' Robert said out loud. And then the last point that was raised by the reporter set him thinking. The youths were emphatic. No, there was no girl with them. They had no idea where she had come from. There was no-one about when they had begun their fruitless search for Archie.

The reporter faced on to the camera and stated that, 'As yet the police have not identified the girl from the river. It is hoped that during the coming day someone will call in to add light to her identity. Meanwhile, the police have issued a description of the girl who was described as…'

Robert sank into his chair eyes, concentrating on the television screen, hoping for a picture, but no, it was just a verbal description, though one that Robert felt surely could have been Joanna.

*

Jamie was becoming more and more frustrated with Robert who, though useful to talk to, had come up with nothing concrete on what to do next. Moreover, he could have kicked himself on returning home from a run to see that he had missed a call from Joanna. On trying to call her himself the line just rang and rang. Staring at the phone, willing her to call again, was ridiculous, but he found himself doing just that.

Deep in revision for his exams (much to his mother's relief), the phone, when it did ring, made him jump. He felt further disappointment as it was only Robert calling. Deciding to ignore him, Jamie turned it to silent. Teased by the fact that the call could only be about Joanna, with his concentration broken and with that inner hope that this might be a significant call about *her*, Jamie pressed redial.

Without any preamble, Robert asked Jamie whether he had seen the news, to which Jamie replied in the negative. Robert sharing his thoughts that the girl from the river might be Joanna didn't help Jamie. Was Robert so desperate to find Joanna that he was finding suspects in the news? Would Joanna have been in that particular village at that time of night and with another boy? Jamie felt sick and yet excited at the same time. Robert's reasoning as to why he thought that the girl on the news was Joanna was a long shot but then, as they had nothing else to go on since she had left, they were both keen to grasp at straws.

8

Having just completed her shift, Maria handed over the notes and observation sheets that she had acquired to Joanna's night nurse. Merrick had only just been accepted onto the intensive care unit. He had spent all year trying to get his status recognised by the NHS, as there was still the requirement to 'prove' himself before his qualifications could be accredited. Eastern European qualifications were not acknowledged as being of the standard required for work in the UK, which meant further exams and training. Having already borrowed the vast sums required for the extra exams as well as the flight and living costs, Merrick had struggled hard to pay back the loan company he had found online. It was not a comfortable situation to be in and now they required a different kind of 'payment' from him than money, as he had disturbingly discovered. On arrival at Dover he had been met and escorted, along with other legal migrants, to a housing estate that had been procured for them. In no uncertain terms it was made clear to him how beholden he and the others were to the security force that stood before them. It was quite clear that they had all been duped into some kind of illegal ring of thugs posing as loan distributors.

Some months down the line, his debt never seemingly reducing, he had now become a trusted and compliant member of the syndicate. Dragged down by fear of the thugs and the power they held over him, he had drifted into the grooming business. What option did he have? Each girl he supplied them with reduced his debt, albeit by the smallest of percentages, allowing him to send most of his salary back home. He struggled to come to terms with his desire to save lives and the pressure he was under to destroy. For what else was it? Convincing himself that the young girls he procured were just foolish, stupid idiots who knew what they were getting into fell flat, but it was the only way that he could justify his actions.

It wasn't always an easy task either. His last attempt at grooming three young girls from West Academy School had failed when they had run scared after the youngest had collapsed unconscious, having inhaled the cheap drugs that he had administered for their pleasure. It took him all his wits to bring her round and bundle her onto a bus with the threat of death if she were to spill the beans. Fortunately, as they were all well aware, the police didn't care for these social misfits, and allegations by young girls were rarely taken seriously. This, his first failure, had upset Assef, who expressed his anger with some violence on Merrick. The hard and aggressive kick to his torso had resulted in cracked ribs. The Russian, Arkady, Assef's business partner, had required three virgins to secure and hopefully seal an important tricky deal. Without the promised 'entertainment' that dealer had backed off. The message to Merrick was clear: find two more young virgins by Tuesday or he would get his knuckles thrashed.

The reckless violence that Assef was prepared to wreak was astonishing. With a broken hand he would no longer be able to work. And that was Assef's top card. Desperation found him scouring the back streets of Maidstone following young girls who were wandering the streets late at night. It cost him, but it was necessary to gain their confidence. These were needy kids. Just kids who were roaming the streets looking for excitement. Desiring affection and kindness (their homes lacked both), they were gullible. A couple of drinks, a hand held, a touch of the hair, a cuddle and they were putty in his hands. He had come on duty tonight with the promise to his latest prey that he would take them 'on an adventure' – a quick train ride to Hastings, where he would deliver them into Assef's hands. He just couldn't believe how simple it all was – and it sickened him. He was angry at the girls for being so naïve and so ridiculously open to accept sexual advances. He was also disturbed by how they excited him! They let him touch their breasts, tiny, plump little breasts, with an eagerness and a desire to which he could so easily have succumbed. In fact, they were vying with each other as to who would give him the most pleasure. Yet he couldn't take them. They had to be untouched for Assef's business deals. Not too sure how much he had left to pay on his loan, he had hoped to be out of this sordid business in the not-too-distant future. Once his qualifications had been accepted he would get a position that would pay him a real salary, releasing him from this vile way of being.

The girl in the bed interested him. She was clearly a vagrant and had no identity to speak of. Nicknamed River Rother Girl, the press had accurately described her pathetic scrap of a body and asked for help in identifying her. He took her observations and wrote them onto her chart. The nurse assisting him complained as to how tired she was and that this was her double shift. Her being a volunteer street preacher when she wasn't on duty at the hospital often meant a few sleepless nights. If she didn't get some soon she would crack. So Merrick told her to go and take an hour's break and he would cope on his own. Desperate for the sleep, Jackie thanked him and slipped into the rest room, grabbing a blanket and curling up on the sofa with the echo of Merrick's voice telling her that he would call her in an hour.

Merrick went from bed to bed checking all his patients, enjoying a feeling of power and control. There were other nurses on the ward, but they were involved with the A&E admissions. His role and that of Jackie's was for the four intensive care patients that had been admitted earlier. They were all mostly stable, allowing the machines to which they were attached to decide whether they would survive or not. Oxygen being pumped in and drips dropping healing chemicals of antibiotics, blood and saline were automatically infusing the infection and internal organs of them all. Checking for the need to add painkillers of morphine and intravenous paracetamol, Merrick made his way around the beds, marking any new signs on the charts as well as marking the temperature charts and blood pressure counts. But it was to the unknown girl that Merrick was drawn. If she was an unknown and if she did survive... well, who knows? She was certainly skinny enough for a future client's dream.

*

Jamie was livid. As soon as he had hung up from Bentley he noticed a missed call from Joanna! Immediately he rang her back, but it went straight to 'this person's phone is currently unavailable'. With clear frustration he threw his phone across the room. But if she had just rang then she couldn't possibly be the unconscious girl in the hospital.

*

PC Jane Winter had taken the bag from Dennis with annoyance. She was irritated that she had been given the task of going to the hospital to interview the River Rother Girl. Jane had been hoping to be assigned the far more interesting and, she felt, more important job of searching for two runaway girls that had been reported just that morning. Ironically, River Rother Girl did not interest her in the least. Not on her patch.

At the station she had had to put up with a tirade of concern from parents who had reported their daughters missing and had no idea why or where they had gone. The rest of her colleagues were involved in many other crimes that were seeping ever more into the fabric of Maidstone society. Drugs and alcohol were the key concerns. The parents of the missing girls were known to the police and had reported them missing several times before. They were very belligerent and demanded their rights to have their daughters found and returned to them. After many man hours and ineffectual searches they always turned up some days later having 'chilled out' at 'a mate's'. The parents then withdrew back to their lives without any sense of trying to control their daughters' behaviours or freedoms. As frustrating as it was, there just didn't seem to be any point in undergoing a massive search. Both girls would inevitably turn up again, in their own time, without undue effort from the police as past behaviours indicated. And so there had been a somewhat mute response this time to the demands of the parents.

Jane hoped to be assigned the job, as she would then have the perfect opportunity to develop a theory she had, that the missing girls were a link to cross-border drug deals between London and Maidstone. She was sure that she was on to something and in the guise of searching for the girls she would have the perfect chance of doing her own investigation. However, much to her chagrin, she was lumbered with River Rother girl.

*

Yvonne was perplexed, thwarted and disturbingly annoyed. A feeling she had felt more and more in the past few weeks. Having now come to face the reality that no-one really cared about her misfits in society, it was a real shock. After the first few hours of Joanna's disappearance the police had stopped the search. Their reason? Well, she wasn't really their problem – no-one was that bothered about a girl who had chosen to run away from a foster home, and clearly the foster mother wasn't that interested about her going and she was probably quite capable of surviving on her own. And she was *almost* sixteen, and that made her not far off seventeen – and therefore not far off being an independent adult at eighteen! Where was the logic in this way of thinking? Yvonne wanted to know.

The retort from the desk sergeant that 'these girls were far more streetwise than the public gave them credit for, followed by moaning about what a waste of man hours it seemed when there was real crime to be investigated, like the new spate of knife crimes, as more often than not they didn't want to be found and would only run off again. Yvonne almost throttled the desk sergeant when he uttered his callous and dubious comments. Even though she had demanded to speak to the community welfare officer and warden, she had received little more help or concern. True, the local community officer who had originally been on the scene seemed perturbed and concerned, but she had little sway with anyone else and was fully occupied in her daily duties to do more than pay lip service to Yvonne's enquiries. It seemed clear that LAC children were at the bottom of the pile as far as care or concern by the police was concerned. Even her own superintendent in social services, Mr Eckersley, seemed less concerned about the missing girl than how many targeted visits Yvonne had managed to log and report.

Her embarrassment over her own daughter's part in Joanna's disappearance had created tension and distress at home. Not to put too fine a point on it, Yvonne was hurt and perplexed by the deliberate aiding of the runaway as well as being complicit in the escape. Their somewhat close relationship had suffered and though it was still very raw there had, of late, been some semblance of reconciliation. It had taken a great deal of persuasion from Clarissa to ensure that Yvonne could allow herself to believe that she had had no idea about where Joanna had gone. Because of that need, Clarissa felt the lack of trust from her mother and she too felt stressed by the tension and distrust. On top of which, she and Jessica had had a big fall-out, which had created a particularly lonely episode at school.

It had been Clarissa who had instigated the upset – she was really angry about how the whole episode had turned out and had verbally attacked Jessica about Jamie. After several days of interrogation at school and not being believed, followed by some really unpleasant bullying by Mel and Sue, Clarissa became defensive and angry, accusing Jessica of keeping Joanna's whereabouts from her. Convinced that Jamie had told Jessica where Joanna had escaped to, she felt left out and hurt that they didn't trust her with the truth. Conversely, Jessica was appalled that Clarissa actually thought that she and Jamie had lied to her by knowing Joanna's place of hiding and keeping it from her. Wasn't that the problem that they were facing with their parents and the authorities? Both girls became highly sensitive and reacted defensively over every remark. Clarissa's projected disbelief fell just short of accusing Jessica of lying. For Jessica that was the last straw.

And so, one bitterly cold November day, both girls had had the most enormous spat in the school grounds. The fact that it was so public meant that Sue and Mel had observed the fight, along with half the school. The bitter recriminations meant that Clarissa was going to be easy meat with no-one to protect her and they took great pleasure, as all bullies do, in attacking her whenever and wherever they could. Games lessons were purgatory for Clarissa until she realised that if she were to really progress in her running skills then she could outwit them on cross-country runs and get herself into school teams for hockey and netball, and as Mel and Sue were quite pathetic at anything physical, it was highly likely that she could reduce her time in their company. As it happened, Jessica and Clarissa found themselves both selected for the school squad, where they were to compete on the South Downs for a place in the county cross-country team.

Initially Jessica had been infuriated that she had to fight for a place alongside Clarissa. Why had she chosen to take up athletics now after all this time when Jess had been trying to persuade her to take it up for years? To spite her? Having refused to have anything to do with her through the many evenings of training that the school provided for them, it was on the day of the actual event that Jessica had observed Clarissa looking decidedly nervous and quite clearly lonely in the school canteen.

As she was about to pass her by she overheard Mel demand from her 'protection' money and noted Clarissa reaching into her purse and bringing out a fiver. Swiftly and without a second thought she intervened, and as Mel's hand touched the note, Jessica whipped it away and into her own pocket. Jessica grabbed Clarissa's arm and, dragging her to her feet, simply stated, 'Right, Clarri, lunch on you – what's it to be? Pasta? Ready for the run later?' And with a swift kick in the direction of Mel's shins, she propelled Clarrisa towards the lunch queue.

With a whispered, 'I'll get you for this, two-tone,' Mel hobbled back to Sue on the far side of the canteen.

Both girls queued in silence at the hot food section and in equal silence returned to an empty table, where they ate their pasta. Nothing was mentioned, and after both had cleared their plates, they rose together and walked out into the corridor and down to the lockers. It was only then that Jessica looked at Clarri and smiled. Clarri took it as a prompt for her to say sorry for not believing her and Jamie. Arm in arm, both girls headed off to the competition with little thought of Joanna and the issues that had caused their upset.

*

Alex, meanwhile, had truly had a foul time. Every day since the disaster had been disturbing and miserable. She couldn't quite forgive Sally for hitting her so hard and for being so weak. Her dad had been pathetic in how he had cried over Joanna's disappearance and the way that Jack had also been taken away. The unnerving silence in the house was tangible. Tears from her dad! A grown man, crying over two children that were nothing to do with him. It was pathetic and on top of it all he had ignored her totally. Having said that he was ashamed of her and her behaviour, he had sent her to bed, leaving her alone. The rows began almost immediately after the police officer had left and Yvonne had taken Jack. It was dreadful. She had never heard her mother, or indeed anyone, screech like she did that night. She tried to ring Laura but then stopped partway through dialling. Too embarrassed by having been shown up by Martha and unable to face the amused sarcasm that she would inevitably receive from her 'friend', she hung up. It had taken her a great deal of effort to get in with Laura and Clare, and now that friendship was clearly blown. School was going to be a nightmare.

*

Alex awoke the following morning just as her alarm was about to trill. Uncomfortable and disturbed by the past evening's events, she lay back in her bed, dreading what she would face when she went downstairs for breakfast. Eerily the house was silent. No radio – her mum always had Classic FM on until Alex tuned in to Heart. There was no aroma of toast either. Wearily she drew back her duvet and felt for her slippers. Pulling them on she wandered over to her basin and began to clean her teeth. The basin was a new item that she had bullied her parents into having because she wanted the same as the foster kids and they had a really nice basin in their room. She had really pleaded hard for her own shower unit – a proper en-suite – but, as her dad had said, there was no spare money for luxuries of that sort. Making do with this little concession, she resented not getting anything more. It did seem exceedingly quiet. School uniform on and blinds drawn up. That was odd. The car was gone!

She flew down the stairs two at a time. 'Mum, Dad?' she yelled, trying each room, but she found the place empty! Unbelievable. They had left her on her own, gone out without informing her! Searching the kitchen for at least a note to let her know why they were absent, Alex found nothing. She slumped in the kitchen chair and gathered her thoughts. A slight nagging guilt registered in her mind. Was she to blame? She felt the kettle – it was cold, so not a recent absence then, for her mother would never leave on a morning without her obligatory cup of tea.

*

Joanna was conscious. She had some vague recollection of where she was and it took her some time to recall why. Her throat hurt and she felt restricted by the tubes and attachments linked to a flashing, bleeping machine by her head. Some kind of fluid was finding its way into her veins via clear plastic transfusion bags attached to a vertical metal pole that too was plugged into the same machine.

Exhaustion made thinking hard and so she drifted in and out of a sleep filled with dreams and nightmares. She sensed a presence over her face and felt the touch of firm hands that wrapped her arm in a cuff registering her blood pressure.

Moments later (or maybe hours) she sensed the light of day flickering through the window until the blind was drawn and artificial light, dimmed and soothing, bathed her face. The presence returned; this time she opened her eyes and noted the friendly, kind face of a male nurse.

He smiled and softly spoke. 'Welcome back, little one.'

But her eyes refused to stay open and she drifted again. Aware of voices, her dreams melded into the distance and she heard snippets of words: '...a vagabond... social services... poor kid... dead...'

Panic welled in her throat. She sat up and started searching for the voices, but the room was empty. The chairs turned towards her bed, empty. Sinking back into the pillows, she wanted to drift away, but this time sleep eluded her. Looking up she noticed that some of the tubes had been taken out, though she could not recall who had done that or when. Then she spied the pipe coming from under the sheet. Edging herself up onto her elbow and glancing down, she spotted a urine bag attached to a wire frame. It was almost full. Feeling pretty rough, she let herself fall back onto the pillows just as the curtain flew back and three medics came into view.

A bald, round-faced man in a white coat and plastic white apron smiled at her and asked her how she was feeling.

Joanna was muted – too afraid to speak.

The woman in a blue dress and pink cardigan came close and spoke to her softly in a gentle Scottish accent. 'Well. wee one. And how are you? We were all getting quite concerned about you.'

Joanna just breathed. A chart from the wall behind her head was lifted and passed around her visitors. As they all grouped together at the end of her bed, their backs to her, she could make out the hushed comments about her incredible recovery considering how cold the water and the night had been. It was her emaciated body that was now causing the most concern. The woman went on to say that she must be a tough little person to have come through so much. She wanted her to stay in intensive care for another twenty-four hours before being transferred to a ward where she could be nursed and nourished back to full strength before going home. Joanna still said nothing. The doctor tried to encourage Joanna to respond, but to no avail. Her refusal to speak and lack of response concerned him. Smiling at Joanna, he patted her hand and left. Speaking to the registrar and sharing his thoughts with the male nurse, Joanna heard just enough to be aware they were saying she was still traumatised but in light of the death of the boy, they recognised that the police needed to speak with her as a matter of urgency.

As all three walked away from her bed the doctor turned and patted her foot. 'Take care, little one, and try to tell us what you can so that we can help you get back home.' And then all three left the area with her notes and Joanna was alone again.

Her mind was fraught. Perhaps she could relax for one more day, but then what? Feeling so very weak, she knew that she didn't have the energy in her to move far. Where was her bag? She looked around – nothing. With great gulps of painful breaths she flung her legs over the side of the bed and stood up. A wave of dizziness and nausea swept over her, and she clung to the bed tray. That was no help. Feeling herself slipping, she crashed to the floor.

Within seconds Merrick had returned and gently picked her up and helped her back into bed. Once he had laid her down he leant over to plump up her pillows while he spoke. 'Your things are with the police. They will be bringing them back later today. But I guess you won't want to be involved with them. So just do as I say and then I can help you. I can get you out of here and somewhere safe.' His accent was fascinating and Joanna looked at him hard. His eyes held her gaze – they were steady and strong. He smiled and released her back onto the bed in a caring, unthreatening way. He smiled and told her that he had realised that she was a runaway. He knew that she could speak because he had heard her mumble in her sleep. Then he winked, went to the table and brought over a bowl of soup and bread. He pulled up a chair and proffered the tray.

In her weakened state Joanna found it hard to control the spoon and liquid soup without spilling it, but Merrick took over and fed her slowly, carefully and in silence. Exhausted by the motion of actually eating something, Joanna refused the yoghurt Merrick offered, but she did drink the orange squash and asked for more by indicating the empty glass. Merrick laughed and gave her a refill. 'Rest now and then in a while I'll come and remove that bag once you are strong enough to get yourself onto a bedpan. That'll make you more comfortable. Oh, and you'll be going to another ward tomorrow, but don't worry. It might be easier to get you out that way. I'm off duty in an hour and then I'll be back tonight – it is my split shift. We can plan then.' And with a wide grin and a wink he left Joanna to sleep.

*

PC Jane Winter arrived at the hospital just in time to interview Joanna before she was transferred to the high-dependency unit. Joanna was asleep when she entered the room, so Jane sat and observed her for a while. Noting how thin the girl was, Jane recoiled from her dirty, matted hair. As she was clearly in a deep sleep, Jane took the opportunity to read up on her notes of the events as described by Dennis.

Her curiosity aroused, she read what little was known about this anonymous creature lying before her. The question for her now was, had the couple jumped together? Had she tried to save the boy? Who was she? The death had stunned the village. The parents of Archie were desperate to know how they had lost their eldest son. Jane, full of empathy for the parents, took an immediate dislike to the girl. Her refusal to respond exacerbated her feelings. A further dilemma for the police was whether to treat her as a suspect in the 'murder' or the hero of a tragic 'accident'. Until she spoke and gave them her version, any charges or recognition of her actions were in abeyance. This delay enhanced the angst of the dead boy's parents, who were desperate for answers.

Scanning the area she noticed a cupboard with Joanna's name on it – well, River Rother Girl, to be precise. Aware the patient was sleeping, she rummaged through it – zilch. That in itself was odd. The absence of cards or personal effects was startling, for even in such cases the general public had always been aroused to send the 'saviour' at least a card of thanks and gifts of sentimental comment – cuddly toys, flowers or just a get-well wish – but this girl had received nothing. She seemed to be truly a non-person. Not even of media interest.

The girl's eyes flickered and so Jane leant forward and in her brusque way said, 'Okay, I think it's time that we had a talk and it would be most helpful to be able to call you by your name… and that would be?'

Joanna, hoicking herself up on to her side, peered at Jane with bleary, hollow eyes. Her voice was thin and waspish. 'I don't really know what happened to the boy but I think he was dead when I got to him. Did he die? Was it all a waste of time?' she whispered.

Jane stood up and dragged her chair closer to the bed, feeling momentarily sorry for this skinny runaway. 'No, it wasn't a waste – it was very brave of you, though perhaps a bit foolhardy too, but you at least survived.' And Jane reached out and took Joanna's hand.

Joanna found herself telling Jane how she had heard the splash and thud as the boy hit the water, how she had realised his friends had been calling for him, but when it became clear that no-one was about, she had jumped. If only she had done so earlier from her boat then she might have been able to hold him up, allow him to breath and not stay face down and drown. Joanna withdrew her hand from Jane's and wiped tears from her eyes. She saw and felt in Jane a threatening presence of authority that had the power to probably instigate her return to social services. That she could not endure.

Quickly she responded, 'Melanie. My name is Melanie.' She lied, explaining how she had been staying on her uncle's boat and that she had expected him to pick her up but that when he hadn't turned up she had decided to hitch back to Hastings.

Jane wrote it all in her notebook, then sucked the end of her pen before saying, 'Okay, Melanie, that's fine, but whatever your reasons are for telling me this story – for that is what it is, a story – I want you to know that I am here to help you. So when you are ready and feel able to tell me the truth I will listen. Unless, of course, you are telling me the truth, in which case I need to know your uncle's name and address.'

Joanna just stiffened without saying anything. Jane then started to talk through a few things with Joanna – very simply she told her that the police were grateful to her and so were the boy's family. She also said that as she was clearly not eighteen then social services would be finding her a safe place to stay as soon as she was released from hospital. But of course if she were to give her home address then they would happily return her there. Jane going on to explain that they had a duty of care for her whatever she may or may not have done was lost on Joanna because at that point the door opened and in walked a nurse with three cuddly toys that had been sent to the River Rother Girl, from well-wishers. Each one had a note. The first was attached to a small teddy bear; it said, 'I think you were really brave and would love to visit you, J.' The second was a dog and attached to it was a note that stated, 'Very brave, call me, Bentley,' and the third was a giraffe, and the note with that just said, 'Be safe, phone someone who cares for you.'

'Well, well – now, I think you might need this.' And with a smirk Jane passed over to Joanna her work mobile phone. Joanna took it for a moment and then realised that she had no idea what Jamie's or anyone's number was as she had not memorised any – in fact, she did not even know Bentley's, or maybe she was to call the dog Bentley? Who knew. She was so confused that she handed the phone back to Jane and turned her head towards the wall.

Jane knew when she had gone far enough and for this first visit she thought that perhaps this was it. So after a few more attempts at trying to get Jo to talk she gave up and just patted her hand and told her that she would be back. 'Oh, and by the way, I've put your rucksack in the locker cupboard, in case you wondered.' And then she left.

*

It was Jamie's idea to send the toys. Robert thought it was just a little too melodramatic and unnecessary, but Jamie had threatened to go it alone if he didn't agree and insisted on keeping Joanna's true identity to themselves – besides which, it was a shot in the dark and the poor girl may well not be Joanna anyway. They had taken a chance by not including any phone numbers in the message, assuming and hoping that Joanna still had access to her phone. Having delivered the toys, all they could both do now is sit back and wait.

*

Disturbed and anxious, feeling hounded and confused, Joanna drifted in and out of nightmares. She woke in a cold sweat. Though the blinds were closed, hiding the winter rain and cold, it was clearly late in the afternoon. Merrick had not come back on duty yet. She had at first thought he might be her saviour. But there was something about him that she didn't trust. He was kind, friendly and with eyes full of warmth… but something wasn't right. But if she didn't acquiesce to his offer of help then what?

A different nurse was fussing around the end of her bed and then she faced Joanna and suggested that she walked her to the shower room. She smiled a no-nonsense smile and held up shampoo and shower gel in her hand by way of invitation. Still weak, Joanna limped, leaning for support on the nurse, feeling utterly ridiculous. How could she have allowed herself to get so feeble and useless? The nurse chatted to her constantly as they wandered down the corridor and into the bathroom. She showed Joanna the red plastic bell pull to use if she felt dizzy or faint and then she drew the curtain across, shut the door and Joanna was alone.

Looking down on her naked body, she was shocked at how skinny she had become. Her hair felt like wool and it took her an age to lather it up and then even longer to rinse it off. Even so, it was just a matted, hardened mess. The cuts on her arms had healed, leaving purple stains as a reminder of how she had abused her body. She felt feeble and exhausted; the warm water trickled over her while she half-heartedly attempted to clean off the grime that seemed to be embedded in her skin. Her mind could think no further than getting back to her bed before she passed out with the dizziness that overtook her.

The nurse had left her a clean hospital gown to replace the emergency paper one that she had hitherto been wearing, but it was not exactly stylish. And that got Joanna concerned over her belongings. Where were her clothes? She knew that her rucksack contained very little – she had left nearly everything in the barn where she was hoping to stay. Then realisation struck – her jumper and bracelet. She cried out in a state of panic. She had to get back there somehow and retrieve her only links to her past.

Towelling herself dry, she was now energised, focused and strong in her resolve to get back to her barn. Exiting the shower, the nurse guided her back to the reception area, where a wheelchair was waiting. It seemed as though she was transferring to a ward immediately. Her intensive care bed was required for another on the brink of death.

And then there he was. Merrick, sitting behind the desk, writing up notes. Looking up and thanking the nurse for escorting Joanna to the chair, he glanced at her. 'Hi, Melanie, isn't it?' he purred.

'That's right.' She dropped her eyes and glared at the floor. There was a mockery in his voice and she knew he didn't believe her.

Merrick dismissed the nurse and called for a porter to take 'Melanie' down to her ward. When she had gone Merrick left his desk and squatted down in front of her. Putting his hand under her chin, he firmly lifted her head up at a tilt. 'Well, my sweetie, you'll be leaving the ICU and going onto a ward. But don't worry. I'll keep my eye on you from afar and will make arrangements to get you free from here as soon as you are fit to leave. Tell the police nothing and you'll be safe with me.' He didn't wait for her to respond, just stood up, ruffled her wet hair and went back to the ward, leaving her alone and shaking.

9

Her arrival to the medical ward was an experience that she had never encountered before. Every nurse, medic and patient clapped her journey from the doorway to her bed. Three cheers rang out as she was hailed a hero for her attempt to save the poor dead boy. Unused to such attention, she felt at first humbled and then a bit stupid. The boy had died! Not only that, he was probably dead before her 'heroic' attempt. Nevertheless, there was a warmth and kindness emanating from those in her new abode. Within the hustle and bustle of the ward, surrounded by women of various ages recovering from a variety of medical conditions, Joanna felt safe and comforted. The warmth and kindness that emanated from these inpatients was like a motherly cuddle. They had all read about the incident on the river and were full of admiration for Joanna's brave attempt at saving the drowned boy. She was overwhelmed by their effusive appreciation of her bravery and survival of such a horror. As they in turn received visitors, who also in turn clapped and placed thumbs up towards her, Joanna began to regain her confidence. What could Merrick possibly do to her whilst she was surrounded by these lovely people?

Yet at the back of her mind was the disturbing fact that she was on the verge of recovering enough to be rehomed by social services. Her one hope was that they were so under-staffed and Christmas was so close that she might be left a bit longer than suggested by the police. At least she thought that she could rely on staying on the ward for a couple more days, especially as she was still pretty weak. Her biggest worry was getting back to the barn where her belongings were safely stashed – if all else was lost she could not lose her jumper.

*

She awoke sweating, surrounded by people glaring at her, curtains drawn closed and a syringe poised, ready to be plunged into her arm; struggling to scream, nothing came from her mouth, which was dry and tight. Her arms felt heavy and weighed down as she attempted to fist her hands to punch out and fight, but there was no response from her body. Merrick's grin leered over her and she could smell his breath.

'It's okay, it's okay, love.' Arms were around her and she was being held by Ruby, the lady from the opposite bed. Her breath came in fits and starts. The dream, the dream, it was the dream! It had all been a nightmare. Merrick wasn't there. There was no syringe, there was no forced pressure on her at all, just Ruby holding her and making soothing comments until the arrival of the nurse, who had been summoned by the alarm bell.

But the nurse in attendance was brusque and commanding. Decisively dismissing Ruby back to her own bed, she turned her attention to restraining and calming Joanna, who in turn allowed the nurse to check her vital signs and give her some medicine to relax her. The nurse comforted her by saying that the trauma of all she had undergone was making its way out of her body, that the sedative she had been prescribed should bring about a semblance of peace and trouble-free sleep.

When the nurse had left Joanna crept out of bed and wandered over to Ruby, who was lying quietly. Joanna sat on the edge of her bed and thanked Ruby, who said nothing except put her arms around Joanna, enabling her to let out all her pent-up emotion in the form of tears. Eventually Ruby guided Joanna back to her own bed. Having laid her down, Ruby stroked Joanna's hair until she had calmed and fallen into a drugged sleep, where she stayed for the rest of the night.

By the third day Joanna had made her plan. Ruby had taken to her and fussed over her with great concern and empathy. She had been a great listener and Joanna had felt able to share with her a little of her life. Careful not to reveal too much, she felt that Ruby deserved some explanation for her support and care, and so it was that Ruby learnt of Joanna's early years and her need to escape from the clutches of the welfare state that had given her so much misery in her life. By still referring to herself as Melanie, Joanna felt in control and confident enough in Ruby to illicit her help. Taking a risk, Joanna told of her mistrust of Merrick and how she felt threatened by him.

Her desperation to get away from authority played into Ruby's sensitivities. A life-long human rights campaigner, she understood the need that Jo had of being free. Between them they prepared for her next move out of the hospital. Ruby insisted that she held off her escape for as long as possible in order to regain her strength both physically and mentally.

But the pressure was mounting when on her fourth night in the ward Joanna had a real visit from Merrick. He slunk in just as the changeover shifts were being debriefed in the nursing station. Apart from Joanna only Ruby was aware of his presence. Joanna was sitting in her chair watching TV when he drew back the curtains and hovered over her. He informed her that she was about to be released into the care of social services – that he had checked her notes and that a visit by her newly assigned social worker was arranged for two days' time.

'The police,' he stated, 'will be renewing their interest in you and will be interviewing you.' He took her hand and whispered that she wasn't to worry, that he would get her out on that day after her interview. He had fixed it all up and she would be safe with his friends. All she had to do was to be outside the ward at the staff change-over of medics and he would take it from there. He squeezed her hand, winked and then left.

*

He didn't trust her. Her eyes told fear. He'd lost her confidence. Having promised Assef that he would provide him with a new girl, a better girl for the Russian, he could not fail again. She fitted the bill exactly. A bit skinny, but then that enhanced her child-like image – which was always the primary choice of the warped customers. He couldn't allow her to slip through the net. He stood outside the ward and pondered. Would she make a run for it? He knew how desperate she seemed and if he was in her shoes then that's what he would do. How to keep tabs on her was a problem. He was on his break with three hours left of his shift. If she stayed where she was until then, it would be simple to come back later tomorrow and try to regain her confidence.

Back in the ward Joanna watched the news on the TV monitor. It was the first time she did not feature in the local spot. Fame was short-lived, thank God. Ruby had had a visitor who was about to leave when she called her over.

With a strong handshake he introduced himself as Barry Masters, Ruby's nephew who worked in Waterstones in Maidstone. Ruby had informed him of Joanna's plight and he offered to collect her from the hospital and drive her to wherever she wished to go. He was working during the day, and in the build-up to Christmas, he would be in the store until eight o'clock. However, if she were happy to meet him at nine o'clock the following evening he would take her wherever she wished, within reason. For once Joanna felt that her luck had turned. Meanwhile, unbeknown to her, Merrick was to get some very important information from a totally unexpected source. On the fifth floor of the hospital the lift doors drew apart and Jamie stepped through into the intensive care unit, where Merrick was at the desk and welcomed Jamie's enquiries with interest.

*

Joanna had gathered her few items of hospital fare – toothbrush, toothpaste, soap and throwaway slippers, all rammed into her rucksack along with her personal items that she had been shifting to the barn on the night of the death. She put her complete trust in Ruby and Barry – two complete strangers but seemingly caring ones. Barry could, of course, be just patronising his aunt and not intending to help Joanna at all. He might well just hand her over to the police once she had left the hospital with him. Running out of options, it was a risk she had to take.

The day had begun with news on the TV of dangerous high winds and rain – amber weather warnings all around the South East. Pictures of high seas at Hastings and the flooding of the River Rother featured on the local BBC news highlighted the conditions Joanna was going to have to face in her barn. She had eaten all the breakfast that she had been offered, though her throat was still extremely sore from the tube that had been inserted when she was unconscious, and that was exacerbated by the acidy grapefruit juice that washed down her toast and jam.

Looking out of her window she noted the flapping of the flagpole where a derelict KCC flag withered and stretched between gusts of really high winds. Bits of paper whirled and eddied around the concourse far below, and people huddled in the smoking shelters as close to the buildings as they could get in order to elicit their right to fill their lungs with the chemicals that had probably been the cause of their visit to the hospital in the first place.

Joanna sank back on her bed, suddenly weakened by the thought of more running and hiding in this somewhat precarious weather. Not just that, though; it was the isolation and loneliness that she dreaded. Here she had been cosseted and cared for and mothered and had laughed at such humour from these lovely women who were all going through a great deal of pain and misery themselves but somehow they found laughter in their plight. This she would miss so much. Not least was the food. While most of them moaned about it, Joanna thought it was amazing. Perhaps she could eke out another day.

Then, true to Merrick's forecast, there stood before her Jane. This time she wasn't in uniform, but she did have a whole batch of forms that she clearly needed to complete. Brusquely she invited Joanna into the small office at the end of the ward where they would not be disturbed. A thumbs-up from Ruby gave her the courage to bluster her way through the interview.

'Okay, let us begin with your real name and date of birth, please,' stated Jane, pulling up a chair and firmly seating herself before Joanna in a cold and efficient manner.

'I've told you, my name is Melanie, Melanie Richards, and I was born on 22nd May in Manchester.' Joanna smiled and leant back in her chair with a defiant look.

The forms were meant to provide information to help establish Joanna's details and her needs, but her refusal to give accurate details of DOB and previous places of residence and next of kin, gave Jane no help at all. Her determined silence and resistance infuriated Jane.

Determined to waste no more time, dispirited, she stood up, put the papers back into her briefcase and placed the chair back on the stack at the entrance to the ward. She walked back to Joanna and, leaning forward, put her hand on Joanna's shoulder and said in a quiet but exasperated tone, 'I only want to help. I deal with so many tragic situations on a daily basis that I cannot begin to tell you. I don't have time to be led on a wild goose chase. However, I shall be back tomorrow with the hope that you will have changed your mind. No matter whether you choose to talk or not, we cannot let you out of hospital alone. You will have to go into care until your parents are found. I can only say that there is an evil world out there and that should you ever need my help...' She slipped a card into Joanna's hand. And with a final, none too friendly squeeze of Joanna's shoulder, she left the room.

Joanna almost called her back but resisted. She looked at the card and saw Jane's name, followed by the words 'Child Support Officer', followed by two different phone numbers and an email address. On the back was the motto 'You don't have to be a victim', followed by a smiley face. In a strange way that helped and gave Joanna a determination that she would not ever become a victim, but that she would go, if Barry was as good as his word, and get back her freedom and live her life. It had been a struggle to defy the officious woman. All the companionship and kindness she had received in the ward had made her soft.

But what really brought her back to her feisty, driven self was Merrick's sudden return visit that afternoon.

He came in and, like a slippery eel, slithered around to her part of the ward, and with a swift glance to ensure that they were alone, he cornered Joanna and, without saying a word, pulled out his mobile phone and flicked the photo shots into view. Joanna's heart trebled in speed. Jamie's face was smiling up at her.

All Merrick said was, 'Well, Joanna, if you don't want anything to happen to him, then I suggest that you do exactly as I tell you. I will ensure his safety as long as you comply with my wishes. If not, well, I cannot guarantee a happy outcome. I'll be back, so be ready to leave here when I say and not before. Get a good night's sleep now – see you tomorrow.' And with that he slipped back out of the ward.

The air cooled; Joanna shivered. She was dumbfounded. *Try to think – what could this actually mean?* He knew her name – he knew Jamie. But Jamie was smiling and seemingly okay. So did that mean Merrick had him somewhere or was it all a bit weird? She was confused and distressed now. Did she have to give up her escape in order to help Jamie? And what was she helping him out of? It wasn't clear, and what did Merrick want with her?

Ruby was sitting by her bed knitting and drinking tea. She smiled at Joanna as she caught her eye. Who could be trusted? What was actually going on? She found herself staring at Jane's card. 'You don't have to be a victim'. Well, she wasn't. And she wasn't going to be. If Jamie was in Merrick's clutches then he would have to get himself out of them. She had to think about herself and she needed to be empowered and not to be bullied or pushed around by anyone else. She had no idea what the photo had meant or how or why Merrick had it – but one thing was certain: she wasn't going to be gulled into Merrick's trap. The more she thought about him the more she realised that Merrick was dangerous and to be avoided at all costs.

She knew what she would do – a flick over the card again and she noted the email address of Jane. The moment she was free from the hospital she would warn Jane about Merrick and the threat he had made about Jamie. But right now it was imperative that Ruby and Barry's plan be put into action.

*

Of course Merrick realised that Jamie was searching and taking a chance to find his 'girl' with the hope that they could be reunited – at least that's what he surmised. It had been so easy to get Jamie to give him the information that he required. In fact Jamie had volunteered almost all he knew of Joanna – well, who wouldn't when faced with a caring, life-saving nurse with little heed of rules and regulations, who 'only wanted to help'? Someone who seemed to want the best outcome for Joanna.

Jamie had asked whether he could see the girl that had saved the boy's life, as he believed that he knew who she was. However, as Merrick explained calmly and gently to Jamie, they couldn't just let anybody into the ward to visit – he had to be sure that Jamie was a relative or at least a person that Melanie wanted to see. A brief description of 'Melanie' was all it took for Jamie to suggest that the girl was indeed Joanna.

She had run away, he had blurted out, and he had had no idea as to where she had been all these weeks; suffice to say that he and her teacher really wanted to help her find a home and to be settled back into their lives. The photograph had been easy to take on the premise that he would show Joanna and if she agreed then he would allow Jamie a visit. Her reaction to the photograph was as he had hoped.

Merrick also suggested to Joanna that the police were suspicious of her and were keeping her under close observation, that they were not so sure that she hadn't been party to the death of the boy after all. Lies tripped off his tongue so easily, and he felt powerful and in control. He knew that he was pushing her, but in his experience, young girls were stupid and believed anything in their fear of being caught out. He secretly suspected that they enjoyed his type of bullying, just as he enjoyed their vulnerability and pleading.

However, he had not recognised the intelligence behind Joanna's monosyllabic responses. Far from being won over by him, he was successfully ensuring that she would have absolutely nothing more to do with anything he had to offer her. His comments that she should avoid talking to the police made her even more suspicious and further supported her idea of telling Jane about him after she had scarpered. She hoped that Jamie was okay and that he could sort himself out – she wasn't going to be drawn in on that score. She just hoped that when he turned up the following day to 'help' her that she would be miles away and untraceable.

10

The mattress was filthy and stank. Alex lay curled up and huddled under a stained blanket. Her head throbbed, and she felt sick and dizzy. She looked around and her eyes took in the half-empty polystyrene cups that had contained cheap vodka. Bruised and sore, she began to whimper. The Russian man that she had had to entertain had hurt her beyond all imagining. In as much as it was a vile memory that drifted in and out of her consciousness, she knew she had been assaulted in the most degrading way possible.

Taking in her surroundings, a wave of panic bubbled up in her head. How was she to get away? Trying to sit up, her head throbbed all the more and nausea swept over her to the point that she couldn't do anything other than just lie down and cry.

The door opened and a cold, accented voice stated, 'You will need to shower and then eat before your next client. Come on, move!'

The man wearing a coarse dark blue jacket bent over and grabbed Alex's wrist. She yelped and pulled back, but he was too strong and yanked her to her feet, whereupon she staggered and fell into his arms. He gripped her wrist still harder and lengthened his hold, keeping her at a distance whilst still securing her upright. 'You filthy little shit,' he spat. 'Don't you dare touch me.'

And with that he dragged her across the room, out of the door into a poorly lit corridor and shoved her through a door to the right from where she had been locked in. This room was bigger, cleaner and there were several futon-type loungers squashed together, accommodating other young girls – all in a state of dishevelment.

A woman sitting at the end of the room on a ladder-back chair stood up and approached Alex. 'Okay, Assef, I'll sort her out,' she murmured and took Alex's hands.

Assef spat and gave Alex a shove. 'Well, sort it – she stinks and she looks ugly! I want her cleaned up and ready for 7.30.' He glanced around the room and his eyes strayed across the futons at the others lying there, counting them as his head scanned the room. 'Eight, only eight!' He drummed his hand on the adjacent wall. 'I need her to make up the ninth, so get her ready. And you,' he added as he took Alex's chin in his hand, his eyes rolling over her face and body, 'stop your pathetic wheedling and get yourself looking presentable and smile!' His final act before he left the room was to point his finger at the woman and grunt at her, 'Sort it!'

After he left the girls began whispering amongst themselves. Some stretched out and lit up cigarettes. Others left the futons and wandered over to the dressing table, where an array of lipsticks, mascara and eyeshadow was littered on the surface. Each girl took it in turns to brighten the faces of the others in garish hues and sparkling grease smears of pathetic Disney colours across eyebrows, cheeks and breasts. Alex realised that they were all her age or younger, and that they looked lifeless and dead. The added makeup accentuated their skeletal appearances supported by the gaudiness of the inappropriate camouflage.

'My name is Maggie, and I'll help you to get dressed for this evening's clients,' Maggie crooned as she steered Alex into the shower unit at the end of the room. There was no privacy. The plastic curtain hardly shielded the spray from reaching the nearest futon.

Alex stood under the lukewarm shower and used the shower gel that Maggie squirted into her hand. 'Best deal with that first...' Maggie intonated and nodded at Alex's thighs. The blood and semen had dried and cracked in small scabs on her thin little body. Maggie held out a sponge for Alex to use to aid the scrubbing. Alex began to cry – silently this time – and made harsh rubbing motions with the sponge, harder and harder until she was almost rubbed raw. It helped, the pain from this defusing the pain from inside her belly.

After a short time Maggie handed her a squirt of shampoo and a pasted toothbrush. All these actions had to be completed in full view of the girls in the room. They, of course, took little notice. They were too busy sorting out their own mini crises.

Once Maggie had inspected Alex thoroughly, the water was turned off and Maggie handed her a rough, grey towel and was steered towards a spare futon on which a sheer, purple silk dress was displayed.

'Dry yourself, put this on your marks.' Maggie handed Alex a pot of cream and indicated her bruises. 'I don't want them visible,' she added.

Alex looked up at her and asked for her underwear.

Maggie just sniffed and stated, 'What on earth would you want those for? Just a waste of time.' And with that she slunk back to her chair.

The rest of the girls ignored Alex. She tried to assess her situation and realised what a bloody fool she had been. Now she was scared. Really, deeply scared and she felt as though there was nothing she could do. She was trapped. She sat on the edge of the futon, naked and hair dripping, head down and eyes welling with tears. Her body shook uncontrollably.

A hand whacked around her legs. 'Get up and behave, otherwise we'll all suffer,' hissed the girl nearest her. 'Put on that shift and dry your hair. Do it NOW!' she urged whilst at the same time curling her own hair.

Alex was galvanised into action, rubbing her hair with the towel and pulling on the dress. It was totally see-through and extremely short. She felt exposed and more vulnerable than she had ever been in her life. She felt shamed and, despite the shower, dirty and horrified.

Maggie beckoned her over to the dressing table and nodded to the rest of the girls who were hovering by the makeup. 'Sort her out while I go and have a fag and get your tea,' she uttered, and then slipped through the door, closing it quietly.

The girls then responded immediately. Each one came to Alex and held her hand or stroked her hair and kissed her bruises. They all spoke in soft whispers. So sorry for what she had had to suffer. They had all gone through the same. Now they were used to it. The trick is to just do what is asked. Don't fight it. Always take the drugs offered and the drink as it dulls the pain and shame. Ellie brushed her hair and curled it in wisps about her head. Sandra took over the makeup and glossed her lips, kohled her eyes and rouged her cheeks.

The one mirror at the end of the room enabled Alex to see her reflection. She shuddered when she saw it. A pathetic, doll-like creature that would have shocked her parents and killed her father had he seen what she had become.

A pair of spiked heels in blue patent leather was her final accessory. Assef returned and called the girls to order. He lined them up and examined them one by one, ticking off on a clipboard their role for the night. He was revolting. He leered at each one. He pinched their breasts and stuck his fingers up their skirts to 'test' the moisture content. Those that were deemed too dry Maggie had to cream up. Alex was told that she had been requested by Vasilli, the man who had robbed her of her virginity the previous night.

Once the inspection was over Assef left, and Maggie went out and returned with a tray of shots that she placed next to the tray of sandwiches she had brought in earlier.

Sandra sat by Alex and told her to take as much as she could stomach because Vasilli was a known beast and did cruel, unspeakable things to his victims. 'Best to know what you're in for,' Sandra stated. 'Be warned, don't fight him. Take everything he buys you in the way of drink and food. But never, ever tell him no, no matter what.'

*

Leaving the hospital was easier than Joanna had hoped. Barry turned up as promised and visited his aunt as normal. The staff had allowed him to extend the time of visiting hours, aware that Ruby had no other visitors and that Barry could only pop in briefly after work. Ruby was improving and it was hoped that she would be able to return home in a few days. As soon as he arrived, Joanna finished packing her backpack with various items that she had 'obtained' from the hospital. There wasn't much, but she had taken several packs of biscuits from the tea trolley, amused that the little cake packs were all gluten-free and almost out of date. She was glad that she was expected to dress each day and not linger in bedwear; it was not a problem to wander into the patients' lounge at the end of the ward. She had ensured that she had done that on the previous evenings to establish a routine that the nurses would observe. Tonight would be no different.

She sat waiting for Barry to walk by. At exactly 9.15 he did. Grabbing her bag, she slipped out behind him. As he went through the security doors Joanna sidled in front of him. All the nurses would see, as they released the lock, would be Barry's back. With silent relief they both stood waiting for the lift doors to open and take them down to the ground floor, where they could escape to the car park. Each floor the lift stopped at created an almost visible tension. But Merrick was not to be seen.

Exiting the hospital, the cold air hit her hard in the face – but that was comforting: it meant freedom. The car was in Car Park A, where Barry logged his ticket and paid the fees. The area being bright and well lit gave further anxious moments, but the security men seemed oblivious to them both. All went without a hitch and Joanna found herself fitting her seatbelt, relaxing and heaving a sigh of relief as the barrier lifted and Barry drove his black UP away from the hospital towards his flat.

*

Merrick, on the other hand, was deciding whether to make his visit to Joanna now or first thing in the morning. Deciding on the morrow, a move he later regretted, he felt jubilant, having had the best bit of luck ever. For he had found an extra girl for Assef. A bonus that would keep him off his back until he could produce Joanna.

The latest 'victim' was another loner, it seemed. A girl who barely set foot in school and who had succumbed to Merrick's 'kindness' in a flash. It had happened almost as an afterthought. He had noticed her hiding behind Tesco, hunkering down by the large wheelie bin. He approached and asked her if she was okay. The poor cow gave herself to him almost immediately. She wanted to get away from her abusive stepfather and Merrick kindly obliged by taking her on the train to Hastings and handing her over, personally, to the abusive Assef. Result! Swift and without a hitch, it was a really easy deal.

He spent the evening preparing the underground room that he used to store his girls, should he need to, before transporting them elsewhere. This time the preparation was simple. For once he had Joanna in his care, a simple sleeper would be all she required.

An evening listening to music with a takeaway Chinese and an early night was the most relaxed one he'd had in ages. The elation of that evening dissipated rapidly when, on arrival at the hospital the following day, he was met by a very disgruntled staff nurse who informed him that the River Rother Girl had absconded.

*

Barry's flat was small and very minimalist, except for the inordinate amount of books that filled the wall-to-wall shelving. Barry had called into Pizza Express and bought them both a takeaway that he now shoved in the oven to reheat. He opened his fridge door and drew out pre-washed, pre-packed salad leaves and popped them into a bowl. He laid the table with two knives and forks and two small teaspoons. 'For the ice-cream,' he said. Within minutes he'd knocked up a vinaigrette dressing using Jamie Oliver's balsamic vinegar and Waitrose extra virgin olive oil. That made Joanna smile! They were items she hadn't known existed outside of TV.

All the while that he was preparing their meal he hummed to himself and didn't say much at all. The journey back to his flat had been in relative silence, except for Radio 4 piping out of the car sound system. Joanna was glad as it meant that she wouldn't be expected to converse; that could have been awkward. Now he seemed so relaxed, as though this meeting was an everyday occurrence, so there was no awkwardness between them.

He pointed out to her the bathroom and which of the two bedrooms was her room for the night. 'Unless, of course, you wish me to take you somewhere right now?' he asked. 'You are welcome to stay here for a bit, and I can drive you wherever you wish to go in the morning. My shift doesn't start until two, so we do have the morning to get you back to wherever, if you like?' He left it all so open and casual that Joanna felt enormous relief. She smiled and took her bag into the room he offered her.

It was a small box room with the barest of furniture. The walls were pale green with a silver spray of oblique lines spattered over them. The lighting was subdued and tinted a rosy hue. The bed was small and fitted under the beam at the end of the room that hung down from the cat-slide roof. There was a cane chair and a small chest of drawers with lights around a mirror attached to the wall above the small corner sink unit. She loved it. A painted white crate stood in for a bedside table, and perched on that was a digital clock and a lava lamp. The whole flat was tastefully and carefully decorated without any pretension but with an air of sophistication about it.

Joanna sat on her bed and hugged her knees and grinned. This was a far cry from the freezing boat! She needed to wallow in this luxury and make the most of it and, if possible, take up Barry's offer of staying for a couple of days before heading out to God knows where.

She joined Barry, when he called her, at the small dining table to eat her pizza and drink a lager and enjoy three scoops of Ben and Jerry's toffee chocolate ice-cream before sitting on the sofa and watching the late-night movie – *Slumdog Millionaire*.

*

Merrick's nasty little ruse had worked in one respect. He had ensured, with his lies and cruel streak, that Jamie felt rejected by the girl. After all his attempts, it was clear that Joanna didn't want to know him. After visiting the hospital and speaking with Merrick, he had felt sure that he would see her again. Both he and Bentley had planned to visit the hospital again that evening, but on arrival Merrick met them with the news that she had vanished. Jamie believed that it was because he had traced her and felt sure that she had run off because of him. Merrick latched on to that bit of emotional angst by stating that Joanna wasn't happy about his visit and that she had said that she didn't want to see Jamie at all! Merrick had had a plan for Jamie's return visit but hadn't reckoned on the older man being with him for company. It made the visit a little more aggravating so Merrick decided to throw them both off the scent and hopefully destroy any chance of their ever being reunited.

His main problem now was finding a suitable replacement. His anger with Joanna was exacerbated when during the afternoon he had received a visit from the child support officer who had been dealing with Joanna's case. What she shared with him made him livid.

Jane had received a phone message on her answerphone from Joanna, warning her that Merrick was not to be trusted round young girls and that he had tried to get her away from the hospital. She also stated that he had threatened to hurt Jamie if she didn't go with him. The call then ended and was subsequently traced to a public call box in Maidstone.

Merrick fobbed Jane off. Joanna, he pointed out, had lied about who she really was, and might well be a key factor in the boy's death which was still under investigation. How could anyone trust anything that the girl had said? As for the photograph he had taken of Jamie, Merrick showed it to Jane and repeated part of what he had said to Jamie, that he only wanted it so that she could say whether she was happy for him to visit. He was trying to protect her, not harm her. He then even suggested that Jamie might well be the person that she was trying to get away from. He pooh-poohed the idea of anything untoward, pointing out that Joanna was a runaway, a street girl and had lied the whole time. Far from being the villain, Merrick suggested that he in fact had only shown her kindness and support.

Jane had to admit that Merrick was probably right, stating that sometimes these girls get themselves into such a mess that they only know how to lie to get what they want, and so she decided that it was just a malicious call from Joanna that they could all forget.

Robert felt as frustrated as Jamie – so close and yet so far.

'I think she really does want to be on her own, you know,' Jamie mumbled as they drew up in the Aston outside Jamie's house.

'Well, I'd rather not just give up on her, you know,' Robert uttered as he eased the car into neutral and pulled on the handbrake. There was an uneasy silence.

'I dunno,' Jamie drawled. 'She has been away ages and hasn't made any real attempt to get in touch. It's doing my head in and I can't believe that she would be so cold as to deny us. Why would she run off like that, eh?'

Robert ran his hand through his hair and then turned to Jamie. 'You know, she is a really mixed-up girl who has nothing going for her – we don't know what had happened on the night of the drowning – so let's not judge her, eh?'

Jamie gathered his coat and the flowers and sweets he had bought to give to her, then he paused, turned to Robert and said, 'Well, you can carry on if you like, but I've had it.' Opening the car door without a glance back, he walked up his path, lifted the lid of the wheelie bin that had been her shield on the night of her escape and shoved the chocolates and flowers into the depths, then on second thoughts he dived in again, retrieving the chocolates. He retrieved the key from under the pot and with it opened the front door, turned and, with a half-hearted wave to Robert, slammed the door shut.

*

Jim downed the second cup of tea and sat staring into space. As that too grew cold he mobilised himself to stumble to the sink and chuck it down the drain along with numerous other half-drunk teas, coffees and cups of water. He sighed long and hard, and sat back down at the kitchen table. He was at his wits' end. Picking up the spoon that lay in a puddle of cold tea, he absentmindedly twiddled it round and round between his fingers. *How has it come to this?* he pondered.

He glanced round the room. Only half past three and getting dark already; he sighed and with an effort stood up and flicked the light switch, blinking at the bright, harsh overhead naked light bulb. It was a reminder of the awful scene whereby Sally had behaved like a wildcat and thrown everything that she could lay her hands on at him. The light shade was the first casualty when it shattered to smithereens as Sally's shoe caught the edge, ramming it into the ceiling, whereby the shards of glass flew in a hail of splinters over them both. It had taken Jim quite some time to quieten her and clear up the shards that had penetrated her arm. The kitchen had the hint of a massacre with streaks of blood splayed over the table, wall and chair. After some moments Jim had managed to get to the hall and phone for an ambulance; however, on returning to the kitchen he was just in time to stop Sally from taking the kitchen knife to her throat.

The memory of that dreadful day pecked at his mind. At least Sally was now in the Conquest Hospital, on a safe ward with locked doors and under the influence of lorazepam, which in itself had helped create a sleepy, forgetful and sad individual that Jim hardly recognised.

The cognitive behavioural therapy that had begun just two days ago had a long way to go and Jim was at a loss as to how his wife had deteriorated so suddenly and so violently before him. Not only that,

Alex had gone crazy too. She had never forgiven him for giving her a dressing-down over the treatment of Joanna and now she was never in the house. In fact, their paths rarely crossed. She had refused to visit her mother in hospital and might well have left home altogether for all Jim knew. He couldn't keep his eye on her as well as be with Sally. He lived a nightmarish existence. Fortunately his work had given him compassionate leave until after the Christmas break, whilst he attempted to keep the home together. Every meal he cooked in the evening he ate alone, watching Alex's congeal on the plate. He ensured that she had her dinner money each day, leaving it on her school bag, but whether she ever went or not he couldn't say. Mrs Bridges supposedly picked her up for school each day and Alex walked home each afternoon. But as to whether this actually happened he no real idea. He could only hope. Now today he was in a dilemma. The school had finally got hold of him to say that they had not seen Alex for over a week. Jim tried hard to recall when he had actually last laid eyes on her but couldn't. All the days rolled into one long nightmare. Sally clung to him at every visit and wouldn't let him go, crying and rocking herself to and fro. It was hell.

He glanced at the clock. He had an appointment with Mr Bentley at ten o'clock the following day in order to discuss the issue. He had been invited to bring Alex with him – but he had no idea where she was. Her bed was a tip, the clothes filthy and smelly. The floor was littered with rubbish and all kinds of junk. But, he noted with a wry smile, one set of her school uniform was still hanging in the wardrobe, clean and pristine as Sally had left it the last time she had actually done the washing and ironing.

The clock struck four. She should be back by now if she was coming. Heavily Jim stood up and wandered over to the hall window and glanced out. The street was littered with schoolchildren of various heights, ages and sizes. Some in groups, some in twos and threes, and the odd one on their own. But no Alex. Okay, he decided to give her till half past four and then he was going out to search. As he rubbed his hand over his chin he recalled that he hadn't shaved for a couple of days – or was it five?

He looked at himself in the mirror and was shocked at how ragged and scruffy he looked. *That's no good*, he told himself, and he made the effort to climb the stairs and enter the bathroom. It too was a tip.

Dirty towels, damp and cold, were piled on the floor and in the bath itself, where a dripping tap had soddened the bath towel. A further wry smile creased Jim's face – for wasn't the face flannel debacle the instigator of all this? Hadn't Joanna done the very same thing? Only this time there was no flood.

With an effort he gathered all the towels and took them to the washing machine, loaded it up, then searched for the powder until he realised there was none. Back up the stairs he rifled through the cupboard until he found a clean towel, filled the basin with warm water and proceeded to shave himself. The water was only lukewarm and yet he felt so much better after he had finished. He then gave himself a thorough wash and changed his clothes. Looking fairly presentable Jim returned to the living room and, seeing that it was now four forty-five, put on his overcoat, grabbed a torch from the cupboard and let himself out of the house.

*

Alex had no idea what had just happened. All she recalled was abject fear and the need to scream. Yet nothing came from her mouth except dribble. Her mind was fazed and she stumbled along the alleyway that she now found herself in. There was blood, that she knew. It wasn't hers. Neither was the parka coat that she pulled around her to hide her shame.

She had grabbed a glass and whacked the vile man on his head as he bent over her. It broke and the jagged edge caught his face as he turned to see what had hit him. The blood spurted from his cheek and he let out a roar. It was that that had saved her. For it had alerted Assef, who was outside the room. It was he who'd rushed in and pulled Alex away from the man who had punched her in her belly and grabbed her by the throat. Clearly they didn't want a dead one on their hands and so she was saved. Her punishment had been a beating and then being dragged into a waiting car, injected with something that made her lose reality, and finally she was force-fed vodka.

It was at this point that she was pushed out of the car. She stumbled and mumbled to passers-by to, 'please, help me, please'. Her voice sounded odd, as she found it hard to formulate her words. People turned away from her. Ignored her. Told her to sober up.

Crying and blubbering, she collapsed in a heap by the Priory Meadows car-park exit. It was warm by the vents and she gave in to the wave of nausea and heaviness that blurred her mind. She vomited and passed out, sitting in her own urine.

*

Jim ate fish and chips that he picked up in the Old Town. He had spent exhaustive hours looking and searching for Alex. Having tried every spot he could think of, he went to the police station to report her missing, showing them her latest school photo. As to what she was actually wearing the last time he saw her, that was impossible to recall. He could tell the older officer on the desk was not impressed with his ineffectual answers to the questions. He had tried to explain that he had spent most of his waking hours at the hospital with his wife, but that just added to the obvious neglect that he'd shown Alex.

Thoroughly distraught, he ended up at Martha's. He knew that she would understand and not point the finger at his ineptitude. But Martha was seemingly unable to help. She had taken umbrage when, having attempted to help by bringing round meals and offering to visit Sally, she was told in no uncertain terms by both Sally and Alex that she wasn't needed, thank you very much! Her pity for Jim was clear and it was her suggestion that Jim should go to the police, but as for having any idea where Alex could be, she drew a blank. The fish and chips stuck in his throat, and as he wandered down towards the seafront, he balled up the majority of it and chucked it in a bin.

The air was cold and windy. As Jim grew colder, so he felt more and more fearful of what Alex was doing and whether she was safe. He found himself standing on the pebbles and watching the waves roll and whiten and glisten under the stars in the moonlight. Christmas was just a few days away. Behind him the streets were brightly festive and happy voices flooded out from opened doors of cafés, restaurants and pubs as people entered and left. He pulled his coat tighter and lifted his collar to cover the back of his neck more. He'd stood for nearly twenty minutes when a street pastor came alongside of him and asked whether he was alright.

'Oh, yes, yes, thanks, I'm fine. Just going home now,' he returned while the pastor patted him on his back and offered him a blessing. With a heavy heart he turned, nodded a 'thanks, mate' and faced the wind and strove home.

*

The following day Robert sat waiting for Jim in his office. He was dreading this interview. He had felt sorry for the poor man after their last meeting, which was the night that Joanna had gone missing, and he, along with Yvonne, had turned up at the foster home where he'd witnessed the quarrel and humiliation of Alex. Robert had no particular feelings for Alex. He had met her several times during her school career, but these were mostly review days when he had discussed her school progress reports. He was also aware that she had been the instigator of Joanna's departure from the foster home. He had gathered that there was an enmity between the two girls, and to some extent he could understand how Alex might resent the intrusion (as she would see it) of outsiders into her home, but he was annoyed with her for her selfish and unkind attitude and spiteful comments about Joanna. Since that night he was aware that the mother had had a breakdown and been hospitalised. Alex had rarely made it into school, and Clarissa and Jessica, the other two girls involved, were more than reluctant to talk (to each other, it seemed, as well) for some time afterwards.

He stood up and walked over to the window and glanced out. The weather had changed and become remarkably mild for the time of year – but that brought rain and cloud and a heaviness that seemed to weigh down on his shoulders.

There was a knock on his door; he adjusted his tie walked over, opened it and proffered his hand as he stated, 'Thank you so much for coming, and how is Mrs Whitworth? Better, I trust? Ah! No Alex then?' He pointed out the obvious.

Jim shook Robert's hand and sat down in the chair by the window.

OF NO CONSEQUENCE

Robert walked around his desk but did not sit. 'Mr Whitworth, may I offer you a coffee or tea?'

Jim shook his head and glanced wistfully out of the window. 'I don't know where she is and I am at my wits' end as to what to do.' He covered his face with his hands and broke down, releasing great heaving sobs. Robert placed his hand on Jim's back and allowed the man to release the tears of fear, loneliness and sadness that coursed down his cheeks.

Some time later Robert watched from the same window the broken father walk aimlessly along the driveway of the school, making his way, by foot, in search of his lost daughter.

In assembly he took the unprecedented step of speaking to the whole school about the missing girl and asked them all to be vigilant as they walked home and keep their eyes peeled for any sign of her. Meanwhile, should any student be aware of or know of anything that could enlighten them as to her whereabouts then they were encouraged to speak out.

Consequently that very afternoon a group of year sevens discovered an unconscious girl in Alexander Park. She was slumped on the ground by a tree and would not have been visible if Flo hadn't had to bend down and do up her laces. As she did so her eyes caught a glimpse of a bare foot half covered by leaves. Terrified in case the person was dead, the children took it upon themselves to run back to the school to inform Mr Bentley.

*

The discovery of Alex in a clearly drugged and drunken state, covered in dried blood and badly bruised, horrified Robert. Fortunately he had had the foresight to engage the assistance of the community warden who patrolled the area. Between them they sat with Alex, attempting to rouse her from her unconsciousness while waiting for the ambulance to arrive. Jim turned up just before the medics and he too was staggered by his daughter's state of semi-undress and drug-induced semi-consciousness.

At the hospital Alex was placed on a drip and her body bathed in order to reveal what wounds she had. By the bruises it was obvious that she had been punched or kicked in the stomach. Her face had a few cuts and there were needle marks on her arms. She rambled in her hallucinatory state, but nothing of any sense could be defined. The police were not particularly interested once they deduced that she had 'self-inflicted' her condition. Jim knew that they thought she had got herself in with a gang of users and abusers, that her body damage was just part of a junkie's life – a point he was ready to believe himself. But just watching her, lying there, so small and vulnerable, made him feel both angry and hurt.

His anger grew, as she clearly had no intention of explaining what had happened to her when she came round. She 'couldn't remember' where she had been but was able to recall 'foreign voices' and 'other girls'. But on further probing she clammed up and said that she couldn't remember anything. She flinched from Jim's touch and wouldn't look him in the eye. The nurses tried to get from her what drugs she had taken, but she was far too out of it to respond coherently – suffice to say that she didn't know.

After twenty-four hours in hospital the doctor released her to be taken home on the understanding that Jim would give her constant support and attention and that he would ensure that she attended the outpatient clinic. The appointment was for two weeks' time. Jim brought her clothes and together they both left the hospital, in silence, sitting in the back of a taxi. Alex huddled right in the corner as far away from her father as she could get. At home Jim prepared a meal for them both, but Alex refused to leave her room, just wanting to curl up in her bed and sleep.

*

Barry had been as good as his word. At 7.30 the following morning he knocked on Joanna's door and called through that he had left some breakfast out for her and that he was just going to the corner shop to get a paper and some bread. If she wanted to shower and be ready for when he returned then he would take her to the barn as agreed the night before. They had discussed the fact that he was going skiing for

Christmas and his cousin was going to have use of the flat over the holidays so that she could be close to Ruby on her return from hospital.

Joanna felt a bit empty hearing this news. Of course – they were a family. Ruby's family clearly cared for her and were all there to support her, a situation she would never know. Barry returned to the hospital dutifully at some point each day and Joanna was pleased to have the time to eat well and get stronger and replan her options. Barry had suggested that his cousin might well be happy for her to stay on, a prospect Joanna insisted wouldn't happen. The fewer people who knew about her the better. She needed to be gone before the cousin arrived. Besides, she could easily get too comfortable and lose sight of her purpose. Barry was to take her to collect her bits and pieces, and she was to stay with him for two more nights. Which got her thinking: what was her purpose? So much had happened in such a short time that she had lost track of why she had run in the first place. She had been surrounded by people that might well have helped her track down her parents. But she had not been brave enough to ask for their help. Barry had been so kind and yet she knew that he could be in real trouble for harbouring her. Yet she had never felt so safe.

The drive to Cranenden took over an hour, passing through Tenterden, where she recalled her first day sitting in the café eating bacon sandwiches and drinking hot tea. The weather was hardly different from that day so many weeks ago and rain began to lash down again. She didn't understand why she felt nervous as they approached Cranenden itself. They drove down past the pub and turned immediately left along Petty Lane and up to the barn. There was no room on the narrow road for Barry to park and as Joanna only wanted to grab her bag she told him to drive up the hill where he could turn; by the time he had she would be ready.

The barn was just as she had left it except for the straw at the entrance, which had diminished slightly. *Good*, she thought. Clearly the chicken farmer had kept to his routine, and this was further supported when she made her way to the wall of stacks she had built and clambered over to discover all her stuff just as she had left it. She glanced wistfully about, reassured that if she needed to then she could return safely in the knowledge that so far this den had been undetected.

On the way back Barry suggested that they pop in the pub for a coffee, but Joanna refused. Bentley had been there and might well return.

During the time Barry was at work Joanna sat at the table in the flat and wrote out her plans. She made a list of all the things that she would need to obtain in order to be free. Heading the list was her birth certificate – without which she had no proof she existed. Next to that she wrote 'contact Yvonne'. She also needed some money. Tapping the pencil on the pad, she glanced round and took in the room. It was perfect. This was what she wanted for herself – her own space and simple but stylish furniture. She grinned. *Really, Joanna, getting thoughts well above your station now*, she mused.

But after an hour or so she was bored and decided that she would go out and look in the shops and perhaps get a hot chocolate. Barry had given her a fiver and so she put on her thin jacket and left the flat. Though it was mild for December, Joanna's clothes were not winterwear and she soon began to shiver.

The first charity shop that she went into was really expensive and she left pretty quickly. The second was in a side street and was much more reasonable. She hoicked her way through piles of coats, parkas and jackets until she found one that had faux fur around the hood and, because it had a paint stain (hardly noticeable) on the right sleeve, was only £1.50. She bought it immediately and wore it over her jacket.

She felt great as she left the shop and wandered along the road until she found a family-run café that sold hot chocolate cheaper than the named coffee shops. Sitting in the window seat, she cupped her hands around the mug and became a people watcher, until out of the corner of her eye she spotted... She froze in her seat! It was him, standing on the road opposite, talking to a girl of about her own age. Breathing fast and with sweaty palms, Joanna shrank back and, placing the menu in front of her face, peered over it. The girl was clearly nervous and it seemed to take a long time for Merrick to persuade her to go with him, for that was what Joanna was convinced he was doing. Then suddenly he took the girl's hand and they walked at a fair speed up the road. What to do? Should she follow?

Within seconds she downed the last of her chocolate and flew out of the door.

The slop of the leftover stew was rancid. Her punishment for having the tenacity to ask if she could see a doctor. The infection in her ankle where the chain had rubbed was coursing through her body with a fever like she had not known before. His response was to pour neat alcohol on the wound and cauterise it with a soldering iron. That was two days ago and it was only now that she had managed to come out of the fever that followed. His grim and sour face leered at her as he forced the vile food into her mouth. He punched her each time she retched it back up again. Amazingly she survived and her heart sank at the knowledge.

11

December

It had been hard. Alex's refusal to talk and her sudden outbursts of tears, her lack of communication and her disinterest in food, created a barrier between Jim and his daughter. She refused to visit her mother and insisted upon her 'lies', as Jim saw them. It was barking mad to believe that there was a gang of foreigners in Hastings 'stealing' girls and making them 'do' stuff with men. In fact he was completely disgusted with what she had come up with. The filth that came out of her mouth infuriated and distressed him. She wasn't the victim. She was the temptress who had let herself be used by whoever, whatever, for her fix, as he saw it. What he did know was that drugs were expensive and Alex had no money, so clearly she had sold herself for the price of a high. He had to face up to it – his daughter was lost to him.

Alex herself was broken. Inwardly she screamed and cried at the injustice of it all. She wasn't believed and she struggled to fill in the blank moments that she couldn't remember. School had been a no-no. She was mocked and berated by her 'friends' for her looks and her withdrawn responses. Spiteful comments about her mum being in the nuthouse were rumours spread by Mel and the gang. No-one was bothered with her except to moan and complain at her lack of work. Inside she felt disgusted with herself. Those men had hurt her, yet no-one believed her. Furthermore, she couldn't eat. Food nauseated her and she found it harder each day to get back into the schoolgirl routine. She found it easy to get her mark in registration and then sneak out to the park for the rest of the morning. At lunchtime she wandered back and got her afternoon mark and then drifted off home. She knew the school knew. That just supported her knowledge that they didn't give a monkeys. The only one who bothered at all was Bentley. He looked for her at various intervals during the day and more often than not wandered out to the park in search for her – convinced that that was where he'd find her. He was easy to fool and after a few days even he stopped the searches.

And so it was that when Assef wandered over to her by the coffee kiosk she almost felt pleased. He put his arm around her and asked her how she was, that they were really sorry that she had left and he had missed her. He further stated that they had reviewed their clientele and the Russian was no longer a customer. Should Alex like to return and stay with Assef? He pulled her close to him and kissed her on the head, nuzzling his face in her hair. It was the first act of comfort that she had received in months. She found herself leaning into him, and he caressed her head and shoulders with a fatherly touch. Nothing to frighten her. Nothing to suggest anything sexual. Still a child, Alex had craved some love and affection denied her by her father. She couldn't go near him when he had collected her from the hospital. She felt too dirty to allow him to touch her. But it had been some time now and she was so unhappy and Assef seemed to be really nice.

'Here,' he said, and took out from his pocket a little yellow pill. 'Take this, it'll help.'

Alex looked at him with sad, dull eyes. 'Help what?' she asked him.

Assef smiled and whispered in her ear, 'That feeling of emptiness that you have. This will perk you up no end.' And he pulled on her chin and popped the pill into her mouth. 'I'm going now,' he drawled as she swallowed the tablet, 'but I'll be here again tomorrow – should you wish to come back to us we can find you some more happiness where that came from.' And with a gentle squeeze of her body and a strong hug, he pushed her down onto the grass and walked away.

The drug began to affect her almost immediately. She saw beautiful colours and felt washes of soft warmth flooding her body. She began to smile and felt as though she were floating, floating above them all…

*

Joanna dodged in between parked cars and hid in shop entrances, keeping her vision on the back of Merrick's head. And then he turned and caught her eye and gave her a huge grin with a gesture signifying cutting her throat. Joanna froze. Merrick turned and continued his walk with the girl up the road, where he then turned off towards the train station.

Joanna slumped to the ground. She hung her head and felt weak and stupid. But her gut was full of fear. Gradually the blood returned to her ashen face and her eyes stopped blinking and shedding tears. 'Pathetic, that's what you are, absolutely pathetic,' she chastised herself. 'Get a grip – he can't do anything, he really cannot get you.' Aware that she had spoken out loud, she gathered herself up and turned back the way she had come and searched for the library.

After a few moments of scanning the street she approached a middle-aged woman who had stopped to swap her shopping from one hand to the other. Having gathered directions from her as to the whereabouts of the library, Joanna began to run. That didn't last long as she was clearly still weak and physically feeble. Making a note to herself to attempt to get fit, she walked at faltering speed to the venue. She gave her name and Barry's address and joined the library so that she could use their internet. It took just a short time to sign the forms and gain her pin number, library card and information on how to avoid inappropriate responses online.

Within half an hour she had achieved her goal and left the library, clasping a book that she had borrowed. It was the Mankell that she had begun to read in Tenterden. Her email to Jane had read:

Hello Jane, you told me to contact you if I had anything to say and I have, twice now. Clearly you have not done anything about Nurse Merrick as I have just seen him 'taking' a child to the train station. He threatened me by sign because I was stupid enough to think he hadn't spotted me when I followed him. He tried to get me away from the hospital and he is a horrible man. I cannot tell you the truth about me because I am scared that you'll put me in a home again! I won't let that happen. But I will help you if you need me to. We can trap Merrick. I don't trust him but I would let him use me if you could follow and catch him. I'll contact you again soon. This is a new hotmail account and should have no traces. I need to know that I can trust you. Melanie Richards.

*

In anticipation of Barry returning that evening from work she had set the table. In order to help Jane catch Merrick she would need to be available around Maidstone. With that in mind she had decided to ask Barry whether she could stay a bit longer. However, the response from Jane put a dampener on that idea.

Whilst Barry was cooking their meal Joanna had asked whether she could use his laptop to read her emails. Barry was fine about it, though confused as Joanna had earlier mentioned that she didn't have an email address. Jane's reply was short and disturbing. She actually suggested that Melanie – or, as she now knew her name to be, Joanna – could get into serious trouble by making inappropriate accusations of the kind that she had intimated. Jane reassured Joanna that Merrick had been questioned after her initial call and was found to be a perfectly honest man of good character. Clearly Joanna had a grudge against the world and had taken it out on someone who was just doing his job that was made more difficult because he was a man. She then went on to offer Joanna therapy for her issues and gave Joanna a helpline number for Depression UK along with a website address. She also advised Joanna to go back to social services, where she could be looked after. Joanna was seething.

Furthermore Barry talked to her about taking her back to Cranenden the following day as he had a late shift at the bookshop. It would be better, he added, as he couldn't see when he could get another chance before he left for his ski trip. He had been so kind to her that she felt that she couldn't now ask for more time at the flat. After all it was she who had insisted that she return to her own life as soon as she could.

But it was when Barry voiced his concern over a neighbour who had asked him questions about her and who she was that she made up her mind to go. Barry had then voiced his own dilemma about how awkward it would be if social services discovered her whereabouts. Though nothing had occurred, he could see how easily he could be suspected of abducting a child. And there was the irony: Barry, kind-hearted Barry, could be in trouble with the police for helping her and yet that scum Merrick was free to abduct and wander the streets with little girls to do God knows what.

Her last evening was fun. She and Barry played cards, talked about books and whether film versions did them justice. Joanna showed him her library book and ate sausages and beans. Barry guardedly avoided questioning about what she was to do in the future. In fact he was so at ease that Joanna felt a little sad that there seemed to be no actual concern about her at all. She went to bed at ten when Barry turned in and read her book until the early hours and then fell into a disturbed and dream-filled sleep.

*

He dropped her off outside the Old Wharfe Inn and gave her fifty pounds. He also gave her his mobile number. 'For emergencies,' he said. Then he drove over the bridge and disappeared out of sight.

Joanna stared after the car feeling hollow and lost. Then she hoicked her rucksack onto her back and trundled along Petty Lane. It was odd seeing the river again – and her boat. The water looked black and uninviting, reminding her of the awful rescue attempt that had nearly cost her life.

As she turned away from the riverbank and faced the bridle-path, clouds drifted across the sky and sleet began to fall. Joanna pulled her hat down over her ears and trundled up the hill to where the barn was waiting for her. The chicken man had not changed anything. In fact she was hard pushed to see where he had taken any more straw from since the last time she had been there. Clambering over the hay bales Joanna slid into the cave that she had constructed so many weeks ago. She was very careful to place her small stove on a slab of concrete well away from the straw, but there was still the chance that a spark could easily escape and ignite the rest. Her first cup of tea took forever to brew as she feared the flame would catch loose strands of hay and so she kept the flame low. Looking around and delving into the recess of the barn, she discovered some broken tiles that she utilised as a surround for the stove, giving it at least some protection. The weather was clearly deteriorating rapidly and it didn't take long for Joanna to spot the holes in the roof and the leaks in the walls as the hail and wind found its way into her hide. Lying in her sleeping bag, she took out her mobile phone and dialled Jamie's number.

The decision as to whether he should respond was taken away from him when Jessica, who was lying on his bed revising for her maths exam, glanced down at the ringing phone and noticed Joanna's name on the incoming call display.

'Hey Jamie,' she called over to him as he was restringing his guitar, 'get this – it's Joanna.'

His grunt and shake of his head gave her the opportunity to answer herself. Yet he put down his guitar and listened as Jessica switched it to speaker mode. The three-way conversation was a little awkward to begin with and Joanna found their questions derived from their feelings of being left out and rejected.

Eventually they both accepted that she was safe and wanted to meet up with them as soon as she could. By her insisting that it couldn't be that soon she detected her rebuff wasn't going down too well. Wanting to see her immediately was heartwarming yet by Joanna stating that she had a few things to sort out first she overheard Jamie utter, 'As ever, always cagey and secretive,' followed by an intake of breath and sigh from Jess. However, she soon pulled them round when she agreed to meet them in Hastings on the following Thursday, the day before Christmas Eve. They hung up after five minutes and rang her back so as not to use up all her credit.

From there the conversation drifted into some kind of normality – how's school? How's Clarissa? And Alex? It seemed so long ago that she had left and yet it had only been a few weeks. She enjoyed the fact that she could enquire after friends whom they shared. Clearly there had been major changes in Sally's home and that disturbed her a bit, but she liked the fact that Clarri had been placed in the school athletic team. She was unsure whether to say anything about her concerns over Merrick but in the end she told them everything and about her escape from the hospital.

After the call Jamie was in total confusion and really wondered whether he could believe the story Joanna told him about Merrick. Had she made it up? He wanted to believe her, but really it did seem rather far-fetched and Merrick certainly hadn't seemed threatening at all – in fact quite the reverse; a friendly and more genuine bloke he couldn't hope to meet. She even admitted that Merrick had shown her the photo he had taken. Also why had it taken her so long to ring them? And who was Barry? How was it a complete stranger let her stay in his flat – in his jealousy he was suspicious; what had she done for him?

Jessica, however, was thrilled at the renewal of contact and immediately rang Clarissa to tell her, whose mother was at that moment at Alex's home.

*

Sally's return from hospital was seemingly a relief to Jim and he had asked Yvonne to be there when she arrived. He had no idea whether Alex would be home or not and wasn't sure how Sally would take the 'new' Alex or even whether she would show up.

They needn't have worried – Alex was sitting huddled on her park bench enjoying the attentions of Assef. He'd taken her back to his place that morning, after taking her shopping for a dress and some shoes. He told her how much he loved her and wanted her and that she would never want for anything as long as he was around. He slept with her. She had little choice, but then, didn't he deserve something after all he had given her? Afterwards he promised her that he would always be there for her. He took her back to the park where he said she would be safe. He told her that she had a great little body and that he could get her more clothes and gifts if she were to make his 'friends' happy. He assured her that he was her boyfriend and that they would make a home together soon, but that for the time being it would be best if she went home and that he would pick her up the next day at the same place. He left her a passing gift of a shot of vodka that went really well with the tablets she had swallowed earlier. She slipped into unconsciousness as Assef took his arm away from her shoulder and walked away from the park.

She was woken by a police officer. He pushed her and asked her whether she was alright. She mumbled that she was fine and was about to go home. He told her to stand up. With difficulty she did. He asked her name and age. Easily she responded with, 'Alex, seventeen, now leave me alone.' She pulled away from him and staggered on up the path out of the park. The police officer watched her go, shaking his head, then he too turned and exited the park on the south side.

The front door looked different until Alex realised that she was on the wrong street. Confused and bewildered, she tried the next turning.

That was when Yvonne spotted her. She almost ran her over as Alex slipped off the kerb and rolled in the road. Yvonne jumped from the car and helped Alex into the passenger's seat. 'Oh, Alex, Alex what has happened to you?' she questioned.

But Alex just looked up, blurry-eyed, and stated, 'I'm fine, I am happy, I have a boyfriend.' And then she slumped over in the seat.

Yvonne drove her down the road. She couldn't possibly take her home to face Sally in this state. Quickly she dialled Jim's number on her car phone and explained that she would be delayed but that she hoped to bring Alex with her later. She then drove straight back to her house.

*

Clarissa couldn't wait to inform her mum that Jessica had spoken to Joanna, that she had been the saviour of the boy who had died, that they were all going to meet up again soon and that she wanted to see Yvonne in order to get some papers that she needed. But that conversation had to wait. Clarissa, on opening the front door when her mother's car drew up, realised that Yvonne had a problem.

Between them and without a word mother and daughter managed to drag Alex up the path and into the house. Not because she was so heavy – quite the contrary, because she was lifeless. The smell of alcohol on her breath wasn't so strong and Yvonne recognised the fact that Alex was pathetically thin, malnourished and virtually starving.

Between them and with very few words they managed to bathe her poor, beat-up body. The needle marks on her arms seemed old and scabbed and infected. The warm water brought her round a little and the tomato soup that they managed to get her to sip seemed to revive her a bit. Alex said nothing. Yvonne, however, recoiled at the fishy smell of sex on her clothes – her school uniform – and was appalled at the change in the girl in just a few weeks.

It took a couple of hours for the soup, bath and hot tea to take effect and then Alex poured out her vitriol on them both. Who the hell did they think they were? They were that cow Joanna's 'mates'. All this was her fault. She stood up and staggered about saying how she was going home now but that she would be moving in with her boyfriend very soon and that no-one could stop her. Yvonne took her by both arms and gently attempted to get her to sit, but it was hard work. Eventually she gave in and sat in the chair and stared ahead, only after Yvonne promised that she would drive her home as soon as she felt better. Clarissa automatically took hold of Alex's hand. Alex let her. Soundless tears leaked from her eyes as she just whimpered out her pain. Her dad no longer cared for her, her mother was crazy and no-one had believed what had happened to her. Now she had found someone who truly cares. He had bought her clothes that she kept at his flat – the flat that they would share together.

As hard as Yvonne tried she could not get out of Alex who her boyfriend was nor where he lived. Indeed Yvonne doubted whether Alex really knew or whether there was a boy at all or just a figment of her imagination. Having promised that she would take Alex home, Yvonne felt honour-bound to do so, but how would Jim and Sally react to seeing Alex in such a mess? At least she smelt better. They had managed to get rid of her stained and filthy uniform and given her some of Clarissa's, though they hung on her limp and shapeless.

After more tea, Alex stood up and demanded that she be taken home that instant and Yvonne agreed. The bitterness and anger, alternating with a child-like whimper, disturbed Clarissa and she was glad when Yvonne left, taking Alex with her.

*

Jim opened the door and put his arm round Alex, an arm that she shrugged off. Both he and Yvonne followed her into the living room, where Sally sat on the sofa watching TV. The tension was eased as soon as Sally looked up and smiled at Alex and patted the seat next to her, intimating that Alex should join her, which she did and lay her head in Sally's lap. Yvonne nodded to Jim and made a hasty retreat.

Two hours later Yvonne received the chilling news from Jim that Sally had told Alex in a quiet but determined voice that she would never forgive her for lying. Alex in return had hysterically sworn, screamed and yelled that she would never forgive her for slapping her and left the house swearing never to return. Yvonne listened as Jim reported to her all the 'lies' Alex had told both him and the police about Russian men and being raped and being forced to take drugs and how he didn't recognise his daughter anymore.

Yvonne's stomach turned to jelly. 'My God, Jim, why didn't anyone take her seriously? I think that she was telling you the truth.'

12

No longer feeling weak and pathetic, Joanna felt more upbeat than she had thought she would. Yes, she was as alone as she ever had been and she certainly missed the company. But she had a new resolve in her and a sense of purpose. Her decision to phone Jamie had been well rehearsed. Wanting to let him know about Merrick, she hoped for an ally, particularly as he had met him. She was determined to ensure that whatever Merrick was up to he would be found out and stopped – she almost missed the hesitancy in Jamie's voice as she shared what Merrick had suggested to her – but the moment she realised he didn't believe her she clammed up tight. *It's okay*, she thought. He would either be on board to help or not, and the sooner she knew where his thoughts lay the better. Again her isolation and realisation that she was alone in the world focused her determination to do right for herself. The barn was not so warm, though, and she felt very chilled when the sky opened and flakes of sleet, rain and snow feathered down and drifted in the cracks. Lighting a fire was hazardous in the midst of all the straw and Joanna was too nervous to do more than boil the kettle.

*

The morning was dark when she woke after a fitful, chilled sleep. Winter, it seemed, was in mid-flow. The water in her bottle was mostly ice and it took an age to heat up in order to make tea. She thought about Merrick and how he had tried to manipulate her whilst she was so very vulnerable; it further supported her realisation that he was a dangerous and cruel man. She had very little to go on and wondered for a moment whether she was being just a bit melodramatic, but on reflection his comments to her, added to his secret visits in the hospital and how he had been with the girl she observed him with in Maidstone, all made her feel uncomfortable. Furthermore she felt a little stupid. She shouldn't have expected the police to even listen to her, let alone take any notice. Authority cannot be trusted. The realisation closed down her desire to keep in contact with the others. Jamie, she now realised, didn't believe her, and what if the girls told Yvonne? Would she be scooped back into a home 'for her own good'? And this place? What a stupid idea. This wasn't going to work at all.

She was frozen and unbelievably hungry. Okay, she would use it as a base to keep her few belongings – she could also sleep here if necessary, but it was not weather-proof enough for her to survive when it turned really cold. The fifty pounds Barry had given her would be easily whittled away just on food and drink – so she needed another plan. Thinking back to her first day in Cranenden, she recalled a couple of houses that were clearly holiday homes. Maybe they were to be used over Christmas, but then maybe not – it was worth a try to find somewhere that could protect her from the elements just overnight. If she were careful she could make her way round the village without anyone knowing. It would be just a matter of getting herself inside and keeping her head down. Then there was always Hastings – worth a try.

Meanwhile, she had a job to do. She wrapped up warm and left the barn. The wind blew cold and icy as she made her way to the bus stop. Country buses were few and far between, and expensive, but she was able to pick one up from outside the Old Wharfe Inn and used the journey to thaw out and catch up on some sleep. She could ill afford the cost of the ticket and was annoyed at having to make two changes. She'd have to find an alternative way back, and a means to make some money. Her priority at the moment was finding and tracking Merrick to see exactly what he was up to with the girls.

*

Yvonne's fears about Alex were real and she couldn't get the girl out of her head. As a social worker she had met many a situation whereby girls had been abused and conned by so-called friends, resulting in abuse and drug dependency that reinforced the acceptance of the abuse with the relief that the drugs brought. It was the area of her work that she found the most intolerable, mainly due to the way her seniors and the police reacted. Rarely were the girls seen as victims by anyone. It was more likely that they were treated with contempt and put away for underage prostitution, drug pushing, shoplifting and minor crimes of petty theft. Now she was in a situation whereby she felt that she could use her little bit of authority with the police and her knowledge of the family to try and persuade them to do something more than what they seemed to have achieved so far.

Her interview at Hastings police station didn't seem to have gone too badly – at least the civilian police worker took down her concerns and, though she didn't ask many pertinent questions, she did promise to pass it on to the appropriate area within the professional police body. If it was felt that Yvonne had something for them to work with then they would most certainly get back to her.

That was a week ago. Nothing had been heard from Alex and the police had not contacted Yvonne. School had broken up for the holidays and it was just two days to Christmas. As Yvonne left her office and wandered to her car, the wind gathered speed and swirled the remaining leaves on the ground around her feet. She tightened her scarf and shivered. Unlocking her door, she slid across her seat and placed her handbag onto the back seat along with her laptop and ring binder file of unfinished reports that she would need to complete before her Christmas could begin. Backing out of the underground car park, she pointed the car in the direction of the one-way system. It was dark and there was no moon tonight.

The shortest day had been and gone but today seemed duller and darker than ever with a sky full of heaviness. As she drove along the coast road the sea seemed angry and troubled, reflecting her own thoughts. She did as she did most nights: scanned the doorways and corners for any sign of Alex. And yet again nothing!

But this night Yvonne didn't go straight home. She went directly to the police station. She sat in the reception area for over half an hour until finally a civilian support worker came out to greet her. But that wasn't enough for Yvonne; she felt shunned and passed by, as though her request for assistance in discovering the whereabouts of Alex had been dismissed and shelved. And so she decided to assert herself by demanding that she see someone in authority – a real police person and not just a civilian note taker! That did not go down too well with the civilian, who took to heart Yvonne's clear dismissal of her capabilities. It was then that Yvonne chose to pull rank from her social worker position even though she was on dodgy ground as Alex was not her case – in fact Alex wasn't anyone's case, though the civilian wasn't aware of that.

Another half an hour passed by whilst she waited and then the door opened from the back room and a tall thin man of around fifty, wearing a dark suit, a white shirt spattered with coffee splashes and an orange tie that supported the stains in smudged variance of brown, came over to her. Brusquely he told her that he hadn't much time – it was close to Christmas and life on the streets demanded his attention, more so at this 'festive' time of year. He almost spat the word.

He did, however, give her the courtesy of taking her through to an interview room, where he invited Yvonne to sit down. He also sat and apologised for the state of his clothes. 'It was,' he stated, 'the result of a truculent young girl who I had "rescued" off the street and her thanks was to spit the coffee I had bought her into my face.' This was not the most encouraging start.

Once DI Skinner had taken note of Yvonne's credentials and confirmed her as being who she was and her professional role, he became more amenable. He found Alex's file and read back to Yvonne what it stated. Basically it was felt that Alex had gone on a rampage, upset her parents, got drunk, had some drugs and tried to pass the blame to a non-existent 'foreigner'. Both the father and Alex had admitted that there had been trouble at home and Alex couldn't really recall what had happened to her.

With a deep sigh, the detective closed the file and shrugged his shoulders. 'Well, that's it,' he stated. 'Case closed.'

Yvonne tried to cool her tone before she attempted to engage with the chap further, but he was already looking at his watch and pushing his chair back with the signal that the interview was now over.

'I appreciate your concern,' he murmured, 'but there is really nothing more to say... unless you have more to offer?' He slipped the last comment in as a response to Yvonne's clear annoyance at his attempt to leave.

'Actually I have, so please could you kindly make a note of what I am going to tell you – I want this interview noted and scribed, in case it is needed for a future hearing... in court.'

Sensing the veiled threat, Simon Skinner clicked his ballpoint pen, opened up his jotter and began to write down the date. 'Full name, please?'

And Yvonne began to explain her concerns and observations. Partway through, just at the bit whereby Yvonne had explained the link between herself and Alex's parents through Joanna, Simon stopped writing and looked at her long and hard. 'So you are not here as Alex's social worker then? You have no real connection or evidence to suppose that Alex is anything other than a runaway. And that is all – I don't mean to be dismissive, as you might call it, but are you aware of how many young people just up and leave home at the merest hint of parental disapproval? No, don't answer that, as a social worker of your grade I know that you most probably are – but look at me.' And here he opened his arms, displaying the full state of his coffee-covered clothes. 'This is the result of trying to help just her sort. I've made a note of what you have said, I have emphasised your concerns, but I am also going to add that this is not a case that I am convinced needs any further input from us, other than a recommendation that all my officers will be made aware of your concerns and that they should look out for a girl of her description – er, do you have a photograph, by any chance? No – well, okay then, should you find one then feel free to drop it in to us at your convenience. Now, I really must end this interview as I have some pressing work to do.' And with that, he stood up, proffered Yvonne his hand that she shook and then ushered her out.

As they reached the exit and Simon keyed in the release code, Yvonne turned to him and said, 'You know, you and I should be on the same side, working towards helping and protecting young girls, and yes, I know you had an unpleasant experience with someone spitting coffee at you this morning, but do you not wonder how or why anyone would be in such a state that they have to resort to doing that? The law, as you know, still views kids under eighteen as that – children – only too many people forget that. Merry Christmas!'

Frustrated and furious, both professionals turned away from each other, each one angry with the other and both in their own way distressed by the inadequacies of their abilities to make life better for the needy and vulnerable. Both felt the other was to blame and yet they recognised the injustice of how their immediate supervisors judged the poor and lower-class 'dregs' of society and how they were unable and unwilling to drag them back out of it.

Yvonne ventured home, her hopes for reuniting Alex with Jim and Sally sunk in the despair of the broken society in which she existed. For even as she put her key into the lock at her home her mobile trilled. As the on-call social worker for the next twenty-four hours she received a request to find an emergency temporary home for a child whose parents had been involved in a drink-driving car crash from which neither were expected to survive. The child was eight.

*

The Christmas break was usually one that Robert looked forward to most but enjoyed the least. Always the disappointment after the hope that this year would bring him some kind of family reunion, he resolved to do what he did every year since his divorce: trim a tree, put up lights, order himself a small turkey and ring round his various family members in the hope that one of them would join him for a festive drink. Last year his brother Donald was to have done so with his wife and two children. He had even agreed to come on Christmas Eve and stay until Boxing Day. Robert had really looked forward to that and bought in delights appertaining to the season – but there had been the most horrendous rain and flash floods in Norfolk where his brother lived and at the last minute they had had to decline in order to dry out their home and salvage what goods they could. It was an absolute disaster for them. They did, however, manage to turn up for the 29th of December so that not all the festive fair was lost, but it was not the joyous of times, though the two nephews were happy enough with the expensive and delightful toys Robert had bought them. As for

Robert, his Christmas Day had been lonely and quiet.

This year he pondered as to whether to go to his brother's, but they had booked a week skiing in the French Alps and as Robert wasn't the active sort he declined their invitation to join them. Then there was his mother – but she always flew to 'somewhere hot' for the event and Robert, though always invited, invariably declined. A hot Christmas was an anathema for him.

Then out of the blue on the last day of term Sybil had asked Robert what he was doing for Christmas and opened up an invitation for him to join her and her husband for drinks and lunch on Christmas Day. It would be just six of them altogether if he were to join them; the rest being Sybil's brother and sister-in-law and a cousin that Sybil hadn't seen for eight years, having just returned from New Zealand after a teacher exchange programme that had been extended twice. Robert felt a bit edgy in accepting and asked Sybil if he could let her know by the 23rd.

Now the day had come and he was still unsure. It could be awkward – in fact, it was bound to be very awkward, if, as he surmised, he didn't get on with the others. After all, Sybil had only just thawed in her attitude towards him and that had only come about due to their uncanny concern over Joanna. And that got him thinking again about the girl and where she might be and what was happening to her.

*

The plastic cuffs around her wrists had no slack, causing small splits that stung every time she moved. The smell of the dank, foetid floor hung in her nostrils, causing her to retch. Joanna was cold. She ached, and she was scared. She heard nothing and the filthy bandage around her eyes gave her no sense of time, be it day or night. And her mouth was like sandpaper.

*

Catching and bundling Joanna into his basement had been unplanned but necessary. The girl had stalked him and was becoming a real pain. He had panicked and knew he had to get her out of the way quickly and efficiently. He was due to fly out the following day and his plans were going well until he had spotted her lurking behind cars and in shop doorways. She was just there – hanging around and bothering him. What choice did he have? Having caught her, he had no time to get her to Assef before he flew out of England for Christmas. She'd be alright in the basement. He had left her water – in a bottle – she just had to find it and work out how to drink it. It wasn't his problem. He'd be back in no time at all.

So on the 24th of December he relished the festivities that he and his family enjoyed together for the first time in years – a real celebration, and it was good! Christmas this year was their best and he knew that their happiness was worth the sacrifices he made – even the taking of the girls to Assef was justified in his mind when he saw the difference his contributions made to his family. The only thing that slightly niggled him was what he would do if Joanna died whilst being locked in the basement of his flat if she couldn't find the water. Maybe in retrospect, he had overdone the bondage.

*

Joanna was beginning to drift again. She was weak and desperate for a drink. Her mouth lacked any moisture and her tongue was sore after several attempts to moisten the duct tape sealed over her lips. Having managed to lever open a small gap was something, but not enough to allow her to breathe through her mouth. As it was, she struggled to breathe at all through her nose, as it was crusting with her natural snotty fluids.

Something, there must be something that she could use to sever the cuff ties that were around her wrists. If only she could see. Get the blindfold off; that must be her first action – shuffling on her bottom as far as she could until she came up against a wall that gave her some momentum. Edging herself up against it, she felt with her hands that it was rough, probably made of brick, that meant that if she were able to rub the bandage at the back of her head, it might loosen. Tentatively she rasped the back of her head up and down on the wall surface where it caught the fibres of the blindfold. It was a painful and hard process, and at first nothing happened. Then after some repeated movements the bandage began to edge upwards towards the top of her head until, at last, her eyes were free.

She blinked several times but the black space did not go – there was no light. She was in what seemed to be an airless, lightless, cold, cave-like room. Even by staring hard there was nothing to see. Deflated and in extreme pain, she walked herself on her knees and then, by leaning her back against the wall, she was able to inch herself up, bit by bit, until she was standing. Exhausted, she made use of the wall as a support and leant back onto it whilst she attempted to feel with her hands behind her the surface of the wall. Little by little she moved along until she reached a corner. Edging along and tracing the next wall, she came to its end. Empty space. She felt a hard surface at the back of her ankles, but nothing behind her back. By bending down she managed to establish that the gap was in fact a stairwell. She sat on the bottom tread and then shuffled her way up to the next, and the next until her head touched the ceiling and she could go no further. With her shoulder she nudged at the edge of the wall. Nothing. Twisting her bottom and sliding her body weight to her left, she worked her way to the other side of the stair. A simple task, but in the dark and with her hands so tightly linked behind her back it wasn't so easy. She then proceeded with her right shoulder to examine the left wall edge, and it was there – a light switch. It was an old-fashioned flick switch that she struggled to drag down. Her body was too soft. But by moving her head downwards, her locked wrists worked their way up the wall and she just managed to touch the switch with her thumb. But she lost the pressure. Sinking down, exhausted, she recouped and tried again.

After several attempts she sank back on the stairs and rested her aching body. She began to shiver and waves of nausea swept over her. Making one final major effort, anger and frustration welled up inside her as she banged her head on the wall, inadvertently catching the bandage that was still wound around her head, on the light switch. She yanked her head back to free herself and the pressure was enough – the light clicked on. The bulb was hanging in the middle of the room.

Her eyes blinked and for a few moments she fought against the sudden brightness. But the bulb was weak and fortunately insufficient to cause much glare and so within a few moments she was able to scan the room and see her prison. It held little hope. Clearly it was a room used as a dumping ground, with rubbish piled in at one end – an old bike lacking one wheel, battered cardboard boxes and a bottle of life-saving water!

Hobbling towards what she now craved, she was frustrated by her inability to drink from it. She could grab it from behind her back and unscrew the top, but then how on earth was she to get it to her mouth? But if she were to carefully unscrew the bottle and place it on the ground she could turn (supposing she didn't spill it) and then upend the bottle into her mouth by her teeth. All she needed to do now was to get the duct tape off.

In a frenzy she began to lick and suck and blow at the gooey, tight tape. She felt a little give from around her lips. As she sucked it inwards she just managed to claw her bottom teeth over her top lip and tear at the tape. It ripped her lip and she tasted blood. It was relentless and exhausting, but she repeated the process in ten-second intervals until, by some miracle, she had punctured the tape with a minute hole that she teased with her tongue for several more minutes. She could now actually breathe through the hole, though her tongue was raw from the harsh plastic fibres that had chaffed her lips. There was little moisture in her mouth apart from the specks of blood that popped from her blistered tongue. Exhausted from the effort, she sat back, planning how to manoeuvre the bottle of water to her mouth without spilling any – if only she could release her hands.

*

Jamie wasn't surprised when Joanna didn't show. He resigned himself to the fact that she was just some crazy loner and a liar. Yet he had been excited at the thought that they would see each other again. All three had waited for nearly two hours and when it became clear that she wasn't going to show, they retreated in disappointed silence back up the hill and began their long walk home.

No-one said anything after Jamie had declared, 'Well, that's it. She's not coming and I'm not waiting any longer – I'm off.'

Both girls nodded and reluctantly wandered back along the seafront behind him. It was just as they had trickled past the Stade that Jessica grabbed Clarissa's arm and pointed to a group standing outside the Fish Café. Both girls were aghast to see and recognise Alex, dressed to kill and with her arm linked to a paunchy, middle-aged man in a grey suit. He was all over her and she, clearly, was happy for him to be so – or so it seemed. But their annoyance at Joanna for not turning up took over their thoughts and Alex was forgotten within minutes of them leaving.

By the time they had reached their respective homes Jamie had deleted Joanna's number from his phone and hardened his resolve to dismiss her from his mind. He had Christmas coming up and their sister Sandi was returning from uni, which both he and Jessica were looking forward to, and there was the party in the Old Town on Boxing Day. It was Jamie's first real event and he was chuffed to bits to have been asked to join the Fundamentalists as their second guitarist. He had also been able to buy real proper Christmas presents this year with his money from working at the restaurant. No, he needed to move on and put Joanna behind him. Again.

Jessica was also frustrated and annoyed – she had stopped thinking up reasons for why Jo could have been so late after the first hour of waiting. It had all become just a bit too dramatic. The attempted 'saving' of the boy off the bridge had become last month's news and the suggestion that the male nurse was a child abductor a little absurd. No – time now to leave Joanna to herself and move on.

Clarissa just wanted to be home. Her mum had been very involved with work of late and she had had to look after her brothers just a few times too many, so now Christmas was really upon them she just wanted to enjoy it. Her nan was coming over on Christmas Day – she was fun, eccentric and mad, but in the very nicest of ways. No, Joanna was now gone and could be forgotten by them all.

Alex had not noticed the girls at all when she stood in her crippling heeled shoes, her arm linked through the blob that she had to 'entertain' for the evening. But she had noticed Jamie. Vaguely she tried to recall where she had seen him before, but then she was ushered into the hotel and whisked up in the lift to the fifth floor, where drinks and a buffet were spread enticingly on small coffee tables throughout the room. Alex knew that she would see very little of the food but would instantly be encouraged to drink as much as she could. She shuddered and wondered why Assef was happy for her to be used by these revolting men, especially as he professed to love her so much. But if she didn't acquiesce then Assef would beat her and slap her about, declaring how much she had let him down. The more she gave herself to satisfy the client, the more presents and affection Assef showered on her, so no contest; she had to do as he asked.

The room was shimmering with Christmas lights and sparkling in the corner, an artificial tree shed silver and blue hues over the room as the cycle of lights alternated between the set programme. A year ago Alex would have loved the magical and pretty décor, but now it had lost its charm. What had once been charming and glitteringly special with the promise of secrets and the excitement of Christmas, now felt shabby, false and with a sense of dark secrecy, hiding the filthy actions of the depraved men that used the girls. The added irony was the nativity scene at the base of the tree with a haloed Mary looking down on the plastic Jesus.

About right, thought Alex. *It's all just a plastic mess.* And then she turned, took the glass of champagne proffered to her from her escort and smiled as he put his hand on her arm, slid it around her waist, then to her breast. He wasn't going to waste much time on preliminaries, she realised as he began to slobber over her, his thick wet lips and disgusting breath covering her face and neck as he drove her towards one of the connecting doors.

A last glance over to her friend Candice, with a wistful raised eyebrow and sad smile, then she was through the door, and before the torture began she popped a pill to appease the pain.

*

Merrick had accepted the offer of the Christmas period off in return for doing double shifts over New Year's Eve and being on call for emergency cover should the need arise, from 27th December. His flight back was booked during the early hours of the 27th and so if he were to be called in then he'd at least be back in town. But when the call came through he was driving back from the airport with no time to return home before his shift began. He drove straight to the hospital. His concern about Joanna was minimal. He fathomed that if she had managed to get the water then she would last until then, but what if she hadn't? Metaphorically shrugging his shoulders, he resolved to put her out of his mind. But he couldn't help musing over the tragedies awaiting him in the intensive care unit and how when Joanna had been one of them, he had fought for her life. Now he couldn't wait to get rid of her – whether she was alive or dead, she would have to go.

*

Her moments of lucidity came in waves. With each waking moment she forced herself to think and act. After a first attempt at unscrewing the cap on the water bottle, the pain in her wrists and the numbness of her fingers panicked her into believing that she couldn't get the cap off. But she did! And the bottle fell, pouring precious water away. Grabbing it from behind she righted the bottle that now only contained two thirds of the precious liquid. Turning, careful to avoid knocking it over, she licked the trickles running down the outside with the very tip of her tongue. She leant back and cried.

After some moments she noticed the old bike and looked it over. There was nothing she could use on it – or was there? The bell – it was an old metal screw cap. Maybe she could get that off and use it as a cup? It was rusty and the more she attempted to twist the bell cup, the more energy she expended and the weaker she got. Desperate now for a container in which to pour the water, she crawled around on her knees searching every crevice. A bundle of newspapers on a battered shelf, an old paintbrush and an empty bottle of white spirit. Nothing of any use.

But the shelf was wobbly – Joanna lay down and, with as much effort as she could muster, kicked and kicked until part of it splintered away from the wall. Just as she had hoped, there were jagged ends of nails exposed. She turned and, finding some leverage, began to drag her bound wrists across the nail. The pain was excruciating, dragging both her wrists and cuffs across the sharp metal. Feeling the warm blood trickle down her arms, she persevered, for she had no choice. Faint with pain, despondency and exhaustion, she doggedly persisted. Fear was her driving force. It could only be a matter of time before he came back for her in order to do what? In a virtual frenzy now, she forced her wrists back and forwards back and forwards until finally she did it! The plastic tore and her hands were free. She crawled back to where the bottle stood and, with trembling bloody hands, ripped free her mouth from the tape, lifted the bottle to her lips and drank and drank. Sinking back, she allowed the water to refresh her body. Ironically, she became desperate for a pee and, too exhausted to do anything else, she just wet herself.

Her wrists were cut deeply and as life drew back into her fingers the pain became a throbbing, persistent, needle-like jabbing. But that couldn't quell the euphoria she felt at having escaped her bindings.

After guzzling more water she began to take in her surroundings. The hatch at the top of the stairs seemed to be just that – a hinged lid. No doubt it would have something heavy over it to prevent her getting out – but it was worth a push. She scrambled up the stairs and heaved her shoulders, but nothing moved. She began to hammer on the hatch, yelling and calling for help. She listened for sound, but there was nothing. Her heightened relief and joy at freeing herself and getting the water turned rapidly back to despair. She stayed on the stair, head down, exhausted, beaten.

*

His shift being over and feeling extremely tired having been up for over twenty-four hours, Merrick drove straight back to his flat. Hungry and facing an empty fridge, he rang for a takeaway pizza. Just as he pulled into his parking space, so did the pizza delivery. He paid and took his backpack and his pizza into the cold flat. Boosting up the heating, he sat down and tore into the box with a ravenous energy. Grabbing his rucksack, he retrieved several beers, stuffed most in the fridge, then bit off the top of one with his teeth and downed it in one. His eyes began to close when he sat up with a jerk – the girl, how could he have forgotten? Fully awake, he ventured out of the flat towards the stairwell. The packing case was still over the basement hatch. That was a relief – but now the big problem to be faced. What was he to do with her? Three other apartments shared this area and all three 'belonged' to others like himself: traffickers of some sort or another. Only he was involved with finding children for sad men. The others were slaves, from Asia, China and Eastern Europe; all had been duped into getting into the UK for a free life. All were bullied and trapped by gang masters and thugs. Furthermore, some poor devils had become slaves to the system and to their 'benefactors'. Rounded up each morning, they were driven to various locations to clean, wash cars or build or cook all day long and then driven back to their shared accommodation. They were all in a Catch-22 situation. Unlike Merrick, though, the other flats housed families, and many of them – aunts, uncles, parents, children, siblings, all smuggled in, all desperate for a new life in the prosperous west, all devastated by their virtual imprisonment by their illegality. None could afford to let their plight be known. Merrick was not illegal, but he had had to borrow money for his way across to England and for his place to live. It was to those people – men from his own country – that he owed so much money. By finding girls he was gradually paying it off – though even he knew that he could never actually be allowed to do so.

What if she were dead? That would be the easy part. Just dump her on the street. Who was going to care? She was a no-one, an anonymous – she had slipped out of society, under the radar. But if she were still alive he'd have to get her ready for Assef. She wouldn't be compliant, that he knew, but enough drugs pumped into her would ensure she would acquiesce. Tonight would be awkward as he needed to sleep and then he was on shift again.

Double-checking no-one was around, Merrick slid the packing case back from the hatch. He lifted the lid and knelt down until he found the light switch that he flicked and then began to descend the stairs. As he reached the bottom tread he first noticed the bloody wrist restraints. His eyes then scanned the floor to the abandoned duct tape and the empty upturned water bottle. But he didn't see Joanna! '*Jabati*,' he swore.

He tore around the small space in a frenzy, crazily upturning the broken shelf, the bike, the papers, knowing she could not possibly be under them but knowing that she had to be there. It was impossible – how had she escaped? How indeed.

He scanned the floor for clues. There was nothing. He began a quick swoop of the cellar. Picking up the restraints and ramming them in his pockets, he took the empty water bottle and the broken bits of the shelf and slung them into a heap amongst the bicycle remnants. Inoffensive rubbish. He looked around; nothing, it seemed, remained of any sign that anyone had been held there.

Satisfied, Merrick began to ascend the stairs when the lid came down with a thud and he was enclosed. He heard the drag of the packing case being drawn across and then footsteps leaving the area. He didn't shout – what was the point? The intention had clearly been to entrap him there. And so he began to think. He wasn't afraid of the police or anything of that nature. No-one from the building would even think of involving them and there could be no connection to him at all. And she wouldn't be believed. He could wait until he heard movement from the other flats across to the main entrance and create a noise to indicate his presence – someone would have to respond, surely? Yet having regularly used this place for his girls the others had known not to interfere and ignore any noise from the cell. He knew the packing case weighing down the trap door was not particularly heavy. What if he were able to put his shoulders and back into it? He could heave and perhaps dislodge it, tilt the case from the lid, and get himself free. He was tired, annoyed and feeling a bit confused by the whole thing, on top of which he had to get out and find the girl. He needed her back.

Angry now and with determination, he lay prone on the hard concrete stairs and bent his knees, fixing his feet on the hatch. Taking a deep breath, he heaved and pushed with all his might. The hatch lifted by a couple of millimetres, then as he exhausted himself it slid back into place. He caught his breath and rolled over on all fours and pushed his back onto the hatch and heaved and struggled against the heavy weight. Again there was a slight shift in the lid, but nothing of any significance. This time he alternated between his feet and his back and made short, violent heaves on the lid.

After twenty minutes, his energy was spent and he was no

further forward. He looked at his watch: almost time for the night-shift workers from the Chinese contingency to leave and for the day workers to return. He listened and waited until finally at just before eleven he heard the van pull up outside and the voices of the drivers and guards as they released their charges into the stairwell. Merrick let rip.

Hammering on the lid he yelled top note. Would they check? Remembering Ling Channi's name and hoping that he was on duty tonight, he yelled out, 'Ling Channi, it's me, Merrick, from number 8. Help me. Please let me out. Ling Channi, it's me, Merrick.' Silence. The shuffling of feet stopped.

Then Merrick heard muffled voices – a door being unlocked. Silence. Then one set of footsteps. The packing case shifted. The hatch was pulled up and Ling Channi's face peered into the cellar. Merrick clasped the Chinese man's hand and shook it with absolute relief. Ling Channi pulled Merrick up and out without a word. Merrick switched off the light and lowered the hatch door, replacing the packing case. Neither man spoke. Ling Channi waited until Merrick had returned to number 8 and then Ling turned towards flat 6, opened the door and escorted out the night shift.

Back in his room, Merrick tried to figure out his next move. He was puzzled as to how Joanna had got out. He'd never had this problem before. The girls he'd kept in the cellar had always stayed put. Mind you, he had never had to tie them up or be quite so brutal. They always had had some effective drug to just knock them out enough and it had always only ever been for a few hours at tops.

Pacing the floor, he began to believe that it had been the others in the flats that had released her. But how? They were all locked in and were trained well to keep a low profile. Perhaps they still had her – maybe she was in there right now. Should he go and search? He fretted over where she had gone and who had betrayed him.

Eventually fatigue set in and Merrick went to bed. He had to be back on the ward in four hours and he was totally exhausted. Setting his alarm for 5.30, he drifted into a heavy sleep.

13

Whilst Merrick had been flying back from his Christmas break, Joanna had slumped to the floor in despair. She had never felt so desperate and bleak. She found herself whimpering like a scared puppy when she heard footfall above. Hearing voices in hushed tones, she yelled out for help. Stony silence followed then a dragging sound of something shifting. As she looked up, the hatch itself began to rise. She backed away, scared.

But then children's faces peered down at her. A hand came towards her, encouraging her to take it and be helped up out of the hole. An older woman took over and helped Joanna to her feet outside of the prison. All was achieved in silence. The children stood either side of the small corridor and she was led into an apartment and all the others followed. She looked back and noted that the one man in the whole group was closing the hatch and replacing the packing case that had held her prisoner.

Once in the flat, and with the front door closed, the children stepped aside while the women came towards her and ushered her into a bedroom that housed several three-tiered bunk beds. The eldest woman indicated for her to hide at the back of the beds and, with her finger on her lips, nodded to Joanna. Joanna nodded back, indicating that she understood. Frazzled through lack of food and water, she fell asleep on the floor next to the barred window.

Drifting in and out of a disturbed sleep, she suddenly woke with a start. There was a hammering on the front door. The woman who had guided her into the bedroom turned towards her and, with fear in her eyes, threw a cover over her and left the room, keeping the door ajar but almost closed behind her. Then there came strident voices, men calling out names and telling the children to hurry up.

Within a short space of time the place emptied apart from the one man and two older women. They came in and took her hand and led her to the kitchen area. Amongst myriad three-legged stools they encouraged her to sit and offered her a bowl of rice noodles to eat that she gratefully took. They couldn't speak English and were clearly afraid. They pointed to a clock on the wall and intimated that she would be in danger when the time reached eight o'clock. Joanna nodded and smiled her thanks.

They all relaxed a bit after that and the older woman took Joanna by the hand and bathed her wrists in warm water. 'You must not tell,' the woman mumbled as she bathed her wrists. 'We let you out – we in danger, you must not tell.' And the woman looked up into Joanna's eyes with a sad yet defiant look.

'I promise, I promise not to tell,' Joanna responded. 'I can't thank you enough, and I will keep this as our secret,' Joanna repeated. 'Our secret.' And she crossed her heart and kissed her hand and clasped the woman's hand and kissed it too. Then she drew the hand to her heart and nodded.

For some minutes they shared a conspiratorial smile and look, but then the woman became agitated and pointed to the clock. It was quarter to eight. Joanna nodded, and though she was weak and unsure as to what she should do once she left the flat, she made her way towards the door.

The woman looked terrified and the man leapt up and dragged her back. 'No – it is lock,' he mumbled. 'Wait here.' Joanna looked bewildered and then the man pointed towards the door and then indicated by his fingers' rapid movements something that Joanna thought meant running.

Somehow, she thought, *I'm to make my escape at eight o'clock.* Maybe that was when the children would return? But that was such a short time since they had been out – she really had no idea.

In the end she was pushed into the space behind the door and made to stand by the hinge edge. The man indicated that she was to slip out immediately the door was opened. And then there appeared from another room twenty or more young Asian girls – all about her age. The man and woman who had helped her lined them up and ensured that they were all there and placed Joanna out of sight, making her kneel near the back of the line.

Just before eight o'clock Joanna heard voices and footsteps outside the room. All the girls moved forward as the door opened and two dark-haired men in overalls stood either side of the door and counted the girls. Once assured they were all there, the girls were led out and Joanna was able to stand. After about half had gone Joanna felt herself being shoved in between the last four at the back by her rescuers. They indicated that she was to run.

Joanna got in line and the moment the girl in front of her stepped into the street and then into the back of the waiting van, Joanna turned tail and ran around the side of the van, hunkering down so as not to be seen. She noticed a row of bins and carefully made her way to them, where she edged herself between the two closest. She heard the driver count the girls in the van and then the door slammed shut and it reversed its way out onto the slip road then took the left turn and drove off at speed.

Meanwhile in the building, Merrick had remembered her. That was when he made his way to the cellar and as he was searching for her, Joanna's rescuer slipped out of the flat, lowered the hatch and replaced the packing case. He looked out onto the street, caught Joanna's eye and nodded, indicating that she could safely leave.

Though now free from Merrick, Joanna was terrified and utterly bewildered, with no idea where to go or what to do. It was late and it was cold and all she had seen made her frightened and afraid. She had nothing. Merrick had clearly taken away every personal item from her – her money, her phone, her bus ticket – and that also made her tremble. If he looked at that he would know where she had come from. Nowhere was safe and he could come after her at any moment.

*

Alex felt ill. Not just the usual comedown from the drugs and drink but really ill. Her face felt hot and her stomach cramped with unbelievable pain. She was back in the 'holding' room with the other girls. Assef had told her that he needed his space for a bit – that he had an important client to entertain and that she would feel lonely stuck in his flat alone. He packed her own belongings (not, she noticed, the gifts he had bought for her) into a plastic 'bag for life' (oh, the irony) and drove her to the grotty hovel where she had first wound up. It was here on one of the truckle beds that she drifted in and out of painful sleep.

She awoke to a hubbub of noise and whispers and crying. She slipped back into unconsciousness, then a hand roughly pulled on her arm. A face, lined and old, leered over hers. Her eyelids flickered and she tried desperately to focus, but double vision made her shut them again. She became acutely aware of further excruciating pain and cried out, gripping the side of the bed. There was a great deal of nervous talk around her and she was conscious of more voices and faces that she didn't recognise. Her body was hot and sweating profusely. Voices and languages she had not heard before rained over her head and then the pain took over and she screamed.

Vaguely, in the haze of agonising waking and fevered sufferance, she became aware of being lifted and carried through the room, until beautiful cold, night air washed over her burning body. She was laid on the hard pavement, which must have been close to the sea as she could hear the waves turbulently crashing onto the stony beach.

Now alone, she sank into the hard ground and gave in to the rolling pain that overtook her. Though burning up, she began to shiver as the cold air trawled over her in waves. *I'm dying*, she thought. Silence. 'I'm dying,' she whispered to the man that leant over her and lifted her head oh so gently.

Now she was moved again, but this time onto a flat, firm surface and hands came down towards her, puncturing her hand with a needle attached to a tube, attached to a bag. A mask was placed over her mouth and nose, releasing cool air into her fevered body. She felt herself lifted up and the next moment she was aware of movement and kind faces speaking to her. But she couldn't make out what they were saying. The noise of the siren and the flash of blue was eerily comforting.

In the hospital both doctors and nurses fought hard to save her. The ectopic pregnancy had burst her fallopian tube and she was teetering between life and death. The operation took over four hours with a cautious hope that she would recover. Realistically her little life hung by a thread.

The hospital had a group of volunteer victim support volunteers. Janine had been part of that group and had loved the work so much that she had applied for and obtained a salaried position as a civilian police support officer and was based at the hospital as a first responder for any victim of violence. She was just about to go for her break when she received a call on her radio to attend the ICU. This was a disturbing case and the staff on duty were quite distressed. A child had been admitted with a perforated ovarian tube, resulting in traumatic surgery whereby she had lost one ovary and part of her colon. She was extremely malnourished and weak and had lost a great deal of blood. The surgeons had achieved all that they had dared and patched her up hoping that she could gain strength before they attempted a further operation to completely address the damage that had been caused. Her deterioration on the operating table meant that they had had to do a quick tidying job to get her stable enough to allow her body to settle down from the trauma of the burst ovum and to try and avoid peritonitis. She was on her third pint of blood and her second bag of antibiotics when Janine saw her. Her body, they felt sure, could not have coped had they completed the procedure; it was a patch-up job that would have to be revisited if she lived.

Now it was down to Janine to stay by her side and hope that she would recover enough to speak, identify herself, then her family could be contacted. Looking at her skinny, stick-like arms, pale as milk and dotted with purple scab marks from needle use, Janine took the child's left hand in her own and spoke softly to her, words of encouragement that she hoped would penetrate her comatose mind. All Janine knew was that an anonymous call had been made to the emergency services informing them of a dying kid that needed an ambulance. There was nothing on her person to indicate who she was or where she was from.

*

Jamie had had a brilliant Christmas after all. His gig with the Fundamentalists had gone down well and he really felt good about his playing and more confident in himself. But the holiday was quickly coming to an end and he knew that A levels were looming. The pressure was on. He would need to achieve high grades in order to get his place at university. Sandi was full of the amazing time she was having in Leeds and Jamie felt that he was ready for and wanted some of that too. The concept of leaving Hastings appealed even more after his shattered hopes of seeing Joanna again.

Even though he had deleted her number from his phone, he did occasionally give it a wistful glance just to check as to whether she had attempted to call him. She clearly had not. But Robert had. There were several missed calls but no texts. Jamie was reluctant to respond as he was a bit unsettled and unsure about how he felt now about the whole thing. He was beginning to think that Robert was perhaps a little bit too interested in his pupil. He had read a great deal lately about caretakers and teachers and priests abusing their positions with vulnerable young people. Even just before Christmas the local primary school IT support teaching assistant had been suspended for what was stated in the media as 'inappropriate images' found on his laptop. It made him squirm, remembering how Joanna had completely trusted him when he took her to his room and how easily she could have been taken advantage of. He did not want to help anyone who might be a pervert. How did he know that Mr Robert Bentley could be trusted? Joanna, for whatever reason, had chosen to avoid meeting up again. When he thought more about it Bentley was odd. A lonely, older man, who insisted on being secretive in searching for a missing girl, gave him an uncomfortable feeling. With those thoughts in mind, Robert's name was swiftly deleted from his phone and a bar put on his number.

He resumed his busy life spending every waking hour between studying and running and cycling and working in the Stade. Thoughts of Joanna faded until she became just a bit of a stomach-churning memory. Yes, he had had feelings for her, but the obvious rejection of him and the loss of what he had hoped would be a romantic involvement was painful; so much so he buried it deep in the back of his mind.

Jessica, on the other hand, was less emotionally involved and wondered casually how Joanna had spent her Christmas. She certainly didn't feature too long in her thoughts until she and her family all went for a long, cold walk along the cliff tops at the Country Park after Christmas dinner. She gazed down at the turbulent and dark sea, allowing a shiver to tremble through her body as Joanna sprang to mind. Where on earth was she? And Jessica just knew that she was in danger. Guilty feelings crept through her thoughts. She had promised to be there for her – but at the first attempt at meeting up when Jo hadn't appeared she just accepted that fact without a concern.

Not mentioning anything to anyone, she made out that she had had enough of walking and was cold and wanted to get back home to open the presents that still lay under the tree. But what she really wanted was to attempt to get hold of Joanna on her phone. She felt shabby that after her 'no-show' a couple of days previously, she had made no effort to try and contact her. Now it was all she could do to stop herself dragging the family back at top speed in order to get to her phone that her mum had insisted be left in her bedroom so it couldn't disturb their family time.

At first she began to step it out, but her dad called her back to take her grandad's arm, as he was struggling on the uneven ground. At last back on gravel pathways, Jessica slipped her arm away from his at the appropriate moment when the path narrowed to single file, and she leapt the stile and motored onward as fast as she dared without losing sight of the family.

She needn't have bothered to race it because it wasn't until 4.30 that Jessica managed to steal away from the family and access her phone. Alone in her room and trembling with nerves at what she might hear, she rang Joanna's old number. Unsurprisingly it was unobtainable. More frustration. *Why doesn't that girl respond?* Then in desperation she wrote a text, begging her to make contact. She was forceful in her demand that she contact her immediately after reading and sent that in the hope that Joanna would do so. Jessica wanted assurance that she was okay and that her worries about the male nurse she had shared with them wasn't true. Feeling very uncomfortable and disturbed, she recalled Jamie's concerns that Joanna was perhaps just a drama queen making up stories about the male nurse that he had seen. But what if she wasn't? What if there was something in it after all and Joanna was in danger?

Having allowed those thoughts to creep into her mind Jessica couldn't get free of them, and she conjured up all sorts of scenarios of life-threatening situations that Joanna had got herself into, yet unbeknown to her none were as awful nor as dire as the actual reality of the circumstances that Joanna was really in. Attempting to discuss this with Jamie had been futile – he had clearly no intention of seeing the possibility that her silence might well be that she was in danger and unable to contact them. Jessica decided to give it one last try, waiting until after all the festivities were over before attempting to discuss it further with Jamie. She trusted her brother and the fact that he had actually met Merrick was important. What did he really think? Did he see any merit in what Joanna had told them? Why had Joanna found him so threatening?

*

Yvonne received the call from DI Skinner at just after 5am on New Year's Eve morning. Funnily enough, she had had a really rough night, one where her dreams became disturbingly vivid and reflected some of the worst cases of child neglect that she had dealt with. This happened periodically, as though her mind couldn't accept the reality of how vile and cruel some people could be to their children. It was always the same. Heart-rendering sobs and screams from behind a cupboard door that Yvonne couldn't reach or open. Then came the begging voices of small children, and the cruel smirks across the faces of those standing in front of the door. She always awoke just as she reached out her hand to turn the handle, but it was always grabbed by the doorkeeper, whose features varied from a tattooed, skull-like face that melded into her mother's and sometimes her own. She always wet herself in these dreams and felt humiliated by her child-like reactions to them. Then came the embarrassment of having to wake Carlos, and the upheaval of changing the bedding and apologising for her infantile lack of control. He never complained. In fact, his concern that she was that distressed by her work was palpable in his attention to her and to ensuring that she showered and settled herself, whilst he cleared away the wet sheets.

But though they were rare, Yvonne had had two episodes since Christmas and this really did concern Carlos. When she nudged him on the morning of the 31st he was prepared for another sodden mess to clear up – but this time she just whispered that he wasn't to worry, but she had been called into work and that she might be gone a while.

He put his hand across the warm space where she had lain and realised in his half-conscious state that her side was quite dry. Relieved, he mumbled, 'Take care,' and went back to his uncluttered and peaceful sleep. Within seconds of her leaving his side he was blowing puffs of weak snores that would gradually build into a full-blown rattling.

Yvonne looked at him, grateful for his goodness towards her yet relieved that she wasn't now lying next to him, having to try and stop the oncoming reverberations from his throat in order to return to sleep. She felt guilty that his perception of her needs when she had such awful dreams was so caring and tender, yet when he woke her with his growl-like snoring, she felt only anger and annoyance. At least this wasn't a battle she would have to face right now. Instead she was deliberating over her phone call.

She ran the call back through her head as she reversed out of the garage and onto the main street. It was dark and she, not for the first time, wished she had bought a car with a heated seat. It was perishing cold. There were still people out on the streets, though, still managing to revel in the season's festivities. She noted, when pulling up at the traffic lights, a group of happy-looking young people meandering across the road, yelling a really early 'Happy New Year' at her windscreen.

The phone call had been from DI Skinner, who had thanked her for dropping off the photograph of Alex that she'd managed to procure, on Christmas Eve. In light of that said photograph, he was wondering whether she would kindly go to the intensive care unit at the Conquest Hospital, where a girl matching the photograph and description was 'recovering from an emergency operation,' and as she had no identification on her they were hoping Yvonne could confirm whether it was Alex or not. Due to the timing of the call and the request to go immediately Yvonne was full of foreboding.

Parking was a nightmare even at this time and after having driven round the hospital grounds twice she finally found a space in the covered area deep in the recesses of the grounds. Stepping into the dark shadows, Yvonne noted how the lights of the hospital twinkled, penetrating the dense hour-before-dawn dark of the night, the reputed coldest and blackest part of the night when statistically most deaths occurred. Yvonne shivered as she took the lift to the ICU.

*

He was making mistakes. Itching for his shift to end, Merrick's anger had escalated beyond control. He was angry at himself for locking Joanna up for so long; he knew he should have disposed of her even if it had meant missing his flight home. She could have been in Assef's hands by now if he had only been a little more patient. What made him even angrier was that one of those bastards in the other flats must have let her out – but who had shut him *in*? Was it her? Or them? He drove back home still annoyed and unsettled.

However, it wasn't Joanna that had created this distress inside him; it was his own folly. For the first time since he'd been employed in the UK he had made a mistake, one that may well jeopardise his future in the NHS. It was an unforgivable and dangerous action that he might well be penalised for, thus ruining his chance of being accredited.

With Joanna and her whereabouts uppermost in his mind, he'd lost concentration and had drawn up a syringe of morphine of a strength treble the required dosage. This was to a post-op patient who had lost his leg in a motorbike accident. Nurse Tilsden, having double-checked the ampules, pulled back his hand from administering the ill-fated dose – the look on her face informed him of the mistake. Thank God she had noticed and reacted before the shot was given. Regrettably it had to be logged and noted all the same – the first error of his career. He blamed Joanna and Assef for ruining his focus. Had he not already inserted the needle into the vein she needn't have done anything but given him a verbal reprimand, but he had had to withdraw the needle immediately and shown that none of the drug had actually transferred. It was a call too close for comfort. She was sorry, but she had to do her job and she would be in trouble if she hadn't noted the error or made note of the loss of morphine that they had now to dispose of and waste. She'd taken over and administered the correct dose herself, ensuring that Merrick double-checked with her that it was correct. Humiliated, he cringed in embarrassment!

Rattled and annoyed, he entered the building. Quietly and with tentative steps he listened outside the doors of the other flats on his floor and heard nothing untoward. Checking his watch, he knew that a changeover would soon be taking place. Leaning against his front door with arms crossed, he waited. As the cars pulled up and the minders entered the stairwell, he made sure that they noted he was watching them. Standing tall and menacing, legs wide, filling his threshold, he glared as the Chinese men ushered out their workers. They were certainly aware of his presence and silently eyed each other. This show of power was not lost on them. An unwritten pact of secrecy was what gave them all security in their dealings. Merrick was declaring that he wasn't happy with their actions. It didn't matter who had let her out and locked him in. Word would get around that he wasn't to be played with. He repeated the stance when the South Asians brought out their workers. No-one was left without understanding a line had been crossed. They all worked on in silence and almost bowed to him as they passed in a servile and subservient manner that they had perfected. After the final exchange took place he drew in a deep breath, turned, unlocked his door and slammed it shut behind him. The echo of the door slam reverberated through the hall.

Satisfied that his message was clear, he slung his jacket onto the sofa, perching himself before the computer, flicking it on. Out of the corner of his eye he caught sight of Joanna's bag slung in the corner. Scraping the chair back on the lino he went over and grabbed it, upending it over the table with a shake. Out flew a scabby little purse containing very little cash but also a return bus ticket to Maidstone from Cranenden. Very interesting. And then there was a phone. An old, battered one with a multitude of dents and scratches. He flicked it open – dead. He opened the back – no sim card. But… there was always the chance that numbers would be held on the actual phone. It was worth a try – it was a bit of an ancient old thing and he remembered that they held a lot of information that wasn't always shifted to the sim. A plan was beginning to be hatched. Worth a try. And he knew the very person who could help with retrieving such information.

Feeling much better, he grabbed a Coke and packet of crisps that quelled his hunger. Finally switching off the living-room light, he went to bed and slept well.

14

Jamie had laughed in Jessica's face. It was followed by a nasty snarl and a pointed finger as he demanded, 'Leave me out of this, will you?' This was followed by his quick exit from the house. Jessica was flummoxed. Jamie wasn't like that. Even if he couldn't be bothered with Joanna now that she had dumped them all, as he put it, his attitude and almost sneering, callous laughter was uncalled for.

Before Sandi left to go back to university Jessica shared her concerns with her. Sandi had patted her on her head in a patronising kind of way until she realised that Jessica was truly concerned about her friend and about Jamie's change of heart. Sandi had seen enough to know that Jamie had been 'involved' with Joanna, though Jessica couldn't see how as they had only been with each other a few hours. Sandi volunteered that she thought Jamie had been attracted to her, had romantically seen himself as her saviour – as a sort of hero-cum-knight. The fact that Joanna had clearly dismissed him from her thoughts had hurt him and he now felt stupid for being so concerned. That's how she viewed the situation, anyway. She told Jessica that he would get over it – eventually – and that if Jessica was really concerned then she should just try her best to contact her via her phone, but if that failed then there wasn't a great deal she could do. If the girl didn't want to be found then she surely would ensure that she wasn't and there wasn't anything anyone could do about it. If the police hadn't found her then what realistic hope did she have?

That was about the truth of it and that was what she was prepared to accept had she not been both surprised and relieved to receive a text out of the blue on the 4th January from Joanna wishing her a happy new year and requesting that they meet up. Too elated by the renewed contact, she gave no thought as to the rather curt and odd message that made no reference to having failed to turn up at their last proposed meeting. Her hopes soared at the thought that Joanna was still a friend. She didn't tell Jamie.

*

Joanna spent the last night of the year in Moat Park. The previous nights since her escape from Merrick had been fraught with danger and distress. She had absolutely nothing but her wits to keep her safe. Having left Merrick's clutches and after hiding behind the bins for some time, she eventually left and meandered about the streets, searching for any clues as to her location. Eventually she made her way through various turnings and landed up in the main shopping square. At that late hour of the night there were several people spilling out from nightclubs and wine bars, and she became caught up in a flow of happy partygoers. Aware that she was an absolute wreck, she kept her head low and tried to cover up her wrists by yanking on her sleeves. But she was cold and hungry and weak, and it wasn't long before she became the focus of a group of very drunk teenagers.

It began when she slipped and stumbled and fell into one of them, a young lad of about seventeen who had his arm around a girl. It was the girl who began to attack Joanna, accusing her of trying to, 'Nick my boyfriend, yeah?' The rest of her friends gathered around Joanna and began to push her and pull at her clothes. Joanna was whirled around by one of them and she stumbled again, this time reaching out to steady herself but inadvertently grabbing, as luck would have it, the same boy. The girlfriend turned on him and accused him of knowing Joanna and the whole situation became violent and petty and stupidly out of hand. Joanna tried to say that it was ridiculous, that the girl was wrong, that she had never set eyes on her boyfriend till tonight. But now, fired up, the girl began to pull at Joanna's hair until a real scuffle broke out with the boy defending Joanna – that, of course, added fuel to the fire.

A foot patrol of community police officers came meandering down the street and moved in on the scuffle. Splitting up the party, they tried to ascertain the issue that sparked the fight. However, after one look at Joanna they realised that she was in fact very unwell and, having had a glimpse of her torn and bleeding wrists, they debated whether to call for a paramedic. Joanna, terrified that she would end up in the same hospital as Merrick, told them that she was fine and just wanted to get back home. Her saving grace came when the officers received a call to attend a disturbance just kicking off outside FatFace in the centre of the precinct. That took precedence for them.

With a fleeting assurance that Joanna was free of the gang of friends, they took to the path and headed for the fight. Joanna, taking her opportunity, turned tail and ran. Slipping down a side street, she nipped into a doorway and slumped down. She shook from head to foot and hugged her knees into herself. Waves of nausea from hunger swept over her and she began to panic. In her head she could only think of getting as far away from Merrick as possible. She tried desperately to think of what to do and where to go, but also how to get back to Cranenden with no money, no ticket and no phone. Then she remembered Barry. He lived in Maidstone. Where was his place from here? She had no idea. It couldn't be far because he worked in the town and it only took him a few minutes to drive back from work to his place. Drawing her coat tight around her shivering body, she meandered up and down the streets, looking for anything, a sign a street map, anything that could help her work out where she was.

*

The street minister found her. They were working in pairs and had just completed their night shift and were walking back towards headquarters when one of them noticed Joanna's foot hanging over the edge of the kerb. Failing to work out where Barry's apartment was, she had stumbled towards a Waterstones, where she knew he worked. Stupid, really, as he would be long gone by this time of night, but if she could find a doorway close by that gave her some shelter then she would just sit it out until morning, when hopefully he would turn up for work. As it was, the bookshop was in a less crowded part of the town and well away from the nightclubs and pubs. The doorway was quite wide but also shallow. It didn't give much shelter but fortunately because of that it was less likely to be a haunt of the homeless. Desperately tired, she'd slept in fits and starts, the cold, hard, step preventing her from relaxing and the chill air disallowing any chance of her fully giving in to her fatigue. What little sleep she did have was hallucinatory and stressful with images of Merrick bearing down on her. She fidgeted to try and keep her circulation going and that was when her foot inadvertently caught the eye of the minister.

They offered Joanna some help that she immediately rejected. Authority, no matter what sort, had left her totally bereft of any trust – even more so when she recognised one of them as the nurse that had worked with Merrick on the ward she had been in. She told them both to 'fuck off' and turned her back.

The nurse, however, wouldn't let it go and moved into the space and seemed to recognise her. Her questioning disarmed Joanna. Cornered, she refused to move and stared straight ahead. Seeing her lack of response, the nurse was about to give up on her until she mentioned that Joanna reminded her of a girl she had nursed in the hospital a few weeks back. Joanna scowled. But when she said that she had spent several nights searching the streets for her, Joanna began to feel less defensive. The nurse/minister pointed to Joanna's wrists and suggested that at least if Joanna were to come back with them to their base she could get her a hot drink and clean up her injuries. 'Then, if you wish, you can leave.'

Feeling utterly drained and weak and devoid of any reason not to acquiesce, Joanna just gave in and without another word got up and followed the two ministers, who both supported her by linking arms and guiding her to the community hall.

The tea was good. The sandwich was even better. The kindness of the nurse as she cleansed her wrists, gently and with care, soothed Joanna's fears. Merrick could not get her here. Even if the nurse went back to the hospital to work alongside him and informed him of meeting up with her, she would be long gone. And so she relaxed and allowed the peacefulness of the hall to lull her into some sense of safety.

As the nurse/preacher worked on her wrists they both remained silent and Joanna looked about her. Quite a few young people were being cared for. Most seemed to be drunk and had passed out on makeshift cot beds. Some were propped up on chairs drinking coffee while the ministers mingled and made hot drinks, proffering sandwiches and cake. But though they seemed caring and kind, Joanna was far too wary. In one respect she felt disarmed as all the 'clients' were clearly young people, but that didn't alter her fear and dread of being sent back to an institution.

Once she had had her wrists tidied and bandaged, and having drunk her tea and eaten her fill, she declined the offer of a bed and chose instead to sit on a chair by the exit until light. She dozed and jerked awake at every movement. Before dawn, however, the night ministers began to pack away their base and gradually people drifted out until it was just Joanna left. The nurse came back to her and offered to take Joanna somewhere – anywhere she wished to go – but Joanna declined the offer, thanked the nurse for her help and left. Refreshed by the food and the snatches of sleep, she felt stronger in herself. She also felt confident that her appearance was so drastically changed that the nurse had not fully cottoned on as to who she really was.

The change in temperature from the hall was a bit of a shock to her regardless of the sustenance that she had received. She plunged her hands into her jeans pockets and hunched her shoulders against the wind. The confidence that she had found whilst in the hall had dwindled and she realised that relying on Barry again might not be such a good idea. He might not even be working today. She wandered around Waterstones, lingering around the area, glancing ever-hopeful up and down the street. Opposite the shop was a hexagonal bench with a tree growing up the centre covered in Christmas lights. She moved her way over, sat there and waited.

Eventually the staff began to turn up and make their way into the store. Joanna watched for any sign of him, but as luck would have it Barry, it seemed, was not working the early shift today. That was a bit of a blow. Now she had to rethink her options. And then she noticed him, ambling up the street drinking from a Caffe Nero Styrofoam coffee cup and eating a bagel. He stood outside the building until he had clearly finished his breakfast and then entered the store. His first day back after his ski trip and he was feeling good. Her plan was actually no plan. She had no idea what he would do or think of her turning up like this after not having had any contact with him since he had driven her back to the barn.

She gave it ten minutes then drifted into the shop. She caught a glimpse of her reflection in the window and wondered whether Barry would even recognise her. She was certainly pretty messed up; apart from her infected and bandaged wrists, her hair was knotted and dirty, and her clothes stained and torn. She was also aware that she had regained that stale, mouldy aroma of sweat that had hung around her when she lived on the boat. Making her way to the toilets, she used the liquid soap to scrub at her face and wash her filthy hands. Next she attempted to sponge her stained clothes as best she could with the paper tissues, which left balled-up scraps of tissue adhering to the surface. Finally she ran her fingers through her very knotted and matted hair. A final glimpse in the mirror delivered a none-too-pretty picture, but it was the best she could do. She fully understood why Barry looked up with horror when she approached him with a feeble, 'Hello, Barry, do you remember me?'

*

Merrick's friend Paulo was a real geek. He had studied at the International School of Electronics and Digital Science. What he didn't know or understand about communication appliances could be written on a stamp. He had been seconded into the NHS to help develop and further the European collective analysis of scans – MRIs, CTs and X-rays – that had been developed using the most sophisticated of readers that were based in Spain. Paulo's job was to link the scanners to the appropriate radiologist specialist in Madrid and thereby ensure accurate and speedy results of high quality and precision. As for mobile phones – that was a doddle. As soon as Merrick had handed him Joanna's phone he charged it and downloaded all the information held on the phone itself. It was simple for him to extract the latest texts that had been sent.

He was infuriated to hear the conversation between Jessica's and Joanna's last communication whereby he had been the focus; it unnerved him. Her comments that she believed Joanna about the 'male nurse' even though Jamie didn't made her a threat. Merrick took a chance and decided to contact Jessica as Joanna. It wouldn't be difficult. He could easily dupe her into a rendezvous, giving him the opportunity to eliminate the threat she posed. What he wanted from this meeting was to shut the girl up for good. Having dealt with Jackie, he hadn't taken on board that there might be others Joanna had told. He guessed that Jamie was the same guy who had visited the hospital and felt assured that he clearly had not accepted Joanna's version, whatever that might have been. But there was danger in Jessica. He had to think fast. If she was gullible he might even be able to use her for Assef, though he would have to be careful. It would kill two birds with one stone. He had to think carefully how he was to reply and where he intended to meet her. Of bigger concern, though, was where the bitch Joanna was hiding.

*

Barry looked Joanna in the eye and emphatically explained that he was at work, extremely busy and unable to help her any further. As he spoke he took in her wildness, her distress and her wizened face. He told her that he was sorry for her but that she was only a child and should go back to where she had come from and stop her dramatic games. Furthermore she had clearly, by the state of her, only got herself into further trouble and he really didn't trust her. If she'd come back for more money he would have no alternative but to call for the police.

Had Joanna not been so desperate she would have left him at that point – but in her deep despair she begged him to just meet her in his break and allow her to talk to him and then she would leave and never bother him again. Reluctantly, to avoid further attention and a scene, he agreed in order to get her out of the shop and away from his customers. She stank and he didn't want attention brought to them both. He slipped her a tenner and told her to sort herself out, promising to meet her at the café Sarah's Sandwich Bar on Blake Street at eleven when he was due a break. Grateful and with eyes brimming with tears, Joanna turned and scuttled out of the shop, leaving an aroma of urine, sweat and dirt in her trail.

Disturbed by this visitation, Barry didn't really connect this apparition with the girl he had helped earlier. He felt annoyed and conned and really didn't believe she'd be at the café as arranged, convinced that she had just wanted the money.

But he'd honour the arrangement, and he dutifully made his way across the street and down the walkway, where he found Joanna lurking by the entrance. She still looked rough, but she had, it seemed, managed to clean herself up a bit and was wearing an old coat that was far too big for her that she had bought from Oxfam. 'They are the only ones that sell at realistic prices,' she confided in Barry as they entered the café. 'Most of the other charity shops put crazy prices on their clothes. Seems like those with money get a kick out of buying retro gear,' Joanna commented, and accepted Barry's offer of soup and coffee for lunch.

The story she then told him between slurps of soup and gulps of coffee was the best yet. He didn't believe a word of it. And after twenty minutes of bending his ear in an implausible tale of kidnapping, near-death experiences, slavery and enforced drug taking, Barry had had enough. He looked at the pitiful specimen in front of him and recognised a damaged and vulnerable human being, though one that he no longer felt he could support. Her lies were just too implausible and though his aunt had clearly been taken in at the hospital (as he had, to a certain extent), it was now clear to him that he had to get her off his back before she caused him any real trouble.

'Melanie, Joanna, or whatever you're calling yourself now, this has got to stop. I can no longer help you and if you come near me again – ever – I will call the police. I am sorry that you are in such a state – and I advise you to go and get help, but not from me. The ten pounds I gave you earlier and money for the food is the last I will give you. Good luck.' And with that he stood up, pushed his chair to the table and went to leave.

Shocked and desperate, Joanna grabbed his arm and hissed, 'Why is it that no-one believes anything I say? Why would I make up such a thing? You have to help me – please, there is no-one else I can turn to.'

Barry shook her hand from him, mumbled an apology and fled the café, leaving Joanna with her worst fears realised. She was utterly alone with no-one to help her at all.

A hanging humid dampness held the midges in the air. Seven hundred miles away from where her daughter was endeavouring to find her identity, in a crofter's cottage on the west coast of Scotland, Mary Cauldwell heard Derick's curses as he bent over the battered and ancient Land Rover, in an attempt to fix the starter motor for the third time that day. Provisions were low and he needed to make the 150-mile round trip to Inverness for their basic supplies. Mary had never been to Inverness. For sixteen years she had seen only the inside of the cottage and as far as her chains would allow her to walk in the yard outside. Once he had locked the door at night he would release her chain, but never in the day. She often stared through the window at the beautiful, hard and uncompromising mountains that held a vision of wild freedom and terrifying danger for her. The road he took to Inverness went through the mountain pass that was often blocked by snow in winter. She had attempted to run one day not long after he had brought her to the cottage. The whipping that followed and the consequent use of the chains meant that she had had no further chance again. Now it was raining, a soft, gentle shower that stilled the midges for a while. She continued to scrub the clothes using the old wooden washboard that her mother and grandmother had used before her. Then she heard him call her name. She stopped and listened again. This time he screeched and then went silent. Deftly she put the brush down, wiped her hands on the tea towel and dragged her way to the door.

How odd. It looked as though he had been cut off from the waist down. All she saw was a pair of fat, jeaned legs as his top half had slunk into the engine. Slowly she edged her way towards the car, and quietly called to him. 'Derick, Derick,' she whispered. But there was no response. Having finally ambled up to the open bonnet she saw that the top half of his body had slammed hard down onto the engine. A gaping wound had spilt blood from his cheek and temple. Tentatively she touched his neck. She listened for his breathing. His lips were blue and his eyes stared like glassy grapes.

She looked at his sad, dead body and fumbled in the pocket of his jeans, where she retrieved a key. With this key she unshackled her ankle from the chain that kept her within six feet of the cottage. A slow smile crept across her face. 'My dear, I do think you have had a heart attack,' she whispered to the corpse. Then she noticed a slight pulse in his throat. 'Oh no,' she determined. 'No-one is going to be reviving you.' And she walked back into the house, closed the door and sank down in her chair.

For some minutes Mary deliberated on what to do. She had thought, dreamt of her freedom for so long that now that idea might be realised she was too stunned to react. Eventually she went back outside. Their place was so remote that very few people passed by and no-one ever visited, but Mary thought it best to bring Derick inside, out of sight of passing travellers. He was heavy and she struggled to drag the fat blob of a man into the house. She had no compunction about whether he could be alive or not as she knew that any flicker of life in him would very soon wane. He deserved no less. She dragged him onto the old horsehair sofa and left him half on and half off, his right arm dangling over the cushion.

15

Yvonne just couldn't believe the total change in the Whitworth family in such a few weeks. Holding the hand of Alex at her bedside and watching for any signs of life, she tried to work out how it had all degenerated so rapidly. She was shocked when DI Skinner ushered her into the cubicle to identify Alex. Admittedly she wasn't a hundred per cent sure that it was Alex – the child had altered so much. But when she approached the bed and scrutinised her face she realised that it couldn't be anyone else. She had not recovered consciousness from the operation and as yet her life signs were pretty feeble. 'They' didn't hold out much hope that she would pull through, but 'where there is life there is hope' – a pretty meaningless platitude but one that she held sway with. She was pumped full of antibiotics to try and ward off any infection from the burst ovary and in an attempt to stage off peritonitis but was struggling to hold her own. Her immune system was weak and her blood levels were dangerously low. Alongside of which, it was clear that she had hepatitis and a low-lying infection that suggested an STD was lurking. Yvonne's confirmation that this indeed was Alex led John Skinner to inform the parents himself – Yvonne wasn't prepared to leave Alex's side until they had joined her.

*

Joanna wasn't so surprised by Barry's response, but it did jolt her confidence. Wandering back through the high street, she allowed herself a quick glance up at the window in Waterstones, where she knew Barry would be. She saw nothing except bright posters for the new David Walliams book. Her wanderings took her to the edge of Maidstone and she found herself in Moat Park again, sitting on a bench in abject despair. Now what? Never had she been so adrift. With absolutely nothing – no phone, no money and no belongings, not even her baby jumper! She stuffed her hands, balled into a fist, into her pockets, drew her knees up to her chin and stared at the ground in total sorrow.

Barry, meanwhile, as luck would have it, had been looking out of the window and noticed Joanna drift by. He really thought she was going to come back in and harass him again, and he had his hand hovering over the phone he intended to use the moment she stepped onto his floor. But she didn't materialise. Relieved and with a very dry mouth, he visibly relaxed and continued with his work, but he couldn't focus.

During his afternoon break he decided to make a call to Ruby, just to check how she was doing and to refresh his mind over what she had thought about Joanna when she was in hospital and whether she had had further thoughts in light of his meetings with her. The outcome of this was that Ruby had become very distressed to hear of the encounter and fervently assured Barry that she was convinced that Joanna would be telling him the truth. She had seen Merrick on the couple of occasions he had entered the ward to visit Joanna and her hackles had risen at the way he had sidled up to her and bludgeoned his way in, and why, if he was such a good man, was he so very secretive? Barry had to realise that Ruby had seen his face even though she hadn't heard his words, and the aggression she noticed in how he expressed himself – well, his whole body language was wrong from the outset. Furthermore, Ruby had heard the story from Joanna herself, which, though pitiful in the extreme, was highly plausible. Even more so, she was of the opinion that Joanna was in serious danger and that if Barry could just go to the police and tell them all he knew then she would feel more comfortable and at ease about her.

Barry hung up and pondered on all she had said. After all, Ruby had been in a vulnerable state herself in the hospital and he still couldn't quite convince himself that they hadn't all been taken in by a street girl who was able to use her wit to get what she wanted. On the other hand, Ruby was quite a canny woman who had lived her life working alongside the dispossessed and had made it her life's work to support the underdog. She had been a fervent feminist, and though often called upon to help others she wasn't one to be easily taken in. If he went to the police, what harm could it do? He would at least have absolved himself of any responsibility and he could begin to feel less guilty about walking out on her – which jolted him into concern at where she had disappeared to.

His intentions had been to go straight to the police station after work and then he imagined that they would go out and look for her. Perhaps they might also find Merrick and take him to task. Naivety, it seemed, was his error.

First of all the police station was very busy. The woman on reception was issuing numbers to people on arrival – like a deli in a supermarket. He, it seemed, was fifth in the queue. Sitting in the waiting area, Barry reflected how this just wasn't going to pan out. So in the end he decided that he wouldn't waste time any further; he returned his ticket and advised the receptionist that he would 'ring in' his request.

Only when he was outside did he notice on the board a list of various numbers for different call centres. One listed was for vulnerable young people. He noted the number and proceeded towards his car whilst both scanning the area for any sight of her and at the same time tapping in the number he had noted. Seemingly they were 'receiving a high volume of calls right now' and he was placed in a queue. When he did get through the advice he was given was to… phone the police! As he had no idea where Joanna was, and because he wasn't able to give her full name or date of birth or the full nature of her predicament, they couldn't help.

All the while this was happening Barry became a little more stressed at trying to find some interest in the missing girl. By the time he rang the non-emergency service for the police he was met by a similar barrier. Eventually he was connected to Maidstone police station, where further notes were presumably made, a request was promised to alert the on-duty officer who was in Maidstone that evening and Barry was invited to accept an appointment for interview the following day.

By now Barry was feeling very frustrated and annoyed. He avoided explaining how he had harboured Joanna in his house over a few nights – he was frightened that *his* motives might be misconstrued – so the story he had to tell was a little disconnected. He didn't dare explain much more and refused to give his full name. In a panic he hung up and ran to his car and drove home.

*

As dusk drew in, people drifted away from the park and the gates were closed. A frightened wastrel squatted in the darkness. Growing ever more cold and tired, Joanna felt pain. It wasn't particularly the physical pain that she had been enduring but the ever-developing pain of worthlessness. It was hard to quantify and voice; all her awareness of herself was that she was of no consequence to anybody at all. She lay down on the bench and tried to sleep. The leafless trees around her provided very little shelter from the cold night to come. Her fingers and face now numb and burning with cold. Already failing to feel her limbs in the dense chill, Joanna reflected how lovely it would be if the frost came and covered her with its delicate icy fingers and take her to the next world.

*

Jamie was ever more annoyed with Jessica and her newfound conspiratorial secrecy that she was clearly not about to share with him. She had flounced into his room and 'borrowed' ten pounds from him for something that she had refused to say. Her irritating chant of, 'Just you wait and see,' followed by, 'Won't you be surprised when I come back,' in her silly sing-song voice she put on when she thought she was being clever, was childish and not worth considering.

However, when she hadn't returned from wherever it was she was going by eight o'clock that evening, and having missed a training session that was the highlight of her week, he was beginning to get a little concerned. Even more perplexing was that Clarissa had no idea where Jess had gone or what she was up to either. Since they had both renewed their friendship they were always in each other's pockets, but not seemingly on this occasion, for Clarissa was out of the loop as well. When Jamie picked up her call on the landline (a rarity these days) it became obvious that she had no idea about Jess's whereabouts. Her only reason for trying to call Jess on the home phone was purely because she couldn't get a response from her mobile.

Dismissing Jessica's absence as a nothing, at that point it became clear that Clarri was more concerned about Alex. Her plight overshadowed everything. The seriousness and danger of Alex's situation became clear when her mum called home from the hospital, where Alex was dangerously ill. Clarissa was aware that something awful had occurred. She now knew her mum had been called in to identify her. Her first reaction was to call Jess. As the evening went on with still no news from Jess, both she and Jamie knew that something had gone very badly wrong.

*

Jess was slightly bemused at how exact Joanna's message was. It made her smile. Clearly she hadn't become used to text speak and had tapped in every word in such precise detail with perfect spelling – must have taken her ages. But nevertheless she was excited about their rendezvous and even more impressed that they were to meet, not in Hastings but Maidstone, where clearly Joanna had moved on and made some kind of life. Maybe she was with the guy from the bookshop. *How romantic,* thought Jess. She hadn't realised quite how long the journey would take nor that she would have to change at Ashford, but it seemed quite a fun thing to do and added to the intensity of the plan. Joanna had suggested that she get out at Maidstone and leave the station turning left and then pop into the little café on the corner of the street, where Joanna would be waiting for her.

Of course, that was not going to happen. Merrick, hands in his pockets, loitering by the newsstand, stood watching for her. Arriving ten minutes before the train was due, he observed every one as they left the platforms. Constantly checking the arrivals board and his watch, he visibly tensed as the Ashford train pulled into platform 12.

Focusing his eyes on the passengers that heaved their way through the barriers, he relaxed when he caught sight of her. It was obvious which one was Jessica. Stupid child couldn't keep the excitement off her face, and when she took a left on leaving the station he upped and followed her.

Two metres before the traffic lights, just a few metres before the café, in the bustle of commuters crossing the road, he made a grab for her arm and in a split second drew her down into the alleyway, frog-marching her to the end. Jessica was so surprised and hurt by his grip that all she could stutter was, 'Hey, stop it, you're hurting me. Let go.' But Merrick's grip only got stronger and he dragged her further to the side street where his car was waiting. He opened the driver's door and propelled her in, shoving her across the seat into the passenger side, bashing her shins on the gear stick as he did so.

With a short gasp and attempt at a scream, Jessica found herself belted up and driven at a steady speed through the town. It all happened so quickly and unexpectedly that she had fleetingly lost her wits, but by the time she had recovered them she was speeding along on the outskirts of the town towards the motorway. In a panic she grabbed at the handle of the door, but it wouldn't budge. Merrick's response was to elbow her face with his left arm and to hiss, 'Just sit back and relax or you can join the rest of the roadkill.'

Horrified, she sat perfectly still, but relaxing was out of the question. At the very next set of lights Merrick grabbed something from the tray in the front of the car and jabbed it into Jessica's leg. Her legs went numb and her tongue felt thick and her eyes rolled as the world blurred into nothing.

Within ten minutes Merrick had left the main road and pulled the car into a layby, where he searched through Jessica's pockets until he found her phone. He opened it up, took out the sim card and pushed it down a drain in the road. He took in a deep breath and visibly relaxed. Now he would be safe to drive her back to his place and to his bolt hole for stupid girls. It was annoying as he had wanted to get her to Assef straight away, but something had happened and Assef had put a hold on any more deliveries. Some trouble had occurred and it wasn't safe to operate with any new girls for the moment. As it was he was shipping out the girls he had in Hastings to various hubs around the country until whatever had gone on had died down. Merrick was again frustrated and annoyed that Assef hadn't filled him in on the whole problem, especially as it had left Merrick with a girl that he would have to deal with, one way or another. Merrick looked at her slumped in the passenger seat. She wasn't bad-looking and he felt that Assef would have really liked her. She had a sweet, babyish look about her, but hey ho. He put the car into gear, indicated and drove carefully away from the layby and made his way home.

*

Jessica's parents were frantic. Midnight came and went, and still no response from her phone. The police had been made aware and a young officer had called at the house to take details. Jamie had given Clarissa the third degree as he wasn't sure that she was speaking the truth in her denying any knowledge of where Jess had gone. He then recalled her behaviour when she had bounced into his room asking for him to loan her ten pounds. He had been only half listening to her irritating pleas and it was that self-assurance that she was going to show him how wrong he had been that nagged at him. Then the moment Clarissa had turned up he knew that it had to be something to do with Joanna. With no proof other than a gut instinct, he informed his parents of his concerns.

Clarissa was not that convinced, as she was sure that had there been anything on Joanna then Jess would have told her. Furious with himself that he had deleted her number, he was desperate for Clarri to ring her – but she had never had Joanna's number, though sure she had got Jess's previous number in her old school notebook, and wasn't that the phone that Jess had given Joanna? Jamie's dad didn't hesitate and drove Clarissa back to her home to try and find it. Clasping at straws they all huddled around Jamie as he tapped in the number. It didn't connect.

*

It happened that the police officer who had called round to Jessica's house had been on duty the night that Alex had been found. It had left its mark. He too had a sister about Alex's age and he felt keen to try and support the hunt for the perpetrators of what was clearly child abuse. Now having learnt that there was some connection between Alex and the missing Jessica with the missing runaway from the same school, he was determined to unravel the unsavoury situation. He finally left the family at half twelve, having ascertained as much detail as he could about the possible reasons why Jessica had disappeared and who she was attempting to meet. Jamie had recalled the name of the guy with whom Joanna had stayed after leaving the hospital, but he only knew his first name and that he had worked at Waterstones in Maidstone. But that in itself was a start. It was agreed that Barry would be their first port of call in the morning as soon as he had permission from Maidstone to interview on their patch.

*

A clock was striking midnight from some distant church. The sound penetrated through Joanna's cold sleep. She moved awkwardly and felt her stiffened body resist movement. So, she hadn't died. But she was numb and very stiff with cold. She shifted her position slightly and attempted to sleep – but sleep wouldn't come this time. Listlessly she attempted to stand up, and that really hurt as she tried to energise the blood to circulate. It was almost comical – her movements were like awkward tribal dance steps, swinging her arms over her head and bending and whacking her legs and arms, breathing great fires of air into the night chill. The silence was searing.

Without conscious thought, wraith-like, she silently drifted through the impenetrable dark of the park. She had no fear of the looming shadows or dark spaces that went before her. Nothing scared her now. The light from the moon came and went as the scudding clouds blocked and then exposed the features before her. Recognising nothing but the endless treeline, her aimless wandering gave her no sense of where she was. A secret smile to herself enhanced her knowledge that she was truly and literally alone in the world and of absolutely no consequence to anyone.

As she stopped, feeling bereft of any fight or desire to live, she slumped down at the base of a huge oak tree. The cold, hard ground penetrated through her thin clothes with a death-like grip. Pulling the coat around her tighter and drawing up the collar, she huddled into it – like a sleeping bag. Eyes open, she stared into the gloom. It was as if there was no other world out there at all. Just her and her thoughts and the dark and the cold. Without thought she automatically and slowly dragged her nails across her sore wrists, opening up the wounds, feeling some relief as the pain seared and the blood dripped. Eventually she slept.

*

This time Merrick decided that he would be a little more careful in how he kept his victim. As long as she was sedated and given enough fluids she would be safely quiet and not bother the other tenants in the building. Though he was still unsure as to who had let Joanna escape, he felt confident that there would be no repeat of that debacle. He felt sure that Channi would have put the word around that discretion was vital for them all. The immigrants were far too vulnerable to be footloose with their interference – scared as rabbits in headlights they were from what little he had seen of them. They were as terrified of Merrick letting on to the authorities of their whereabouts as he was of them telling on him. It worked. No-one said or did anything – but many watched!

As Merrick drew up in his car Jessica began to come round. Her vision was blurred and her tongue felt heavy and fat and furry. She could hardly get the words to form, though she knew that she wanted to yell and scream and kick out as she was being lifted in a fire-fighter's carry, but her body would not respond to her efforts. Merrick opened his front door and carried Jessica into the living room and dumped her onto the sofa. Within seconds he had grabbed a sleeping bag, a blanket and an old half-drunk bottle of Coke, which he emptied and filled with cold water from the tap then disappeared, leaving Jessica alone.

She struggled to stand. Her feet would not go where she wanted them to. Her arms tried to propel and push herself off the sofa, but they had no strength. With a great deal of effort she just managed to slip onto the floor, where she drew herself up onto all fours. She aimed for the front door, dragging herself forward, desperately trying to mouth words and scream out for help. Nothing materialised that was audible.

Just as she reached the door, Merrick came through it. All her efforts had been to no avail, for he just unceremoniously picked her up like she was a doll and carried her, not back into the flat but out to the corridor, where, through blurry vision, Jess could see the opening of a chasm in the floor.

Merrick steadily took each step one at a time and dropped her onto the sleeping bag. All the while he said nothing. He indicated to her the bottle of water and then with a cold, deliberate glance around he kicked the bag of bread he had brought (as an after-thought) towards her, then scrambled back up the stairs, dropped the door and slid the packing case back over it. Once back in his flat he sat down with a can of beer and caught his breath. He was troubled. This could not continue.

So far he had avoided anything too sinister – no-one had died. But he had an uneasy feeling about this latest problem. Assef was becoming more and more evasive. He was also not sure how much longer the others in the building would be keeping their silence. How much could one person stand being cooped up in one place only being let out for work? At least the girls he procured were having a happy time. Those lucky bastards who could afford them he almost envied. But the groups next door they were doing all kinds of filthy work with very little pleasure. No, he concluded, it was time to try and get out of this whole situation.

Going to the fridge he pulled himself another beer. The hiss of the ring pull whetted his thirst. Can in hand, he wandered over to the window and gazed down onto the street. What was he going to do about Jessica? And where was Joanna? He needed to get them together, but how? Joanna's phone was no longer with her and as far as he could tell she was uncontactable. He mused over his Christmas that seemed so long ago now but was in reality only a few days ago. He smiled to himself as he turned back from the window and sat back down on the sofa. His mum had been so happy to see him, and the difference in his whole family from the few extras and luxuries they were now able to have because of his contribution – it was all worth it.

Putting the can on the table, he leaned back, running his fingers through his hair and his hand over his chin. Mmm! He hadn't realised how stubby his beard growth was; he would need to smarten himself up a bit before his next shift. But just for now he took out his mobile and ordered himself a takeaway, to be delivered in thirty minutes. An evening alone, watching TV without thinking or caring about anything else, looked good to him. Jessica would be fine and Joanna wasn't worth the worry.

16

The moment Barry saw the uniformed officer approach he knew. As Kate, the ground-floor manager, ushered him towards Barry's counter he began to shake. How had they traced him? If Joanna was underage then what kind of trouble would he be in? He felt sick. His mouth dry, he was unable to do more than nod as the officer affirmed that he was the man called Barry who had sheltered Joanna when she had left the hospital. Kate took over his desk and in a dream-like state Barry went with the officer to the office, where they both sat on the swivel chairs and Officer Ken Beech began his questions.

He informed Barry that as he was from Hastings Police in East Sussex he had applied for and been given permission from Maidstone to make a few enquiries and that if they proved fruitful then he would like Barry to come with him to Maidstone police station, where a Kent police officer would join him in the interview. Barry spilled it all out. How he had attempted to contact the police yesterday, how he felt scared because of Joanna's age and how his motives might be misconstrued; how he had helped Joanna escape from the hospital because of her fear of Merrick; how he had listened to his aunt Ruby's concerns and offered Joanna shelter for a couple of nights; how he had not touched her or attempted to touch her; how she had insisted on returning to Cranenden, how he had driven her there, how she had turned up out of the blue looking bruised and hurt with a story of kidnapping and being tied up and how she had feared Merrick was a child abductor and of how he had not believed her and turned her away; how he was now concerned that she might well be in real danger and how he was anxious about the whole state of affairs.

'You read so much nowadays about men who have been alone with girls and they then get locked up. I've done nothing to her, I promise you – I only wanted to help. That's why I turned her away yesterday and now she could be in real trouble and... oh, what a mess.' Barry buried his head in his hands and drew in a deep breath. 'I should have minded my own business – best to not interfere and keep your head down.'

Ken's response was to immediately encourage Barry to help further by stating that in all probability Barry had saved Joanna from an assault with his sheltering of her and not leaving her to Merrick if what she had told him was true. At that comment Barry interjected with recalling the last thing she had said to him that had echoed in his head ever since: 'Why doesn't anyone believe me?'

Finally, at Ken's request, Barry, more confident now, volunteered to go to the police station and give as much detail as he could about everything he knew and of all that Joanna had shared with him. Ken was reassuring enough to convince Barry that as long as Joanna was able to verify his side of the story then he didn't think anything would be brought against Barry. However, there was a chance that another girl was in immediate danger from the same perpetrator and anything that Barry could give them would be useful. Just as they were about to leave the store Jamie, his dad and his mum entered the shop.

With some distressed interactions and bewildered conversations Ken managed to persuade them all to make tracks to the station, where he hoped to unpick the events leading up to the disappearance of both girls.

*

Merrick woke from his sleep at around four thirty in the morning. His head was thumping and he was thirsty. The debris from the takeaway lay littered on the floor and the five empty cans of beer were strewn among them. The vodka bottle was on its side and what was left of the contents had trickled over the coffee table and dripped onto the rug. The room was disgusting. He felt disgusting. Grabbing a glass, he drank three lots of water, took two paracetamol and crawled into bed, where he slept for the next five hours.

Jessica had woken up. Merrick had not returned to top up her sedative and she was beginning to feel her limbs and her voice. She was nervous of the water in case it was also drugged, but her mouth was so dry she gave in and drank it down. Feeling no ill effects, she sat back on the sleeping bag and tried to ascertain what had actually happened. The light from the bare bulb threw shadows around the space. She noticed a pile of rubbish at one end, split bits of wood, an old bike frame, and odds and ends.

After allowing the water to revive her, she noted the stairwell up to the trap door. She went to climb it until her head and shoulders were touching and then she tried to heave it up. It wouldn't shift. With a heavy heart she poked about in the rubbish to see if she could find anything that could be used as a lever or screwdriver. The hinges were rusted into the wood but might well be easy to unscrew if she could get a grip to it. But there was nothing that could be utilised for that purpose. Then she thought about shouting. Obviously whoever had put her in here must have been assured that if she were to make a noise then she wouldn't be heard. Also she didn't want to alert the man as to her revival and bring him back down before she had a chance to work out what to do. But then again he might believe her to still be incapacitated. So she took a chance, opened her mouth and screamed. She heard nothing. She tried again. Still no movement or response from above. Screaming hurt her throat and took a surprising amount of effort.

As she lay back on the steps wondering what she could try next she glanced up at her prison gate and noticed that the slats near the edge of the door had tiny gaps near where the hinge was screwed in. Feeling in her pockets, she found her train ticket. She had nothing to use as a pen but the fact that this was an unused return ticket might just make someone inquisitive enough to pick it up, and then if she yelled as they did so, they might help her.

She didn't hold out much hope at this rather tenuous idea, but with little other options it at least meant she was being proactive in getting attention from a passer-by. Jessica poked the ticket up through the slit. The dust and filth that had gathered in the gap prevented the whole edge from popping through, but part of the ticket lodged itself, which meant that at least a third of it was standing upright on the other side. That was a start. Rummaging through her pockets, she found the ten-pound note that she had borrowed from Jamie. If she were to poke that through also then someone would surely be tempted. It was hard because there were no other spaces that she could see.

Going back to the rubbish in the room, she discarded it all until she noted the trashed shelf that had a nail protruding from the splintered wood. After several hard pulls, she managed to release it from the wall. Laying on the third step with her face towards the ceiling, Jessica worked on the tiny gap around the other hinge. She scraped and tore at the detritus and dust that filled the space until a little glint of light showed through. Excited now, she worked with renewed energy until, by folding the note into four, she was able to squeeze most of it through. She didn't want it to go all the way as she needed to see if anyone grabbed it – then she could yell.

*

Getting access to PC Jane Winter's file that she had created on Joanna had been progress for Ken. As soon as he had read up on the conversation they had had and the notes that were made in the hospital when she was under the name of Melanie, as well as reading a copy of Joanna's email alongside a transcript of the interview that Jane had had with Merrick, Ken's suspicions were alerted. Ken had had dealings with victims of abuse before and he could hear the tell-tale signs in the notes. Jane herself was to join him as soon as she could and together they would officially interview Barry, but Ken knew that Jane would be very much on the defensive and dismiss him out of hand. Jane had also listened to the retrieved recorded phone call that Barry had made the previous evening; the fact that she had not acted upon it spoke volumes. Ken would have to be careful how he dealt with this officer who was bound to hold firm in her original beliefs about Joanna.

Jamie and his parents were put into a small waiting area and left on their own, having been informed that they would not be allowed to be party to Barry's interview. Frustrated by this lack of involvement and determined to do something, both Jamie and his dad made the decision to go to the hospital and confront Merrick, leaving his mum to deal with the police. Though the police station was in the centre of the town, the hospital was quite a trek to the other side of Maidstone in a place called Barming.

Even so, Jamie and Alan drove out to the hospital in super-quick time, parked and entered the reception area, where Jamie was able to direct his dad to the zone that housed the ward that Joanna had been on and where he had met Merrick. The ward was extremely busy and it seemed to take an age before anyone from the other side of the closed doors responded to their request to be let in. Security, it seemed, was a prime feature. It took a visitor to finally respond to their constant ringing of the attention bell, who then scurried back to where she had emerged from behind a curtained bay. Several auxiliary nurses came and went and then a male nurse came through the side door and sat at the desk.

Alan took his chance and, having ascertained from Jamie that he wasn't the nurse Jamie had met, approached him. He answered Alan's questions without a flicker of interest – no, Merrick was not on duty today, as far as he knew. After much prompting by Alan the nurse reluctantly looked up the duty shift and was able to confirm that and also to inform Alan that Merrick was not due on until later that evening. However, his concerns arose when Alan asked the nurse for Merrick's address. Now the nurse was interested and began to question Alan and Jamie as to what they were doing there and who they were.

As luck would have it two junior doctors came through the double doors and requested the nurse to accompany them to see a patient and to bring the notes. Alan and Jamie took advantage and pressed the release button and escaped the ward.

'Well, that was a bit hairy,' Jamie whispered to his dad as they hot-footed back down the stairs to the car park.

'Well, at least we know where he'll be later today. Come on, we'd better get back to your mum – maybe the police will have his address by now anyway. I'm not a praying man, Jamie, but I think we'd better do so long and hard right now as I've a really bad feeling about all this.'

*

Ken and Jane were having a discussion following their interview with Barry. Jane was very defensive and attempted to pick holes in Barry's statement – concerned, as she shared with Ken, that in fact it was Barry who was the perpetrator all along. His protestations that he hadn't touched Joanna were a little too defensive, especially as no-one had suggested that he had. It also didn't make sense to her that a nurse of Merrick's status and calibre and doing the job that he did as a specialist in intensive care would then systematically go about 'getting girls'. It all seemed pretty improbable.

Ken, on the other hand, could see that there was a delicate balance here with Jane not wanting to acknowledge how she had missed what was really staring her in the face. Joanna *had* returned her call and *had* expected to be believed. She *had* also attempted to contact Jane again but Jane *had* suggested another agency for her to contact, without giving her the time of day. The adult had been believed against the protestations of the child. How often had he seen that in his everyday work? Now it was up to him to get Jane to recognise that she might have been wrong and that there was a connection between the two missing girls and furthermore Merrick was somewhere amongst it.

*

Alex began to regain consciousness. Both her father and Yvonne were there when she spoke her first words. Her mum couldn't face it and had had to be taken back home by taxi. The shock of the state of Alex and the reason for Alex's operation was far too much for Sally. Facing up to what Alex may have been involved in was beyond her ability at present. To accept that Alex might have been a victim of abusers was unthinkable. Guilt would rear its ugly head at her failure to support and protect her. The alternative was even worse: that Alex had voluntarily prostituted herself. Neither could be contemplated and Sally withdrew into her lorazepamed mind. So much easier and simpler not to think at all.

She paid the taxi driver, stumbled up to the front door, opened it and went straight to the kitchen, where she made herself a cup of tea and swallowed far too many of the little blue pills, put the heating up to twenty-five degrees, staggered into the bedroom and lay fully clothed on top of the duvet and allowed her body to sink into oblivion.

Meanwhile, Alex opened her eyes to see her father's worried face searching her own. She turned her head away in shame and whispered, 'I should have died.'

Relieved that she had come round but recognising that the danger had not yet passed, Yvonne left Alex's side to allow Jim time to reunite with his tiny scrap of a broken child. Questions and hopefully answers could come later.

As she left the hospital, Yvonne breathed in the crisp January air long and hard before she found her car in the car park and paid an extortionate amount of car-parking fees and drove home. She had to have a break before going back to the hospital. She needed to regroup and think about how all this mess had occurred and somehow retrace her understanding of what signs she had missed.

She entered her house and called out for Clarissa and Carlos and the boys, but no-one responded. *Now where on earth could they be?* she wondered. Slipping off her shoes, she opened her bag and pulled out her dead phone and plugged it into the charger that was laying on the kitchen worktop. Within fifteen minutes she had showered and changed into clean clothes and made herself a turkey mayo sandwich. She sniffed the meat and, though rather dry, it seemed to still be okay, amazingly so when mixed with the mayo her mother had made. She also poured herself a gin and tonic, sat at the kitchen table and enjoyed the few moments to herself.

Then she heard a frenzy of pings as her phone came back into life and alerted her to several missed messages. Allowing herself the luxury of finishing her sandwich and sipping her drink first, she eventually leant over towards the worktop and flicked her phone open. There were seven missed calls and thirteen texts.

*

Robert was in school. He liked to get back a day or two before the inset day prior to the first day of term. He had had an interesting break. The day he had spent at Sybil's over Christmas had awakened his interest in women. Still damaged by the cruel sniping of his ex-wife and her ability to reduce him to a quivering mess, he had found meeting a woman who had not been so derisory and who in fact seemed to find his wit amusing rather empowering. The unattached sister proved to be very feisty but very knowledgeable and they had engaged on interesting and fascinating diverse subjects for discussion. Though he had no interest in her at all in a romantic sense she had raised his awareness of what it was like to be in the company of others who had similar intellectual opinions and abilities in discussing them.

Feeling very adventurous and slightly guilty at using the school's equipment, he sat down in his office and googled dating sites for the mature intellectual. He was amazed at how many there were and how expensive they were too. A little in awe of the whole enterprise in the end, he decided to check out local societies and clubs that focused on his interests and see what that might offer before entering the cyber world.

As he scrolled through the BBC web page and hit the home news link, he was astounded to see right in the corner of the web page a small headline under Hastings – 'Unexplained Death of Missing Child's Mother'. He went cold as he clicked the link that took him to the article. Within the last few hours police had been called to the home of local foster parents to discover the dead body of Sally Whitworth, wife of Jim and mother of local missing schoolgirl Alex Whitworth. It was, it seemed, an unexplained 'accident' – Mrs Whitworth, who had been under considerable strain lately at the loss of her daughter, had, it was believed, inadvertently taken an overdose of anti-depressants on her return from having identified her daughter as the child discovered on the beach at Hastings. A police spokesperson was unable to give any further details but established that there would be an inquest following this tragic death. It was also noted that Alex, though now conscious, was still very much on the critical list.

Robert couldn't think. He paced the office like a caged lion. Running his hand through his hair, he screwed his face up in a desperate attempt to go back over in his mind all that he tried to do to help the family. To his utter shame he realised that he had done nothing! His limited authority in the school didn't allow for him to spend time chasing around Alex or supporting Jim when Sally had had her breakdown. No, his immediate thoughts had only been for Joanna – and a fat lot of good that had been. A wild goose chase with Jamie no longer returning his calls. The stupid attempt to play clever when they suspected her of being the rescuer of the dead boy from the river embarrassed him. Instead of marching in there straight away, what had he done? Sent cryptic daft messages via soft toys. He knew Alex was distraught. He had seen girls hurt and upset before and their parents' inability to understand. Yet he had failed. Failed to alert the police to Joanna probably being the girl from the river. Failed to tell them what he had thought about Jamie's involvement and, worst of all, having Jim in his office over Alex's truancy. He had not done anything! Ashamed, he closed the dating websites and rang Hastings police station to make an appointment with the safeguarding officer.

*

Not believing what she was reading, Yvonne scanned the texts and listened to the frantic phone messages that were garbled and often incoherent. But what she did manage to decipher left her cold. Regardless of the gin, she immediately grabbed her coat and boots and got into her car and drove to Hastings police station.

*

Jim knew, as soon as he let himself into the house. He could smell death. She looked so peaceful and young – all trace of the lines that had puckered her pretty face now had dissolved and seeped back into her flesh, giving her a child-like quality. He didn't even want to disturb her as he felt for a pulse and breath, knowing there wouldn't be one. With a heavy heart he rang 999. The paramedic, who arrived within minutes by motorbike, was kindness itself. He affirmed that Sally was dead and called in for police assistance, due to the circumstances, he mouthed to Jim, with his hand cupped over the phone. Jim felt nothing much. He took the proffered tea from the paramedic and sat in the armchair without drinking it.

When Yvonne hadn't returned as she had said she would, Jim felt he couldn't leave Alex alone. Only when the nurse had suggested that he needed to go home and get a bit of a rest and see his wife did he finally let go of her hand and leave. Could he have saved Sally if he had got home earlier? Had she intended to end it all? It was of little consequence. Wracked with the horror of his daughter's damaged body and now his wife's death, he became too numb to feel.

He answered the questions put to him as if on autopilot – monosyllabic, simple responses. The private ambulance came and took Sally away. He turned down the heating automatically, drew himself a bath, scrubbed his body as hard as he could until the red welts became too sore to touch, dried and dressed himself in fresh clothes, left the house and walked back to the hospital. He didn't tell Alex. He just sat with her, encouraging her to talk, to tell the truth about what had happened to her and who was to blame. His promises that he was now ready to believe she had been telling the truth all along fell like stones. Alex said nothing.

No he couldn't survive this. Mary went up the stairs and stood before his room, a room she had never been allowed to enter. The key was on the same fob as the house key. With a deep breath she turned the key and entered his hallowed space. It was full of filthy pornographic magazines and hundreds of photographs of women doing the most indescribable things. She went to the wardrobe and opened the double doors. Out fell the instruments that he had used upon her. She staggered back and heaved. Turning to the drawers she yanked them out of their holdings and tipped them up, rummaging through until she found the cash box. The key to that too was on the same fob and with trembling hands she opened it. Wads of rolled-up paper money were wedged in together with a few photographs. The photographs told her nothing – faces of people she had never met. The money she pocketed. Then she turned and left the room, locking it behind her. Turning towards her own room she lifted the latch and entered it, viewing it now as if for the first time. She replayed in her head the violent scenes that she had had to suffer with him in his perverted and sick fantasies. She sat down slowly on the bed.

It was difficult to really comprehend her new status. What to do next? As every second ticked by she envisaged him returning to life. He couldn't – could he? She had to leave, and leave as fast as she could. It was almost midday and the postie would be by at one. Derick sometimes took the postie bus into the village, where he drank and met his mates. The idea penetrated her thoughts and became a plan – quickly she gathered her few possessions together and piled them into an old holdall that had held the porno magazines. She filled the kettle with water and heated up several whereby she could have a thorough wash at the sink.

By ten to one she was clean and dressed in her oldest but cleanest clothes, bag packed. She unfolded a few of the notes and popped them into her pocket – she didn't have a purse – and put the rest in her bag.

Her final act was to say goodbye to the three little mounds behind the coal shed. The babies he had deprived her of. There was one he hadn't managed to kill. The one that she had wrapped in her best jumper and left to be hopefully found and loved. That was now her purpose, her goal, to find her daughter, however long it took, for there was nothing left in her life but that hope.

17

Merrick awoke with a thumping headache. He really did not feel at all well. Knowing his shift began in just two hours' time, he lay back on his bed and groaned. Pulling back the duvet, he attempted to get up, but nausea swept over him and he sank back down. No way was he fit to go on the ward. Even if he managed to stand, the hot sweats that engulfed his body told him that he couldn't possibly be in control of doing any procedures on patients. For the first time ever since being in England, he knew he would have to call in sick, and the sooner he did so the better. He knew more than anybody how hard it was to get staff at the eleventh hour.

Scrabbling about for his phone, he found it down the side of the sofa. He spoke to Meryl, who, though understanding from his shaky and fevered voice that he was truly sick, was rather curt and 'disappointed' that he hadn't contacted her earlier. Merrick reminded her that he had never called in sick before and that if he could stand he would be in, but as it was he would be a liability in his state, and then he hung up, drank a glass of water and fell back into a heavy sleep, with no further thought about the girl he had locked in the cellar.

She, meanwhile, was beginning to panic. She had heard nothing from above and her two feeble attempts at being noticed were still wedged in the hatch. Realising that she would be a gonner if she didn't get some help pretty soon (how long could one live without water?), she began to pace up and down the room desperately trying to keep herself focused and alert. And then she heard the noise of many feet shuffling overhead. She stopped and looked up; the ticket and note were still there but then in a flash both had been snapped up.

'Oi!' she yelled. 'Help me, come back and help!'

The silence that followed was almost unreal. All shuffling stopped and then a mumble of voices and the shuffling began, but quicker this time until the noise faded into the background, then nothing. Both her ticket and precious money had gone! She now knew that whoever had found her money had no intention of discovering its source. A stupid, stupid idea; she berated herself for expecting anything different. She was abandoned again. No water, no food and no means of getting help. Desperate for the loo, she just weed in a corner. Distraught and terrified, she sunk down in tears.

*

The evening air was calm and chill. A strange quiet had settled over the town as if the past few days of high celebrations had sated people, and so they had retreated into the darkness of the night, exhausted and keen for some homely comforts before work and school began again after the festivities.

Jackie had felt relieved that the worst of the drunken revelries were over and that Maidstone would just have the normal drunken binges to deal with at weekends. As opposed to most nights, she was free over the holiday period. Her work as a street minister was essential to her Christian faith, but right now she was glad that she was on duty at the hospital and not on the streets.

She alighted the bus just outside A&E and made her way through the side door into the cloakroom, where she left her cheese wrap and her personal bits in the locker that she shared with Merrick. She changed into her uniform and checked the duty rota and her assigned ward. Making her way to intensive care, she chatted to the others that were just coming on duty. However, when they had gathered round the nurses' station to be briefed on their patients, she was quite taken aback to hear that Merrick had called in sick. In fact there was a bit of a mumble of disbelief from most of her colleagues, as they had not known him fail to attend a duty before, no matter how ill he seemed.

Then, as George was leaving after the handover, he turned and mentioned the odd incident of a couple of men earlier on in the day who had come onto the ward trying to get Merrick's address. 'Odd, they were, and pretty shifty – they didn't hang around long after I asked them what they were doing here or why they wanted Merrick.' George then shrugged his shoulders and left the others to their work.

So Merrick was ill, was he? Jackie too was surprised – not by the illness – 'We all get sick sometimes,' she uttered – but by the fact that he hadn't even turned up for work. She had been rather concerned about him recently, certainly since his return after Christmas. Though she couldn't put her finger on it, he wasn't quite the same. And hadn't he nearly made a serious mistake a few days back? Well, this was her opportunity to find out what was wrong. Aware that Tilsden had reported the one mistake Merrick had almost made, Jackie wondered whether he was under a caution. She had the perfect excuse to call round to his flat and see how he was. A simple case of checking for his address on the files would have to wait until morning because right now she had to get on with her job.

*

By four in the morning Joanna awoke to rain lashing down. She ached and her arms throbbed. Moving her head created sharp shards of pain shooting down through her whole body. All effort was now beyond her; she really just wanted it all to go away. Trembling uncontrollably, she forced herself to stand, causing herself even more distress as her feet came back to life. Pins and needles shot through her legs as she staggered back towards what she thought was the centre of the park. To keep moving was really all she could do. Now not caring whether Merrick found her or not, she worked her way through the park and out of the gate, limping along the street that she had ran up earlier.

The houses were all in darkness, but looming ahead was a tower block of flats which may give her some protection if she could just find a small space to lie down out of the incessant rain. Scouring around the grassed foreground, it was difficult to see where to try. The first three entrances were dark but the fourth had a courtesy light over the doorway. At least by being there she could see what was around.

Pushing open the heavy door she was met by a cold, concrete corridor, stairwell and lift door that had a NOT IN USE sign sellotaped to the glass. Heading for the walkway, she made her way up the first flight of stairs, avoiding the rubbish that had accumulated in the bend on the stairs, and worked her way along the corridor of closed front doors. Lacking space or corner nooks or anywhere to sit down that wasn't directly in front of a numbered door, she shuffled from one end to the other. All she wanted was some space to get out of the weather and a chance to curl up and sleep. Climbing further up, she trundled through the second, then the third and finally the fourth floor.

It was here that she heard some noise: melodious music quietly drifting through number 125. It wasn't loud or raucus but melodic and hypnotic. It certainly gave Joanna a sense of some peace and in her exhausted state she hunkered down on the concrete floor just outside number 125, allowing the music to simmer in her brain while as she drifted into a light sleep.

Inside 125 the Sharma family were celebrating the return of their brother from Pakistan. He had arrived at Heathrow at nine o'clock the previous evening but had been held by immigration for some time before being allowed back into the country, which was why, due to his having to find transport back at such a late hour, they were quietly celebrating in the early hours. Half an hour after Joanna had arrived outside their door, the Sharma family put away their instruments, hugged each other one more time and crawled into their beds, unaware of the child on their doorstep.

*

'Hey, you what are you up to?' the rough hand shook Joanna's arm and pulled her to her feet. Joanna opened her eyes and wildly took in her surroundings. She had momentarily forgotten where she had ended up. The woman who had dragged her to her feet had clearly come out of 126, as that was the only door open on the landing. 'I... I...' she began, but the woman didn't wait to hear more but propelled Joanna into her flat and shut and bolted the door immediately.

*

So slowly, and Alan was furious. There seemed to be no rush to find Merrick. What were the police doing? Not a damn thing about him. Apparently both he and Jamie had been 'out of order' in going to the hospital. They were to leave it to the police to find and question Merrick when they felt it was the right moment to do so. As it was he might have been frightened off by their earlier visit and they could have delayed any chance of seeing him until Maidstone believed it was appropriate to talk to him.

Ken, it appeared, was having trouble getting Jane to accept that her earlier understanding of Merrick might have been wrong. She had insisted that they interview him at his home as opposed to going into his place of work, where he would be under the public glare. She also reasoned that he had not altered his behaviour at all and his records showed that he hadn't deviated from his duties apart from the planned break at Christmas and returned to his duty since on his return. What obvious chance had he had of getting Jessica? She really felt that perhaps Ken should be concentrating on his own patch where Jessica had last been seen. And as for there being any connection between the two missing girls and Merrick – well, that, it seemed, was highly improbable. Reluctantly, the cooperation between the two counties had dissipated.

'It's nothing like the TV programmes, where police forces all storm troop together on a potential kidnapper,' bemoaned Alan.

On their return to Hastings both Alan and Carlos, desperate for some kind of answer, made the decision to act alone and disregard the advice from Ken – an action that gave Jamie, Clarissa and Jessica's mum some hope. They would both return to the hospital and await Merrick's arrival for work and force him to explain himself. It was about all they felt they could do. They had to do something and the longer time went by without hearing from Jessica, the worse they all felt.

Ken himself, frustrated by the response he had received from Maidstone, returned to Hastings, whereupon he was given two independent reports taken from both Robert and Yvonne earlier that day. He immediately hunted both down to clarify what he thought were two very interesting perspectives.

Jackie had had a really long and busy night. They had not found a replacement for Merrick and so she was totally exhausted. Drained with fatigue, she decided not to go to see him until after she had first had some sleep. But she felt she ought to do just one thing, and that was phone him and warn him about the two men who, it seemed, were persistently searching for him. Not long after her shift had begun the two middle-aged men had come up to the ward. They had encountered Staff Nurse Rigby, who gave them short shrift. But the men were very insistent. Jackie only overheard part of the conversation, but they clearly wanted to know why Merrick was not at work. Where had he gone? Were the hospital aware that he might be in trouble with the police? Again they demanded Rigby tell them Merrick's home address, which clearly she refused to do, adding that she would call security if they didn't leave immediately. Both men passed Jackie on their way out and one of the men was quite visibly distraught and crying and threatening to 'kill the bastard if he has touched her'. Jackie only overheard the threat, not the latter part of the comment.

Invariably her thoughts were for Merrick's protection, and by completely misreading the situation she rang Merrick as soon as she had left the hospital building. It went straight to his answerphone. Her message was simple, just warning him about the visit and the threat she had overheard. She offered to come over after she had had some sleep in case he was in some difficulty and needed help.

*

Janmai, always alert, had noticed the ten-pound note sticking up from the floor as she sidled out of the flat in the queue of workers heading for the transport van. She niftily yanked it up and clasped it in her hand, then her eyes glimpsed the ticket – she swiped that too. Within seconds yelling came from underneath the packing case. Everyone froze. Trembling with anxiety in case anyone had noticed, she slid the two pieces of paper into her back pocket. Ignoring the noise from beneath, Channi put his finger across his lips for silence and then beckoned them all to move on.

Janmai stepped up into the van and crouched down with the others for the short trip to the hotel where they worked. Partway through the night Janmai, alone in the corridor of the hotel, pulled her 'finds' from out of her pocket and examined them. She was not stupid and had learnt English in China in preparation for what she thought was going to be a career in England. Her enforced slavery of six months had drained her of any hope of that. The ticket she could tell was for a train and the note was real English money. For the first time she felt as though she stood a chance if she were to break loose and run for it. These were small symbols of hope that she felt were signs she could be free. She could get on the train and go somewhere – anywhere, away from these barbarous people. Ten pounds might be a lot of money or very little; she didn't know, but it was something. One good thing was that the hotel she was working in was very close to the train station. All she had to do was run out, get to the platform and use the ticket to get on the train and get as far away from the gang that had imprisoned her as possible. It was a dream that gave her hope.

She popped the two pieces of paper inside her bodice and kept them very close. A thread, that was all it was, but it could mean liberty at some point in the future, if she could run. The hope was all she needed. Locked away, later back at the flat, she lay on her bunk bed, planning.

18

Joanna had her hands clasped around a dirty mug full of hot sweet tea. She could hardly believe the state of the flat that she was in. The woman mumbled to herself constantly, clearly in a half world of her own drifting back into the real world in fits and starts. 'If I'd left you out there any longer they would have gotcha.' It was some time before Joanna realised that 'they' were the people next door who had drawn her to their door by the lovely music. 'Only me, only me is safe from them,' the old crone stated as she handed Joanna her tea. 'I have them in my power,' she added.

The room where Joanna was sitting was littered with old newspapers piled in several staggered heaps. There was a sofa, but it was showered in envelopes and advertising leaflets that had clearly been collected for many a month. There was very little real furniture, but several boxes had been divvied about the room with odd scraps of material draped over them and in turn more printed leaflets on top of that. The woman busied herself shifting piles from one area to another and stopping now and again to sit and read them whilst mumbling to herself.

Joanna was forgotten for a time until at about six thirty there came a knock on the front door. A voice called through: 'Hi, Mrs Webster, it's me, Salmond, with your breakfast.'

The woman jumped up and picked up a wooden spoon and yelled, 'Stop it – I'll getcha, leave me alone.'

The voice didn't give up. 'Salmond, Mrs Webster, it is okay, it is me with your breakfast. Look through the door and I'll wave.'

The old woman with the raised spoon in her hand went to the door, pulled back the net curtain and peered out. In utter surprise Joanna realised that of course the door was solid. There was no glass to look through, but the old woman peered at the solid mass as if she could see right through it. 'Salmond? Is that you? Don't let them getcha... I'll let you in if no-one's watchin.'

The old women unbolted the door and turned the lock and pulled the door back a few inches. A man in a white shalwar kameez stood smiling with a small tray. Furtively the old woman looked both ways down the corridor and then he stepped through the door.

The old woman slammed the door shut and looked at him intently. 'Youse still in your jimmy jams then?' she quipped.

He laughed and cleared a space on the table and placed the tray in the space. Then he noticed Joanna. His face became quizzical and he looked back at the old woman who was perched on a pile of newspapers, chomping into the toast that he had brought. 'You have a visitor, madam,' and his eyes turned to Joanna.

'Yes, had to get her in or they'd have got 'er.' She then carried on eating, oblivious to the man and Joanna.

He then turned his attention to Joanna. He folded his arms and fondled his beard as he looked her up and down. 'May I ask who you are and what business you have with our Mrs Webster?'

The way he said 'our Mrs Webster' gave Joanna a yearning inside. Clearly Mrs Webster was seen as belonging. He cared about her.

After a brief pause, with Mrs Webster chuntering away to herself as she spooned into her mouth the porridge, Salmond half smiled and said, 'Don't worry, she won't take any notice, not while she's eating.'

Joanna put her mug down on the floor near her feet and began to stand up. 'I don't want any trouble, I just need to go now, thanks.'

Standing, she tried to make her way towards the front door but Salmond put his arm out to try and stop her. Half expecting to be halted, she ducked deftly under his arm and aimed for the door. She hadn't reckoned the speed of the old woman, who spun niftily from her porridge and slapped Joanna across the face hard. It wasn't clear who was more shocked: Joanna, with the bright red stinging welt across her cheek, or Salmond, who grabbed the old woman's arm before she attacked again. This time the old lady allowed herself to be guided back to her food and Salmond had the wit to instantly take Joanna's hand and push her out into the corridor and into his own home, where he quickly closed his own door.

The difference between the two flats was mesmeric. No rubbish and filth here. It was serene and calm and beautifully pungent with perfumes of lavender and jonquil pervading the air. Far from being cluttered, the whole ope- plan area was sparsely furnished with simple cane loungers and stools. Huge pastel cushions encircled the floor space that in itself was layered with vibrant coloured matting. In odd spaces beautiful ceramic bowls were balanced in between the cushions and loungers, releasing the aromas that had challenged Joanna's sense of smell as soon as she had entered the room. She ought not to be here in this sanctuary. So beautiful, untainted and clean, as opposed to her own filth and stench.

If Salmond felt the same it didn't show, for he ushered her in and encouraged her to sit on one of the cushions. But she refused and stood with her back to the room, edging towards the door to make her escape. Salmond smiled at her, recognising her discomfort.

The contrast of her personage with his home was not lost on him, and with a kindly nod of his head indicated the kitchen. With very little choice, Joanna turned and went through the white cotton screen into a basic, clinical kitchen. On the worktop were the remains of a cut loaf that Salmond had used to prepare toast for Mrs Webster. On the hob was a small saucepan that had, she presumed, held the porridge that Salmond had also given to Mrs Webster. Turning, she realised that this was not a good move, for Salmond stood in the entrance, blocking her exit and trapping her in the room. Not for the first time, she felt cornered by those bigger and stronger than her.

He stood with his arms folded and asked in hushed tones, 'Now, I need to know who you are and what you were doing with Mrs Webster. Please be aware that my wife, brother and children are still sleeping and I don't wish them to be disturbed.' He smiled and nodded, encouraging Joanna to speak.

However, she wasn't having any of it and she too crossed her arms and closed her mouth, staring at a point beyond Salmond's head.

Salmond leant back onto the wall and nodded again. What did he expect? Did he really think that she was going to confide in him? Enough strangers had wheedled their way into her confidence and expected her to just confess all. Not this time. Joanna stood her ground and waited. The air grew tense and Salmond kept cocking his head towards the living room as if expecting to hear something.

In the end he sauntered over towards the sink, turned on the tap and filled the kettle with water. But when Joanna made an attempt to skip by him he stepped in front of her and took her by the shoulders. 'I am not sure how or why you ended up in Mrs Webster's flat, but if it was to steal her money then you'd be very unlucky as she doesn't have any.' He gripped her harder and she stepped back to try and get clear when he pushed her down onto a chair. 'All I can say is that you have been very fortunate not to have been hurt. She is a vicious old woman. Don't be fooled by her. Social services only allow her to stay there if she gets fed by her carers and pays her rent.' Salmond released his grip but kept the intensity of his staring and verbal attack. 'The carers refuse to go in anymore as they struggle with her violence. A care home would have to be more like a prison and other residents would be at risk. So it is best that I feed her twice a day and collect her groceries and see to her needs. That way no-one gets hurt and she can carry on in her own world.' He then stepped back as though realising for the first time that he had been pretty intimidating. 'But I won't have her preyed upon by youngsters like you. So tell me what you were doing in there.' He crossed his arms.

Joanna was just about to speak when into the kitchen burst a pretty little boy of about two, who clambered up onto Salmond's feet with arms outstretched, crying, 'Daidi ji, Daidi ji!'

Salmond bent down and picked up his child, and in that fleeting moment Joanna jumped up, brushed past, pushed Salmond and his child to one side, and ran across the room, grabbing the door handle and yanking it open. Fear gave her strength and she ran along the corridor and down the concrete stairwell until she reached ground level and out into the open.

Fresh air and rain hit her like a wet flannel and revived her energies. She aimed for Sainsbury's that loomed up ahead. She ran in and headed straight for the ladies. In the toilet she sat on the seat regaining her breath and tried to think. It was all so very bizarre. Had she dreamt it all? Was she hallucinating? The change from the old woman's disgusting room to that of the purity of the white and coloured exotic shades in the next apartment was surreal.

Unlocking the loo door, Joanna turned on the hot tap and filled the sink with warm water. A squidge of soap from the dispenser foamed up nicely and Joanna luxuriated in the opportunity to cleanse the dried blood from her hands and wrists. Unfortunately there was only an electric hand dryer instead of paper towels which she could have used as a flannel. As she improvised with several sheets of toilet tissue, they just balled up into small bits and made it hard to use. Nevertheless, she managed to get rid of most of the dirt from her face and hands, and the water was so warm it reddened her chapped hands. Drying herself as best she could, from the air dryer, she cleared up the mess and left a mountain of sodden paper tissues in the bin.

From there Joanna walked through the store. She watched people and they, unfortunately, watched her. She was desperate to grab some food, but security, it seemed, was everywhere. Strategically placed by the exit was a large charity stand for contributions to the food bank. Being so early in the day, there was hardly anything in it, but it was worth noting and maybe worth trying later in the day when she could grab something edible and run away fast.

But in the meantime she ambled back around and up the escalator to the clothes section. She picked up four items and slid into the changing room when the assistant was dealing with a customer. Inside she stripped off her clothes and pulled the tags off the T-shirts and jumper she had just lifted, pulling them on one layer on another. She had three and then her own top and coat. The fourth item she took back out and handed to the assistant, stating that 'it didn't fit'. With a smile she turned and made her way back down to ground level. So now she was a thief.

Emboldened, she wandered around the store with a basket, in which she placed various items of food. When she arrived at the checkout she fumbled in her pockets and let out a loud, 'Shit, I've lost my purse.' Handing the basket over to the cashier, she asked her to hang on to it for her to collect later and walked out the door. She walking slowly and with deliberation until she was sure no-one was after her; her mood lifted. The extra layers were worth it and helped warm her body. The bar of chocolate that she had managed to smuggle into her pocket she wolfed down in seconds. But what she really needed now was proper food and drink, and then she could decide what the hell she was going to do.

*

Merrick had slept on and off for hours. He was also aware that he had not done anything about the girl in the basement. But what brought him up with a shock and chilled him to the marrow was the text message from Jackie. The horror that Assef was after him brought him back to his senses. He recalled his earlier encounters and threats from Assef and his gang. Was it Assef who had tracked him to the hospital? What had he done wrong – he couldn't think of anyone else, unless... but he had been very careful; no-one could have traced the girl to him, surely.

He felt so ill. His head throbbed and he was running a temperature that heightened his fear of Assef. He knew that if he had actually gone to the hospital to find him then it wouldn't be long before he turned up at his home. Maybe the 'issue' was with him, why the network in Hastings had closed down. He racked his brains to think. But he couldn't do that properly. His head thudded. He began to shake. What to do? What to do?

He found himself packing his bags, ramming all his clothes in a rucksack. He searched wildly for his passport. He went through all his pockets, drawers and wallet, grabbing his cards and cash. Then he calmly sat down in front of his computer. He searched for a flight back home. He needed to get clean away as soon as he could. He had seen what violence Assef and his 'friends' could inflict, and Merrick was tired of it all. Flying from Gatwick would be all too obvious, but if he flew from Newcastle or Manchester... there it was, a flight from Stansted to Dubrovnik in five hours' time. He could just make it. If he drove it would take him about an hour and a half – but then his car would be a giveaway. He looked up the trains – that would take an hour longer with two changes – but that could be useful. Within minutes he'd bought both his train ticket and booked his flight. He'd leave his car – Jackie could have it… he'd text her. It was a shame, as he'd really loved that car; it had been his first purchase on arriving in England, and if it could talk what a tale it would tell.

Now thinking on his feet, he scanned the place: nothing untoward. Mercifully the rent was paid last week so he'd have plenty of time to flee without being looked for and then he could cancel the direct debit. He'd lose his deposit but then he had smashed a few items so what's the difference?

The knock on his door threw him. He dropped down to the ground and shuffled to the wall, hugging his bag. He expected the door to be hammered down and Assef to burst through. Instead the knock was repeated and after a few moments, silence… footsteps retreating away.

Sweat poured from him now, and it wasn't just his fever. He shook and gasped for breath. This was real fear. He peered through the slats in the blinds and noted a police car. A plainclothes officer was looking over his car, and then looked up at his window. He ducked. He heard a car door slam and as he sneaked a further look he observed the police car driving away. He gave it five minutes then he let himself out of the front door, flew out into the street, remembered the girl, ran back in and shifted the packing case, before scuttling out into the crowds, making his way to the station on foot.

*

Fatigued beyond all care, Jessica had fallen asleep. The loss of her money and ticket had shaken her and she was so scared that she gave in to the wave of despondency that crept over her. Whimpering at the bottom of the stairs, she drifted into a semi-conscious state, then a sound above her brought her back. She wasn't sure what it was, but something had changed. There had been the sound – she was sure of it – of something shifting over the trap door. She moved herself up higher in the stairwell and peered up, but to no purpose. Should she try yelling again? She had no idea of the time or day but thought she would have another go and, taking in a deep breath, she screamed top note.

Jackie had tried to contact Merrick again by phone, but it again had just gone to voicemail, but that didn't worry her as she was almost at his place. As she turned the corner into his street she noticed his car parked by the side of the road in a parking space next to the bins. *Good,* she thought, *at least he's still in.* She made her way up the opening two steps and into the lobby of the housing block. Glancing at her phone where she had keyed in Merrick's address, she checked the number of his flat when an ear-piercing scream assailed the air. At the same time beneath her feet she could feel a hammering and movement of the floor; both things had come from the same place.

She jumped back and glanced down at the space where both the noise and the movement had emanated. Anxious about what she might discover, Jackie hooked her fingers inside the loop of metal that was hinged in the wood and pulled up the trap door. At the same moment half a bicycle came flying up as Jessica gave one more attempt at battering the lid from inside.

Within seconds Jessica, recognising the fact that she could be free, hurtled herself up the final steps and with a swipe at Jackie shoved her to the ground and ran straight for the exit.

Winded and totally disorientated, Jackie lay stunned on the floor for a few moments before being able to stand. When she did so she went straight to Merrick's door and hammered hard and cried to be let in. It didn't take her long to realise that Merrick was either not there or being stopped from responding.

Unsure as to what to do next, Jackie ran to the exit to see if she could see the creature that had knocked her down. Oddly there was complete silence over the whole place. Apart from the earlier scream and shouting, now there was nothing. Was there absolutely no-one in behind all those other closed doors? Someone else must have heard the scream.

Then she heard the sirens, the screech of brakes and the running of feet. It was almost like being in a movie: she was immediately surrounded by police, one with a battering ram and several with batons raised. Totally bewildered, she allowed herself to be taken by the arm and escorted out onto the street. She heard one urging Merrick to open the door and finally the thud and splitting of wood that denoted the smashing open of Merrick's front door. Several moments later, she was asked to give details about herself and asked brusque, interrogative questions suggesting that she was involved in something that was both unpleasant and disturbing. Suspected of being an accomplice, she was handcuffed and driven away to face further enquiries.

*

Having ascertained that Merrick was not at home earlier, though his car was parked just outside the entrance, the police thought very little about it and had determined to roll on by again later. Jane had heard from her superiors that she was to pull out all the stops on this one as it wasn't looking too good with their counterparts in Hastings. Ken had suggested that their lack of cooperation was thwarting ongoing enquiries about a missing child; however, Jane determined to quash the link to Merrick as soon as she could. Then Hastings would return to their world and she could resume her work on her patch.

However, alarm bells rang when she personally called the hospital to speak to Merrick. It was quite clear that for the first time in his employment he had not attended his shift, and furthermore he wasn't responding to their calls. Jane had a sinking feeling in her stomach. She put a call out to the squad car to get back to his flat and break in if necessary and make a thorough search of the place for any evidence of abduction. She then grabbed her coat and a car and made her way to Merrick's flat at the speed of light.

19

A gathering at Jessica's home was anxiously awaiting news from Ken the DI. Along with Jamie, his mum and dad, Yvonne, Carlos and Clarissa, Robert had joined the worried group. As it happened they had received some news that was positive – Maidstone Police had at last attempted to track down Merrick. An update was desperately needed to allay their growing angst and fears as to what action the police were planning to take in regards to the nurse. Yvonne and Robert's conversations had enlightened the investigating officers in Hastings to determine a link, albeit vague, to the two missing girls. Ken's superior officer DI Skinner had contacted Maidstone and added a bit of weight to Ken's request, resulting in Jane's phone call to the hospital and eventual search for Merrick.

Ken was on his mobile as he entered the house. The others allowed him the privacy of the hallway, while they waited in the living room with bated breath. His face seemed unperturbed and without much emotion when he finally came into the room. 'Well, it does seem as though the nurse from the hospital is somehow involved in something – though whether it be Jessica's abduction or in fact anything to do with Joanna at all is still to be established.'

They all commented under their breath and Alan interrupted the mumbles with, 'So what have you found and what is the progress? And where is Jessica? And just exactly what is happening? What action is being taken to find her?' Jessica's mum sat wringing her hands with Yvonne's arm around her shoulder, dropping silent tears.

*

Jessica had had escaped through her ingenuity and determination. She'd surmised that if she kept up the screaming someone would eventually hear and come to see what the issue was. People had been walking above her while she had just feebly yelled out now and again; obviously her yelling and their walking didn't coincide. It was an opportunity missed that she wouldn't let happen again. Poking around in the cellar, she grabbed the strongest, toughest thing she could find, the bike frame, and, with a determination she only ever reserved for running races, screamed top note while jabbing the frame on the hatch lid. Consequently after her initial attempt she couldn't believe it when the hatch lifted. Terrified that she was going to be grabbed and taken elsewhere by her abductor, she swung the bike frame for all she was worth. As she let it go flying across the gap and lunging at the person bending over the steps, she hurled herself up the steps, lashing out with her fists at anyone or thing she could reach.

Having knocked down Jackie with the full force of the flying bike frame, she sped as fast as she could through the door and out onto the street. She took in two deep breaths and ran fast to distance herself from the block of flats and headed in the opposite direction. She aimed for busy main roads.

Once in what seemed to be a busy shopping precinct, she stopped and leaned against the wall of WH Smiths and slid down on to her bottom. Her eyes searched – of course there were no telephone booths, and neither could she see a police officer. What was she to do for help? She certainly didn't trust anyone.

Then she spied a group of schoolgirls in uniform. That would be her safety. Kids you could trust. Faltering to her feet, she ambled over to the crowd, lingering by a 'bus only' drop-off point.

Focusing on the ones looking at their mobiles, she honed in on the loner on the edge of the group. 'Hey,' she offered with a smile, 'my name's Jessica and I've lost my phone and my mum needs to hear from me pretty soon or I'll be in trouble – can I please borrow yours to make the call?'

Rosie looked up at Jessica and smiled. 'Sorry, my phone only accepts calls, I can't ring out – except the emergency number.'

'Oh, but that will be fine – that's what I need. Please, please can I use your phone?' Jess pleaded, holding out her hand for the phone.

OF NO CONSEQUENCE

Reluctantly Rosie handed her phone to Jessica. Nervously and with shaking hands Jessica tapped in 112 and waited. There it was – the voice asking her what she requested: what was her need? She could hardly get the information out: 'I'm Jessica, I've been grabbed by a man and locked up,' then she began to sob uncontrollably. 'I-I-I d-don't know where I am, there's a Smiths and a Greggs and...'

Rosie was gesticulating at Jessica and asking for her phone as her bus had just turned up. Jessica begged the girl for more time, but Rosie needed to get home and was becoming concerned that Jessica wouldn't return it. Just before she handed it back to the girl Jessica had the foresight to let the phone run on, enabling the operator to hear her acknowledge that the bus number was 657 and she was at bus stop HJ1, before handing it back to Rosie, who was desperate to get a seat on the bus and close the phone down. The last thing the operator had told her was to not hang up. Jessica backed away and looked after Rosie as she entered the bus that disappeared down the street, hoping that the operator would track her down, having heard her direction pointers.

People were scurrying past as rapidly as they could, avoiding getting anywhere near her. Jessica caught an image of herself in a shop window, recognising only what looked like a scruffy down-and-out wearing filthy clothes. She now noticed a pungent aroma of urine emanating from her jeans. On top of which, she looked down at herself and with utter embarrassment realised her period had started, leaking a dark stain down the inner thighs of her jeans.

Humiliated and without thinking, she backed away from the main street and slumped in the alley that she recognised as the one Merrick had dragged her down. Would he be here? Wildly she eyed every entrance and exit. The train station couldn't be too far away. But she had no ticket or money. Why wasn't there any police about? Losing her phone restricted her ability to think. How else did one make contact with people without a mobile? The alleyway was suddenly filling up with people who began to queue outside the back of Greggs. A shutter was raised from the adjacent building and the Salvation Army Soup Kitchen opened its doors.

Orderly and quietly several people shuffled along collecting a Styrofoam cup of soup and a hunk of bread, then shuffling off down the street to the main shopping area, where the benches and tree-lined seats acted as dining tables. Realising how terribly hungry she was and knowing that she could maybe tell these people what had happened to her, she joined the queue when suddenly looking up towards the front of the queue a face she recognised was looking wildly in her direction.

'Jess, is that you?' Running towards her with open arms came Joanna.

*

Jane and DS Marsden, meanwhile, were questioning Jackie at Maidstone police station. The air in the interview room was stale with a leftover sharpness of body sweat and old coffee. The realisation that Merrick was not the man she thought he was came as a huge shock, resulting in Jackie's trembling and shaky responses. Added to which, her knee throbbed from where she had landed awkwardly when Jessica knocked her off balance in her escape from the underground cell. She had a cut on her left cheek where part of the rusty frame had scratched past her and a blue reddy-brown bruise began to emerge just on her cheekbone.

It was, therefore, some time before she understood how she might be implicated in the abduction. Her texts to Merrick warning him of the men asking after him at the hospital gave the police ammunition against her. For what purpose would she have in advising him of this if she wasn't involved? Why would she be concerned over someone trying to see Merrick unless she knew that he was in trouble or had something to hide? Was that the reaction of an innocent person? It was only when DS Marsden invited Jane to begin questioning Jackie over the runaway she knew as Melanie, but who, it turned out, was in fact Joanna, that Jackie clicked as to how it all must look to the officer sitting before her.

Added to it all was the text that buzzed into her phone that the officer invited her to read out loud, from Merrick himself, advising her of the fact that his car keys were in his flat by the cooker and that she could take them and the car as a leaving gift. He, it seemed, was flying home to look after his family following his mother's stroke. At any other time this would have been a godsend. Merrick had known how hard she had struggled to exist on her nurse's salary and that a car for her was not in the equation. They had talked about her struggle using public transport, particularly when she worked shifts in unsocial hours. It was probably the most stressful aspect of her life, and one she had discussed with Merrick frequently. Ironically his generous parting gift had inadvertently implicated her in his skulduggery.

The police were very unsure of Jackie. Her role as both a nurse at the hospital and as a street preacher meant that she had the means by which she could link Merrick to the vulnerable. Horrified by what all this implied, Jackie became hysterical, imploring both Jane and DS Marsden to believe her, stating and affirming that she knew nothing about what Merrick had been up to. On the ward he was one of the best and most diligent nurses she had worked with. Looking from one disbelieving face to another that seemed to hold a little friendliness, she implored them that she should be free to go as she was due on duty very shortly. As it was, Merrick would not be turning up; with the ward already short-staffed, there would be real issues if she failed to do her shift.

Jane was reluctant to let Jackie go – she so wanted Merrick to be clean. Jackie was clever, bringing in the emotional angle of 'her duty' to escape interrogation, and then there was the juggling of two jobs, both giving opportunities to draw in the weak; she must be the perpetrator. Jane would not accept otherwise. Feeling under scrutiny herself as the two forces engaged together over the abduction of at least one girl, she was determined to save face. They had not liked her dismissal of Joanna's emails warning her of Merrick. Refusing to take the pressure off Jackie, Jane firmly believed that she was a calculating, clever key worker in the abduction. If she was wrong about Merrick then at least she would not be faulted in losing his co-worker in the crime.

With dogged belligerence she cross-examined Jackie, ferociously badgering her as to how she knew that there was a girl in the basement if Merrick hadn't informed her. The focus shifted to her reason for calling on Merrick that very moment and then homing in on why she had felt the need to alert Merrick to people enquiring after him at the hospital – questions that Jackie found impossible to respond to without getting deeper into a plot of which she had no concept. The car was clearly a huge dilemma for the inspector. Was it payment for deeds accomplished?

*

Merrick had sweated with true fear. Assef's cruelty and violent outbursts he had witnessed, and he did not want to ever be a part of them again, neither in the giving nor on the receiving end of his cruelty. Memories of what he had witnessed brought about further tremors and sweating as those visions were recalled on his journey to the airport. The journey on the train seemed laborious and slow, creating its own tension. Everywhere he looked he saw Assef's face.

He couldn't even relax once he made the airport lounge, and it was his sweating and shaking that alerted the check-in security. His edginess and awkward body movements were somewhat suspect.

With quick thinking, Merrick assured the guy on duty that he was a fearful passenger who hated flying but had had an urgent call to fly home to see his ill mother. He laughed and made out that he would usually get a sedative for flying, but the urgency of the call and his luck at getting a seat on the plane in such a short time meant that he was ill prepared.

The officer believed him and let him through, wished him well and advised he have a drink on board to calm his nerves. 'Not too much though.' He winked.

Smiling, Merrick walked through into the departure area and entered the gents' toilet.

*

Jackie was possibly telling the truth. Not only that, she seemed truly anxious about the need to get into work. Jane reluctantly allowed her to go back to work her shift, with the proviso that she would be available for further questioning, when necessary. Fingerprints taken and also a swab from her mouth for DNA matching, Jackie was gratefully released and she stumbled from the police station, bewildered and traumatised. Making her way across town to the hospital, she couldn't believe what had just happened. The first hour of her shift meant that she was little less than useless, having to hold back the tears that seemed to well up inside, until an RTA offered her a boy whose life-threatening injuries meant that she had to give one hundred per cent concentration. A true nurse, Jackie retrieved her control and focused totally on her patient, with little thought about her now-throbbing face and sore knee.

*

News of Jessica's call reached Maidstone police station a mere five minutes following Jackie's leaving. Jane and DI Marsden both headed out for the shopping precinct, where they found both girls huddled on a bench drinking soup.

Ken received the news just as he was trying to placate Jessica's parents. Relief was acknowledged all round and the family travelled back to Maidstone to collect her. Yvonne followed. Joanna may well be the other girl that Jessica had been with and she wasn't going to let her go this time.

20

The 23rd of May found Jessica, Joanna, Clarissa and Alex sitting their first GCSE – their English Literature exam. For Alex this was a profound moment in her life, as she had not entered school at all since her escape from Assef. Jim and the school had arranged for her to be home-tutored. Furthermore, her teachers had all been generous with their time outside normal school hours. Robert had ensured that this was the case. Her option choices were limited but there was enough support to enable her to get five passes if she focused. Though her body was frail and weak, her mind seemed to have revitalised and shown a strength and aptitude to achieve academically. Haunted by remorse and guilt over the death of her mother, her studies gave her a much-needed distraction. In a strange way it helped her to come to terms with the suicide and in a sense her desire to achieve well was a kind of offering to her mother's memory and gave her father hope for her future.

What she had learned about Joanna's and then Jessica's encounters with Merrick, and her angst over her 'friends' who were still, as far as she was aware, under the influence of Assef, gave her the incentive to give as much information as she could to the police now that they had finally listened to her story. They in turn had passed her on to victim support and it was their help and support that gave her back some self-esteem. That it was Assef in the wrong and him who had committed a crime against both her and the other girls she now believed to be a fact. Alex was able to accept Assef as a villain. Now when she had the desire to inflict self-harm to herself, in order to alleviate the pain and struggle that her mind was going through, she was able to use a 'safe' self-process shown to her by her counsellor. Her body would no longer be at risk of further mutilation; instead she relieved the pressure by other methods – still painful but not damaging. Ice burns are far easier to heal than knife cuts. Gradually the need to even do that became less and less.

Clarissa and Jessica were fully focused on their expectation to do well in their exams and revised continually, working alongside Joanna and Alex whenever possible. Joanna joined Clarissa and Jessica in their running and, though she was not as fast, became fitter and stronger for the exercise. Alex never joined them – her body was not strong enough and her mind certainly couldn't handle going out to public areas yet. Instead she built her strength up by swimming with her dad every Tuesday morning.

Reaching this collaborative acceptance of one another was no easy feat and the girls encountered further issues before they reached this relatively stable situation.

*

Having discovered Jessica in the alleyway in Maidstone, Joanna realised that she could not continue to run. Instinctively she was ready to keep up her anonymity and stay free, but how could she leave the poor girl who had ended up at the mercy of Merrick all because she had been tricked into believing that she was going to help Joanna? Jessica had clung to her like a limpet, crying and shaking in a real state. She in turn had clung back. Both girls fed off each other's unspoken experience at the hands of Merrick. The kind Salvation Army officers gave them the much-needed hot soup and bread that they both took time in drinking, after which both girls limped back onto the main street where two squad cars had pulled up.

Four police officers ran, eyes searching, the main square. Joanna recognised Jane and held back as she came towards her. She was in half a mind to release Jessica's hold and then sprint for it, but the police officer next to Jane reached out, offered her his hand and, smiling, asked, 'Are you Joanna? We've been looking for you for a long time.'

Though it was a complete lie, and Joanna knew it was, she was thankful enough to see that for a short time she might well have a small chance to get her voice heard and Merrick stopped. With that in mind it was easy to go with them, Jessica in one car and herself in the other.

At the police station the girls were given mugs of tea and sandwiches. There were three people supporting them when they gave their statements. With Jessica was her mum, and two plainclothed detectives, one male and one female. Joanna had to wait until her support arrived and at the insistence of DI Marsden Joanna was asked whether she would be happy to accept Yvonne in the role of guardian. Considering the only other option was to wait for someone from social services to turn up whom she wouldn't know, Joanna accepted.

That day and night became a veritable blur for both girls. Yvonne fought hard to get Joanna released into her care and not be sent to a hostel. She insisted that she had a placement where Joanna would be safe. As her former social worker, she pulled familiarity and authority to take her back to Hastings, East Sussex, and not use the resources of Maidstone, Kent, which the police were happy to go along with; less money out of their budget and responsibility shared. Martha came to the rescue and Joanna spent the next few nights and weeks staying with her.

Over time Jim, with the help of Yvonne and a rape crisis support group, was given the skills by which he could try and give Alex the security and safety that she needed. Her fragility was obvious. He learnt that what her body needed was to recover and heal as well as her mind. He learnt to cook nutritious meals and didn't let himself be fazed when Alex couldn't or wouldn't eat them. He knew it was all part of her healing process. But gradually, bit by bit, she began to respond and, encouraged by his kindness, didn't let on that she was vomiting food in the toilet after his back was turned. He feared for her. At first she seldom left her room and even when she did it was to sit in the half-light of the kitchen looking at nothing. The times they ventured out together were when Jim took her to her victim support session.

Once a fortnight for three months they both attended and both learnt how to get back control over their own lives. The therapy was as much for Jim as it was for Alex. It was here that Alex was given strategies to cope and a place whereby she could share her desperation and needs. They made plans for the next few weeks of her life but focused on one day at a time. Gaining back control and power over her future was hard. It was Jim who struggled over the fact that Alex would never be able to have a child. For Alex that was a thought, a situation, too far ahead in a future she didn't believe in.

In February Alex had to have further surgery. Yvonne used this as a means by which she could try and bring Alex and Joanna towards a kind of reconciliation. Joanna had been constantly devising ways by which she might trace her parents and was begging Yvonne almost daily for help. It was help that Yvonne knew she couldn't truly provide. On edge and, as Yvonne mused, about to run off again, she felt that there might be something in giving Joanna stability if all the girls involved were to bond somehow.

With that in mind, the day prior to Alex's return to hospital Yvonne drove Joanna to see both Alex and Jim. It was Jim who responded to the doorbell and he ushered them both into the hall, informing them both that if Alex refused to see them then he would not allow the meeting to take place. But part of the work covered by the social services, counsellors and victim support had been to try and allow Alex the opportunity to place aspects of her earlier life in perspective. It was a vital part of moving on. Joanna had never felt any animosity towards Alex, believing that if she'd had a mum and dad she would not have wanted them to be shared with anyone and so actually understood why Alex disliked her so much. Alex, though, was now a much-altered girl; her maturity and understanding had come from bitter experiences. The counsellor had suggested to Jim that she could have gone either way – into a hard, locked-up angry person or one that recognised need and empathised with others.

The meeting was short and stilted, with Alex saying very little and Joanna even less. But when leaving Joanna asked Alex if she could visit her in hospital. Alex uttered a quiet, 'Yes.'

*

Martha had been very troubled by all the events that had occurred to her friend Sally's family – not least the death of Sally herself. She had often wondered if by her dragging Alex back that night she had triggered the breakdown of both Sally and Alex. Sally's decline had been clear to see – she realised that now – and her mind was troubled over how she had failed to do anything to help her. She recalled the moment in her kitchen when Sally had poured out her troubles and her need to 'get rid' of Joanna. What help had she been to her then? She had done absolutely nothing to support her friend. And when Jim had called her when Alex had gone missing – what had she done then? The very same – nothing. She grasped the opportunity Yvonne gave her to make some amends back in January – would she please consider taking on Joanna for an emergency foster placement for a few days until a proper place had been found? She didn't hesitate. At last there was something that she could do.

*

At eight o'clock on a Friday evening Joanna arrived skinny, filthy and with a haunted look about her with nothing to her name. Yvonne had dropped her off, promising to return with some emergency items for her, and within an hour she was back. Clothes and toiletries for the night, and a T-shirt, jeans and a jumper for the following day as a stop-gap from Sainsbury's.

A much-altered child stood before her now. It wasn't the skinny body or the hollow eyes that melted Martha, but the change in her character. Where was the quiet, silent child that had stood and accepted all that was thrown at her? Anger and bitterness streamed from her in both her body language and verbal actions. Touching was forbidden. No cuddles then. Furtive and sullen, her eyes never stayed still. Sitting still was a complete no-no.

Martha's only way of getting some kind of stability was when she offered to help Joanna search on her laptop for ways and means of trying to trace her parents. This was the whole focus for her now, it seemed. And to Martha she was seriously troubled about how to cope when Joanna finally realised her dream had no hope of coming true.

*

227

Joanna's anger at having to give herself up was assuaged by the way the interview had gone at the police station. They actually seemed concerned and not so quick at blaming her for the situation she was in. Seeing Yvonne in the interview room made her very nervous – where was she about to send her now? But she was impressed at how strong and firm Yvonne approached the interview and stood by her. During one of the many breaks in interrogation, Yvonne shared with her the situation with Sally and Alex. Joanna felt little for the loss of Sally, sad, but not overly distressed. However, she was really angry at what had happened to Alex.

That was why, on their return to the interview, Joanna turned on them all and let rip about how stupid and wrong the authorities were. She shared with them how she had been treated back in Barnet. How it was so obvious that girls in care were easily abused and that no-one, least of all the so-called carers, gave a damn. Had they any idea about the Asians living in the building where Merrick's flat was? What, she wanted to know, were they going to do about it? Fired up, she swore at them and told them all to just eff off.

'Too late now, isn't it? He's gone and I bet the police frightened off the Asian jailers too and there will be an empty flat waiting to be discovered. You all believe in yourselves. "Us adults must be right. We must support each other." Well, you are wrong. Children don't lie! Children trust and will do what they are told to do *because* they trust, whether what they are told is right or wrong. Yet all you can do is blame the kids. Even Barry was too scared to help because of the way you twist everything. So you can all sod off. I'm saying no more.' She gritted her teeth, crossed her arms and hunkered down in her chair, lips firmly sealed. Nothing would persuade her to say another thing.

After a prolonged silence where it became clear Joanna meant what she had uttered, Yvonne suggested that she take Joanna into her care and that any further discussions might be had after Joanna had had time to recover from what had clearly been a horrendous ordeal. Reluctantly the police agreed and Yvonne made the call to Martha.

*

In the car on the way back to Hastings Yvonne tried to get Joanna to talk – not about the case but about anything. She asked whether it had been Joanna who had tried to save the boy in the river and what a really brave and courageous thing she had tried to do. Joanna said nothing. But as they began the drive through Cranenden, Joanna's eyes picked out the road where she had last spent the night in that village.

She turned to Yvonne and begged her to go up the lane to the barn so that she could retrieve her bag. It was pitch black and Yvonne had no intention of deviating an inch. The girl could just disappear if she were to let her out of the car. Having lived for some weeks in the area, Joanna clearly had some connection to the place and would know her way about; besides, with no torch, fumbling about in an old barn in the dark would be futile.

So instead she turned to Joanna and smiled and said, 'I tell you what, I'll bring you back here tomorrow in the daylight and help you find what you're looking for. But only if you will just give in and not try to run off any more. I promise I will not place you anywhere that you don't want to go and I will stand by your right to have your story told. I also need you to help me get Alex back into the land of the living.'

With a grunt Joanna agreed. She was knackered anyway and hungry and far too drained to do anything else. 'Alright, but if you put me in a hostel I'm off.'

*

The police did return to Merrick's block of flats and, as Joanna had predicted, the rest of the flats had emptied. With no cause to break down doors or gain forced entry, the police could only rely on knocking and waiting for someone to respond. Their interest in Joanna's description of the comings and goings of the people in the flats became a major point in their enquiries and so once they had determined that Merrick had fled they observed the area by placing a small camera in the spyhole of Merrick's front door that conveniently faced the corridor leading to the two 'vacant' flats. Merrick's was left empty at the request of the police as it was integral to their investigation and the landlord complied with that request on the understanding that it would be available to relet after Merrick's final payment had come to its end. The basement also was a source of evidence that shared the DNA of both Joanna and Jessica, along with traces of several other human. As far as Merrick was concerned, there was no sign of him. It was presumed that he had left the country, though there was no record of him landing back home. His place on the plane had not been taken. To all intents and purposes, he seemed to have vanished.

*

True to her word, Yvonne drove Joanna back to the barn and helped her retrieve her stuff. There was very little to find. Someone had been there and had wrecked the small area that Joanna had secluded off from the rest of the barn. Kids, she assumed. Her precious jumper she found stuffed in a corner, but there was no sign of the bracelet. She retrieved the jumper that had been further reduced by nibbled holes and a covering of mice droppings. Yvonne immediately put it into a plastic bag and informed Joanna that she wasn't to touch it until it had been through a wash. Cold though it was, Yvonne asked Joanna to sit on one of the bales and tell her how she had lived here. With the air noticeably chillier and the light darkening, Yvonne listened with some distress to Joanna's calm yet concise explanation of her world as she had lived it since running away.

For fifteen years Yvonne had been in social work. Poorly paid and with an overstretched service that meant corners were often cut, she had still believed that she was doing some good in the world. But listening to Joanna and all she had described, Yvonne recognised the fact that, far from helping, her institution actually perpetuated the devastation of children like Joanna. Knowing how hard it was to get good recruits, how many times had references not been taken up or shelved applicants been brought back into play to support an already crumbling service? Was she too guilty of closing her eyes to the appalling failure they were to children in need?

By the end of Joanna's story, Yvonne made a firm and strong resolve to both herself and Joanna – that she would raise her concerns at the highest level and make it her priority to get someone in high authority to listen and make good what was clearly a broken-down service. Yet in her heart of hearts she knew she'd be only pissing in the wind as far as that was concerned.

Her arm around Joanna's shoulders, Yvonne walked her back to the car parked at the top of Petty Lane with a very heavy heart. How many children had they all missed? How many children like Alex, like Joanna, had been prey for the evil, twisted minds of the likes of Merrick and Assef? More importantly, how were they to get anyone to listen and to do something about it? Joanna's outburst at the police station rang so very true. We don't listen to kids, they are of no consequence and we ignore them at our peril.

*

That evening Yvonne called round to Martha's and brought with her Clarissa. Both girls went up to Joanna's room and caught up with Jessica through FaceTime on Clarissa's iPad.

Yvonne and Martha were both attempting to find a workable solution out of the whole sordid mess. Yvonne shared with Martha the absolute absurdity of the way the social service was letting down so many children. Martha shared with Yvonne the fact that no-one had really recognised the breakdown that Sally had endured. Furthermore, after their second glass of wine they both focused their angst on the way the police were reluctant to recognise that children under eighteen were vulnerable to the preying of men. Now that the girls were being taken seriously, Assef and Merrick had both vanished. Alex had so very little recall as to the place where she had been incarcerated with the other girls, that the police attempts to discover them failed. Consequently, in light of a reduced workforce and other ongoing crimes, their case began to lose momentum and urgency, so it was placed on the backburner. What ultimately concerned both women the most was how many of the girls who had been with Alex were still out there being used and abused. Reluctant to let this go yet fearing lack of support from an already overloaded police force, both women made a plan.

With backup from the local council they offered their services to voluntarily try to track down any missing girls that had been reported in the past year. Though a drop in the ocean, this at least seemed to be a start. Ken Breech seemed to be the one to contact at Hastings Police as he had been instrumental in getting the girls back. Furthermore, they thought that Mr Bentley would be in favour of joining in on getting something started in light of his very obvious concerns over both Alex and Joanna. The concept was hatched. Yvonne was to book an appointment that was convenient to all four and propose the setting-up of an action plan and a commitment from all to wipe out overt child abuse in Hastings – as a start.

Later that evening Joanna and Martha were curled up on the sofa, having just eaten a Half Man Half Burger takeaway, when Joanna shared how she wanted to be allowed to live for herself – to not have to go back to school but to be able to search for and help the girls that Alex had been with and spending more time researching for her parents. Feeling it the right moment, Martha shared with her the concept of the action group, making it very clear that Joanna was far too young to be part of it and that she had to attend school by law.

Joanna pulled away from Martha and stared her in the eye. 'At what point was this law enacted upon when Alex and I failed to attend school? No-one was bothered then. We can at least go on the streets and be bait for the pervs and then you can pick them up.'

Drawing her back to herself, Martha explained the fact that they were both far too vulnerable and young to be used as 'bait'. That would never happen. Besides which, these men were extremely dangerous and only appropriately trained officers could hope to infiltrate the gang. But if she did go back to school and get her qualifications, then in time she could join the police or such like and be part of the investigations into such crimes.

Joanna's retort was to comment, 'Well, that's just bollocks! Far too late and not dealing with the situation now!'

Used to her unworthy language and outbursts, Martha just shrugged and let her go to her room.

*

However, Joanna did go back to school, and she did her own investigative work with Jess and Clarissa, and, to a certain extent,

Jamie. That all came about after she had left Martha's and gone to live with Jim and Alex – at Alex's request.

*

Robert Bentley had been so relieved that Joanna and Jessica had returned to Hastings that he wanted to do all he could to keep them safe. The concept of such trafficking in his hometown revolted him. The moment Yvonne approached him with her idea he was in and eagerly awaited the invitation to meet up with Yvonne, Martha and Ken to initiate the support group. At last he might be able to do something proactive for once. He and Sybil had already come to an agreement over the education of the girls involved. When Alex was being home-tutored, with their respective parents' agreement, if the topics coincided with any the other girls had chosen to do, then they would join her at her home.

As far as Joanna was concerned, her situation was more awkward as she had had very little schooling to speak of. She was also very determined about what she wanted to focus on. Adamant that she would not repeat the year and fearing that she would just up and run again if forced to do so, the decision was taken to allow her to reduce her subjects, focusing all her school time on those in which she felt confident, in the hope that she would at least pass something. The study of literature was paramount to her accepting her fate. She and Alex struggled through *Silas Marner, Othello, An Inspector Calls* and Carol Ann Duffy's poetry. But surprisingly these were the very texts that enabled Joanna to express her deepest concerns. It was the discussion over the fate of Daisy Renton, Desdemona, Bianca and Molly that brought home the appalling way women were treated over centuries. Duffy's poem 'Valentine', that had sparked off the initial incident that brought the girls together, was now superseded for Joanna by her poem 'Whoever She Was'.

As her study days in Alex's home lengthened, she often stayed over and became a comfortable and caring companion to Alex. Towards the end of March Alex asked Joanna if she would move back with them permanently. Jim was delighted as he could see how the friendship of the two girls was enabling Alex to gain confidence and strength.

It pleased Martha too. Though she had become extremely fond of Joanna, despite her somewhat newly found colourful language, there was a real sense of good to be recognised in this new relationship and Martha happily accepted the fact that her role in the care of Joanna had completed this part of its course. For Jim it was a tremendous relief. It meant that he could begin to think about returning to work and to attempt to get some kind of normality back into his life – though it did take him more than eight months before his firm would accept him back. albeit on a reduced salary.

*

The setting-up of the lost children unit that Yvonne, Martha, Ken, Robert and now Sybil had founded took far too long. It wasn't until a country-wide scandal of trafficked and abused children came to the media attention that any credence was given to these professional people who had a wish to keep the lost and desolate children of the country safe.

Finally in June of that year all founder members were given access to the details of missing children – boys as well as girls – from the Hastings area. All five adults took great care in searching, researching and finding links to those who had disappeared. They interviewed family members of the lost and spent time with school friends and began to build up various portfolios that may or may not be linked together.

Meanwhile, the four girls had made a pact that after their exams during the long school summer break, they would attempt to find the place where Alex had been so brutally abused. Alex herself was more than a little reluctant. She feared ever seeing Assef again.

Joanna also had new plans. Yvonne, true to her word, had made several enquiries into Joanna's past. There was no further evidence for her to share but there had been a strange development that might give hope and maybe a tenuous link to Joanna's birth. The meeting was going be held in Yvonne's office between herself and a lady called Margaret, who had travelled down from Scotland in search of her lost child. Of this Joanna was not aware. False hope would be too much to bear. For the time being Joanna was just told that they had found the whereabouts of the lady who had found her.

*

The 4th of August began with a mini heatwave – the first really hot day of summer. After much tempting and coaxing, Alex had allowed herself to be persuaded to venture to the beach. The heat was almost tropical. The sky was a mesmeric, soft blue with nothing to break the burn of the orange in its centre. Twinkling reflections of both danced on the cool water as the waves gently trickled back and forth over the stones. They were in T-shirts and shorts. It was an idyllic way to celebrate their exam results – none too brilliant but in the circumstances, enough.

Abandoning their trainers, Alex, Jessica and Clarissa paddled in the cold, salty inrush of waves that licked the shoreline. Joanna had queued at the ice-cream van, where she bought three cones and a choc-ice. Joining the others with ice-cream dribbling down her fingers, all four leapt and danced at the water's edge. Joanna was looking forward to finally having the opportunity to speak with the person who had found her. She also had support from Yvonne, who had been contacting colleagues from the district where Joanna had been found. A particularly friendly lady known as Maddie, having been intrigued by Joanna's story, committed to help. Joanna was due to meet her the very next afternoon.

It was a delicious day. The sun was beating down warm, instant heat, melting the ice-creams with speed. As Alex bent to lick the drips off her hand, she laughed, lifted her head and caught a flash of sun glinting on metal. The air held a humid moment.

She looked again. His watch. Assef. Arm around a girl no older than twelve. Leading her. Leading her away down the road, past the hotel with its flags out, past the Italian café, past the water fountain and then down. Down into the abyss of her past. She dropped her ice-cream and crumpled to the ground, shaking and whimpering, 'He's back.' She sobbed. 'He's back.'

But the scream that reached Jessica, Alex and Clarissa's ears was not that of Joanna. The sirens of several police cars cut through the air. Assef was running hard and fast; having released the girl, he stumbled and fell into the trap that she had set. Arm held firmly behind his back, he was clipped neatly into handcuffs and ushered into the back of an unmarked police car.

Murdo drove his postie bus up towards Fat Derick's. He had hoped that he would want a lift into town today, as they always had a great rapport. With a sense of humour that was both wicked and crazy, Derick could be relied on to entertain.

But as he pulled up to the path and gate of the cottage Murdo had the surprise of his life. A woman hailed him. Never in the ten years delivering Derick's post had he ever known him to have a visitor. Aghast and intrigued, he helped her into the back of the bus. Her complete silence unnerved him and he also said nothing.

She clutched her bag to her chest for the remainder of the journey, only moving her glance away from the window as she allowed another passenger to board and sit next to her. A weak smile emanated from her in acknowledgement of the other passengers and then her eyes returned to watch out of the window until she too left the postie bus at Achnasheen, where she picked up a commercial bus to Inverness.

As each mile took her further away from her harrowing past, Margaret felt a tremulous fluttering in her belly as she drew closer to where she birthed and abandoned her first-born. Looking down at her hands and then the red wheels on her legs, Margaret felt ashamed of her appearance but recognised that these physical signs of her imprisonment would make her story all the more real to those she would have to tell. They would then help her, she assumed, help her to find her long-lost baby daughter, and even if it took forever she would not give up until she could be found.

Relaxing now in the reality of her newfound freedom, she took in the beautiful views of mountains, hills and heather. Laughing out loud, she rejoiced at the sight of those hills, for in her tortured mind that was the name she had given her lost child: Heather.

The bus trundled along, and the further away from her prison it went the more empowered Margaret became. At Inverness she would go straight to the police station and ask for their help. All would be well.